Luna Sol Amat

FOUAD FARAJ

Visit our website at
www.StillwaterPress.com
for more information.

First Stillwater River Publications Edition.

ISBN: 978-1-965733-27-1

1 2 3 4 5 6 7 8 9 10
Written by Fouad Faraj.
Cover illustration by Nelson Navarro.
Interior book design by Matthew St. Jean.
Published by Stillwater River Publications,
West Warwick, RI, USA.

Names: Faraj, Fouad, author.
Title: Luna Sol Amat / Fouad Faraj.
Description: First Stillwater River Publications edition. |
West Warwick, RI, USA : Stillwater River Publications, [2025]
Identifiers: ISBN: 978-1-965733-27-1
Subjects: LCSH: Interpersonal relations—Fiction. | Battles—
Fiction. | Peace—Fiction. | LCGFT: Romance fiction. |
Fantasy fiction.
Classification: LCC: PS3606.A674 L86 2025 |
DDC: 813/.6—dc23

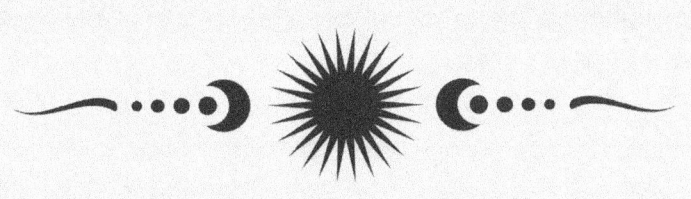

I dedicate
this book to my parents,
Fouad Faraj-Musleh & Gail Faraj-Musleh,
as a thank you for making
me who I am.

Radric Wartox, Ruler of Sol

It was a warm afternoon as the artificial sun burned in the gloomy, smog-covered skies. A tall, golden-skinned man made his way into the throne room of the king. His tired hazel eyes bore the sadness of many years of war and loss but managed to shine with a slight glimmer of hope. He fell to bended knee as he respectfully lowered his gaze.

"My Lord, is now a good time? I was informed you summoned me." He addressed calmly as he remained on bended knee. The king stood looming over the rail of the palace balcony, staring into his vast kingdom. Upon hearing the voice, he turned with a slight smile.

"Ah, General Wasukah. This is actually a perfect time." He responded warmly as he returned his gaze to the kingdom. Wasukah made his way to the king's side and peered up at his colossal figure, awaiting him to speak. "General, I've often wondered why I was born so different." He continued, raising his hands and staring into his ruby-red palms. "And I don't just mean being the largest Uçebian ever to grace this planet. I'm sure that comes as no surprise, seeing how my mother was a Mountain Giant. No, I mean this unique red skin complexion that neither of my parents nor their ancestors have possessed. I believe our great Father Gi has blessed me with this aesthetic as a mark of my importance to the kingdom."

"My king, are you implying that the sun-god himself has selected you over all your predecessors for—" The general began to speak, but Radric looked down at him with a raised eyebrow.

"Is it that hard to believe?" He interrupted. "Not only were the circumstances of my birth unique, but my complexion is as burning as the raging sun himself. I truly feel that I will be the one to bring an end to the conflict with Luna that has raged for countless centuries."

"Forgive my earlier tone, Lord Radric. I agree that your deeds in battle and accomplishments thus far separate you amongst the pantheon of Sol's rulers...but can such a feat truly be achieved? How do you plan to do this?"

"I'm rather hurt, Wasukah." The king responded with a playful grin. "You, of all people, should have full faith in me. That aside, I didn't summon you here to boast about a potential plan. I already have something that will turn the tide in our favor. One the likes that has never been achieved. Long has it been that the rulers of all kingdoms of Uçebar have been blessed with unique powers by their respective gods. But what if I were to tell you that I have discovered a way to share my powers with the marines. Would that lessen your doubts?"

"Well, I wouldn't call my reservations doubt, but what are you implying, my lord?" The general asked with widened eyes. Without a word, Radric reached into his pocket, removing a small red sphere and cradling it between his thumb and index fingers. With a gentle flick, he tossed the glowing gem into the air and snatched it up quickly with a boastful smile.

"I call this the Ignisque talisman," Radric replied, holding out his massive palm and allowing the gem to glisten before Wasukah's awestruck eyes. "Now, as I harness the flames of our golden lord, so can anyone bearing this talisman."

"Your grace, this is—unbelievable! How did you manage such a feat?" Wasukah responded with energetic disbelief. Without a response, Radric fell into a fit of maniacal laughter, sporting an unsightly and rather cartoonish posture. His flame-orange eyes bore the pride of ages as well as complete lunacy. "My king, please!" Wasukah pleaded with embarrassment and unease. "You must control this intense *fake laugh* that you still seem to be doing. It's unbecoming of our noble leader." Radric sighed slightly as he took a deep breath and tried to calm himself. "Really, your majesty, it was one thing when you were a child; I merely thought it was a phase. At this point, I'd expect you to be more mature, with all due respect."

"Forgive me, Wasukah, but can you blame me for beaming with pride at this moment?" Radric responded calmly. "I have accomplished what none of my predecessors could have even dreamed of. Now, the Lunian marines won't stand a chance on the battlefield with Sol's finest."

"Truly, this is an indescribable accomplishment, my lord...so, how does it work?"

"One must simply have the talisman on their person and envision the light of our lord burning within their soul. They should be able to harness it at will; however, it does draw on the body's physical energy. It can be tiresome, so I will need the men to train in using it for a while before they can be entrusted with it in the field. For that and the fact of how difficult it will be to mass produce these, I find they should only be entrusted to the battlefield commanders." Radric paused for a second and let out a deep sigh before thinking quietly to himself. "I only hope we don't have to use these talismans against Luna, but we do need to maintain the upper hand while I try to find a way to end this war. I guess they could still prove useful against the Wasteland monsters as well."

"My king, is there something wrong?" Wasukah asked, snapping Radric from his thoughts.

"No, my friend, don't worry. Anyways, my plan is to have the blacksmiths forge rings and mount the talismans to them. It will be easier to keep track of them and obviously make them more practical."

"Lord Radric, this is excellent. Father Gi has truly blessed you with great cunning. Perhaps you just may be the one to put an end to this perilous war."

"Yes, the great burning sphere has given me much wisdom, but let's not forget to give credit to our dear Octonia," Radric responded warmly as he looked to the sky where the majestic, giant phoenix of Sol was gracefully flying by. Upon hearing her name, she gently glided down towards them. Radric looked at her with a bright smile as the enormous bird touched down before them, dwarfing even the mighty king. He lovingly stroked her flaming feathers and praised her in a high-pitched manner that anyone would to a beloved pet. "Yes, that's right, you heard your name. Yes, you did. Who's a better kingdom guardian than that pompous wolf of Luna? It's you, it is." Radric continued to gently pet her as his voice fell to a normal tone. "It's hard to believe that you have been watching over this kingdom since its birth. Nearly a millennium. What an amazing creature you are, my beauty." Octonia chirped affectionately as she gently nibbled at one of Radric's shiny horns, causing him to chuckle playfully. "Seems only yesterday that you emerged from the ashes of your most recent reincarnation, yet you're already so big. And, of course, I never could have made these talismans without you and your ruby ashes." Wasukah watched on with a warm smile, witnessing the king in child-like bliss.

"Anyways, my lord, how long do you think it will take to create enough of these rings for the commanders?" Radric ceased his praising of Octonia, and she gently took flight, returning to the skies.

"Now that I've got the technique down, I'd say it would take me no greater than three months." He responded with confident pride.

"Very good, sir. Shall I make my leave and inform the commanders? Or was there something else?"

"No, you are free to go." He responded softly, returning his gaze to the kingdom. Wasukah bowed his head and promptly made his way out.

Radric remained in deep thought as a passing breeze caused his chestnut hair to float along the gentle gale. He peered into the smog-covered sky and felt his eyes grow misty as his thoughts raced. "I truly wish for this all to come to a swift end. What are we even fighting for anyway? I wish for a better life for my people. A life where the true sun, our great Father Gi, is able to grace the fields of Uçebar with his majestic rays, unimpeded by this endless fog. And where our artificial sun is no longer needed." He began to envision the world as he believed it to be in the past. "A world where the skies were once a brilliant baby blue, and the air was clean. So fresh that a deep inhale filled your lungs with a crisp wisp that would elicit euphoric satisfaction and ease the stress of the day." He took a deep inhale, imagining he was tasting that fresh Uçebar air. For a moment, he was overtaken with happiness. "Small, winged creatures, not much different from Octonia, filled the skies and graced the hills with soothing lullabies. Where many large and small bodies of water covered the land, apart from only existing in Aquaria. Children could play out in the sun, enjoying the comfort of Gi as he embraced them in loving light. Where Uçebians the world over lived together in peace, harmony, and without segregation." His dream-like state faded, and the dark gloom of reality filled his burning eyes.

"Ah, but can that truly ever happen? As confident as I feel and the purpose that burns in my heart...it's frustrating to think it may not happen for many more generations. But, even if it can't be me, it starts here. It begins with me. I must find a way to work towards change. To silence the fighting and vanquish the hate. I will make it my life's ambition to begin the climb towards peace, tranquility, and the return of beauty to our planet. But for now, I must continue to fight. My people aren't ready for change. I suppose, neither are Luna's. Somehow, I will plant the idea in all Uçebians, that we can live together, in peace." His eyes grew heavy, and he released a slight yawn. "A new morn comes tomorrow, with a new opportunity for change." With this final thought, he lifted his hands into the sky and pulled them down slowly, commanding the artificial sun to set. A peaceful silence and darkness fell over the beautiful kingdom of Sol as her inhabitance welcomed a needed sleep.

Three months later, Radric had finished forging the Ignisque talismans. In the late afternoon, a group of marine commanders made their way into the grand throne room, falling to bended knee and lowering their heads. The highest-ranking amongst them, Major General Gorg, was to address the king.

"Good morrow, highness. We bring news from the recon teams tasked to the borders of Luna." Greeted by nothing but silence, Gorg lifted his head to notice that the king was not currently seated on the royal throne. His face brightened with a tint of cherry as he was consumed with embarrassment.

"It's no use major general." An exhausted-sounding voice echoed from the rightmost corner of the room. "The king is in one of his daydreams about what he believes the world was like before the smog. He's been babbling to himself for hours." The man said with a slight sigh. Gorg's eyes shifted to see the general leaning against the wall with his arms crossed and staring towards the balcony where the entranced king remained. The commanders quickly sprung to their feet and stood before Wasu-kah, rendering him a salute. "At ease." He calmly instructed as he rendered a returning salute.

"General, we had some news for his majesty. However, seeing how you are here, I have news from the Luna Recon team." Gorg announced, pulling Wasukah's gaze from the king.

"Have they figured out any weakness to Queen Lycia's power?" Wasukah responded with wide eyes of intrigue.

"Colonel, please report the intel to the general," Gorg ordered as he gestured to the recon commander.

"General, we have learned three major facts about Queen Lycia of Luna. Firstly, her ability to shape-shift into her dire wolf form is only possible at night, under rays of moon light." The colonel began.

"Excellent, this is valuable news!" Wasukah responded as he clenched his fist with excitement, and a fiery determination glazed over his hazel eyes. "So, she is not as dangerous as we thought; there are limits to her abilities. Anyways, continue, son."

"Secondly, we have learned that the elder dire wolf, Silver Fang, is deceased. They burned his body three nights ago."

"I don't see how this is relevant to Lycia," Wasukah responded with a curious eyebrow. "But I guess that's good news; the other dire wolves pose no threat. They are merely transportation at this point. He was Luna's last defender; their strength grows weak."

"About that, sir, there is relevance to Lycia." The young marine continued. "There are rumors, that we have determined to be true, that Lycia herself...has given birth to the new guardian dire wolf pup of Luna. It has remained a secret for the last two years but has recently come to light."

"What? That is absolutely barbaric, colonel; it can't be true!" Wasukah shouted with disbelief. "Are you truly sure of this? It's just not natural. Even that accursed goddess Mana would never allow something like that. Would she?"

"Sir, I'm afraid we have very reliable sources that have provided us with this information." Gorg replied, joining the conversation.

"This is heinous..." Wasukah responded as he placed a thoughtful hand on his forehead, vigorously massaging his temples. "It's disgusting. It's bestiality! Do her people know of this? Perhaps we could use this to take her down? Even they would not accept her after that, it would be the downfall of their noble line."

"Well, sir—" Gorg responded with a sigh. "Despite how it may seem, and not to defend her...but it would seem Queen Lycia never laid with the beast."

"But how?" He responded, looking over to Gorg with shock. "If that were truly the case, goddess Mana has gone too far this time! She is too actively involved in Uçebian affairs. How dare she do something like this?" He recomposed himself, taking a deep breath. "No matter, we can still use this to our advantage. We can find a way to taint her reputation by making this public to her people. Only we do so in a way that implies she did lay with the beast."

"You see, sir..." Gorg said, clearing his throat after a nervous chuckle. "Her whole kingdom—already knows." Wasukah's eyes widened with disbelief. "Apparently, they are calling this "The Mystical Miracle." She is now more revered than ever before. They are calling her the true queen of Luna."

"This is madness!" Wasukah shouted before recomposing himself once more. "Colonel, I believe there was one more fact that has not yet been said. Might as well lay it on us now. I'm two more conversations away from a mental shut down, so let's get this over with."

"Well, sir, the last thing is..." The colonel's cheeks began slightly flush. "Her beauty is beyond compare." The listening commanders were stunned into silence. "I was instantly awestruck. From her majestic silver hair to her twitching wolf-like ears and tail.

But mostly, that luminescent eye, free of her swooping bangs. I personally find her beauty is her most dangerous attribute. How will the men be able to focus through such radiance?"

"Colonel, compose yourself!" Wasukah commanded with irritation. "This is utterly embarrassing! You dare to stand amongst the highest respects of the king's royal military and behave in such a disgraceful manner? What's worse, to hold such tender emotion for the enemy!" The colonel recomposed himself professionally and apologized as he was forcefully pushed back by Major General Gorg.

"Imbecile!" Gorg shouted. "Colonel, you have earned yourself—"

"What's all this then?" A booming and commanding voice cut into the squabble.

"Your majesty!" They shouted simultaneously as they fell to bended knee.

"Forgiveness, my king, we were having quite an *interesting* conversation," Wasukah responded, remaining on his knee.

"Very good then, on your feet, men. General, fill me in. The rest of you are dismissed."

Wasukah learned that Radric had completed the Ignisque talismans and began to fill in the king about what he was told regarding Queen Lycia. Obviously, leaving out the buffoonery of the young colonel. Wasukah was dismissed, and as he made his leave, Radric gently shook his head.

"Only at night, they say? How foolish!" He thought to himself. He traced his finger across the large claw-like scar across his upper body. "Have they forgotten when she gave me this?" He chuckled as his thoughts continued. "My artificial sun burned through the dreary sky that day. How easily things are forgotten with time...all but our hate, unfortunately." He rolled his eyes. "No, there is no limit to that woman's great power! Those fools." He retreated to the balcony and fell back into a daydream.

Lycia Wulfina, the Wolf Queen

The little queen of Luna stood on the balcony of her majestic palace. Her gaze into the smoggy night sky as she addressed her goddess.

"Mother Mana, bless you for gracing this pitiful gloom with your radiance. You are too proud to allow yourself to be hidden by the never-ending smog, as does Father Gi. It is your beauty and blessings that keep me and my people going." The moonlight began to shine hard on her as if she stood in a spotlight. She closed her eyes with a warm smile as she felt the tender, maternal embrace of her loving goddess, the light seemingly massaging her soul. Lycia's skin began to glow with her own pale luminescence as her heart was overcome with joy. As the encompassing glow faded, she returned her gaze to the sky.

"I can't help but feel sorry for the Solyans." She began to think to herself. "Their god neglects them, allowing them a mere sample of his majestic beams. It is a wonder they still even worship him. Ah, Sol, why must we fight? I may be good at it, but I hate to kill." A tear formed in her visible eye as her bangs gracefully hid the other. "I can still see them, all the faces of the men I've killed! Enemies or not, they are still Uçebians. Why must we fight? It won't always be like this, right? Eventually, the gloom will be triumphed over. I can feel it deep within my heart, for with every beat, I feel we draw closer to restoring our planet to how it was in the beginning." She returned to her throne room and approached a large, very old mural. It was painted by the Uçebians of old, many generations prior. Staring at it intensely, her tears slowly rolled down her soft cheeks as her majestic glow faded. She fell to her knees, maintaining her stare. "Uçebar, my beautiful Uçebar." She uttered weakly. "What have we done to you? Your crystal blue skies, all your wonderful creatures. The grass was once so green throughout the land. Trees bore colorful flaps on their branches. From what Mother told me, as told to her, Uçebians never used to be this way. No hate, no violence...no segregation. I long for an Uçebar like that. My people deserve an Uçebar like that." She gently rose to her feet. "If I cannot lead to change for this generation, I at least need to pave the road that will eventually be traveled down. We are all Uçebians, after all, so why must we be this way to each other? Besides, why must my love have to be that of secret? If only we could get past the hate, I can see it now. My strong husband swooping me off my feet and carrying me into our new home. Away from the palace, away from the noise. We would have beautiful children with whom I could spend every waking moment under the warmth of the true sun. At night, laying in a soft bed of grass under Mana's glorious light." She reached out a hand and placed it tenderly on the mural, shutting her eyes once more. Suddenly, she was snapped from her thoughts as a knock sounded from the enormous throne room doors.

"It's okay, please come in." She shouted in a welcoming manner as she used her tail to quickly dry her eyes. An elderly maiden and a small child made their way in.

"I'm sorry, highness, but she was just begging to come to see you." The maiden explained respectfully. "Is it alright that she is here?" Lycia looked down upon the little blonde-haired child who was staring at her with a smile of admiration. A warm smile formed on Lycia's face as her skin began to glow brightly.

"Of course it is!" Lycia responded happily. She gently fell to her knees and opened her arms wide. The small child's large brown eyes glistened and quivered with excitement. Lycia's adorable little peasant flew into her arms, and they enjoyed a quiet cuddle. The little girl opened her eyes and looked up to Lycia with a bright smile.

"Queen Lycia, you're so nice! I love you, Queen Lycia!" Lycia's wolf-like ears twitched playfully as her cheeks grew flush.

"Aww, well, aren't you the cutest!" Lycia stood to her feet, lifting the small girl and holding her gently in her arms. "So, to what do I owe the pleasure of a visit from such an adorable little princess?" The child energetically hopped from Lycia's arms.

"Oh, but your majesty, I'm not a princess. I'm a warrior, just like you, Queen Lycia! One day, I'll be the strongest in the kingdom!" She hopped up, kicking into the air, shouting, "Hiyah!" She didn't know how to land properly and came crashing down on her little bottom. "Ow!" She shrieked as her eyes quickly filled with tears. "Aww, I can never be a warrior if I get hurt trying to kick the air!" She pressed her tiny balled-up fists into her closed eyes and sobbed. "I just want to be like you, Queen Lycia, but I never can! I'm too weak!" She spoke brokenly through her tears. Lycia's glow slowly faded as she gently fell to her knees beside her sobbing little friend. She wrapped her arms around her, resting the little one's head against her chest. The little girl calmed down slightly, enjoying Lycia's warm embrace.

"Little one, it's too soon for you to give up." Lycia spoke in a tender and encouraging manner. "You are still young; you're just not ready yet. One day, you will be the great warrior you strive to be. You'll see, just never give up. Always keep trying to do your best." The little girl smiled as she looked up into Lycia's revealed luminescent eye. Slight, unfallen tears still glistening in her large eyes, Lycia dried them with a gentle sweep of her fluffy tail.

"Thank you, Queen Lycia, I promise to do my best!" The little girl responded as she waved goodbye, quickly spinning around and skipping out of the throne room.

"Oh wait, dear! Please don't run off!" The maiden shouted as she made chase. Lycia closed her eyes and giggled slightly. Her smile gently fell into a determined frown as she looked back towards the moonlit sky.

"Good night, my dear goddess, please continue to give me the strength and wisdom to rule." She made her way to her personal chambers and drifted off to sleep.

The next morning, Lycia awoke well before dawn, as she always had, and began to make her way to the training grounds. Mana was still gracing the skies with her presence and had not yet turned over ownership to Gi. As she walked outside, the guards standing watch bowed, rendering proper honors.

"Good morrow, your majesty." They announced in unison.

"Good morning, boys!" She responded as her wolf-like ears twitched playfully. One of the guards turned bright red and struggled to maintain his composure as he watched her skip away.

"Queen Lycia must be the daughter of Mana herself! To think a mortal being could be so radiant and perfect in every way! I never get tired of watching her train, I love this watch!" The second guard rolled his eyes and let out a frustrated sigh. He balled up his fist and uppercut his dazed partner in the chin, returning him to a proper, straightened posture.

"Compose yourself, corporal, we are on duty! Besides, you sound like a pathetic virgin when you speak like that." The corporal looked around frantically in embarrassment as he slid behind his comrade's back, covering his mouth.

"Hey, first off, I outrank you, so show some respect private!

Second, watch how loud you say that!" He began sternly, quickly switching to a nervous whisper. "She might hear you and mistake me for an adolescent!" The private's eyes widened with amusement as he began to chuckle. The corporal slid back to his post, releasing his hand from his comrade's mouth. Their eyes met, and the private's eyes narrowed as he continued to chuckle through his teeth.

"Well, now, corporal, I didn't realize you actually were." The private teased with a mischievous glare. The corporal's face grew hot as red steel.

"No! That is not what I meant. I just, I just, you know, don't want her getting the wrong impression!" Corporal stammered rather loudly. The private kept his judgmental stare with a gaze of disbelief.

"Hey guys," Lycia said gently, making her presence known. They both flinched and looked over to her. They were shocked not only because she was suddenly there but also because of how close she was to them, and they didn't even notice. "Are you two alright? You weren't scared of cute little me, were you?" She giggled playfully as she teased. The guards tried to act poised as if nothing had happened and stood professionally.

"No, highness, I merely thought there was a bee in my armor, and my jumping must have surprised my comrade." The corporal responded with a nervous chuckle. "But as you can see, I was clearly mistaken, as there is no bee here." The queen became puzzled, placing a thoughtful finger on her cheek as she gazed at the sky.

"Bees are extinct though, aren't they?" She responded impishly. Corporal's cheeks grew red with embarrassment. "Mana keeps what little flowers we have in the kingdom alive now." She lowered her head and smiled playfully, awaiting his response. He remained silent, and she released another playful giggle. "Anyways, boys, is everything alight? I heard quite a bit of commotion over here."

"Well, my queen, the corporal had something he wanted to tell you, and I was trying to encourage him to do so." The private announced with a devious smile. The corporal froze with nervousness as her revealed eye fell to his gaze. His thoughts began to race frantically as he pondered what to say. "Oh no! Why would he do that? What do I say? Oh goddess, don't sound like a virgin, don't say anything stupid. I have to say something. She's just staring at me...staring with that big, beautiful silver eye." He fell into a daydream where he confidently confessed his crush to her. He suddenly felt a sharp elbow to his side, snapping him to reality as his frantic thoughts continued. "Shit! How long was I daydreaming? Her ears twitched; she's looking at me with confusion as to why I'm not talking!"

"Go on...say something." Private whispered through his teeth.

"I...we...majesty...I mean...he..." Corporal stammered pathetically. Before he could get out a coherent sentence, Lycia giggled.

"Well, it's okay; nothing seems to be wrong here after all. I'll get back to training." She responded as she drew her axe and began twirling it with impressive speed until it began to look as if it were a solid circular blade. She happily skipped away, as she maintained her twirling speed.

"You're an idiot! How did you ever make corporal?" Private said bluntly.

"I'm hopeless." Corporal thought to himself as he slouched and sighed weakly.

Back in the training grounds, Lycia fought as if she were in the very heat of battle. She pushed herself to the last of her limits with everything she had. Her mind was a blank state of concentration, with random thoughts of her people and children flashing through her mind. As her intense session came to a halt, she fell to her hands and knees, sweating profusely as she struggled to catch her breath. The artificial sun now warmed the skies as a maternal voice gently floated in the air.

"My queen, you work too hard. Please, do take care of yourself. You are already the most powerful warrior in all of Luna." Remaining on her hands and knees, Lycia lifted a fist to her face and stared at it intensely. Her grip was so tight that her hand began to tremble.

"In Luna, yes..." Lycia responded to the woman in a frustrated tone. "But if I'm to keep our kingdom safe, I must be the most powerful in Uçebar! I may have scarred Radric in the past, but that was only because he had not yet experienced my wolf form before. He still bests me in my Uçebian form, and now he's learning to best me in my wolf form!" She slammed her fist into the ground.

"You make our kingdom proud, my queen." The woman replied warmly. "However, every good warrior needs to eat to keep up her strength. Come inside and have some breakfast." Lycia's frustration seemingly washed away in an instant, and she hopped to her feet happily.

"Coming, Mother!" Lycia responded as she skipped over to the middle-aged woman.

"My queen, I've said it before; you don't have to call me that." The woman responded in a soothing, respectful tone. "Elizya works just fine." Lycia wrapped her arms around Elizya and rested her little cheek against Elizya's chest. Lycia began to glow brightly as she gently shut her eyes, looking like a small teen in Elizya's embrace.

"But you raised me, Mother. So that is what you will always be." She responded with a warm smile. Lycia's parents were killed on the battlefield two years after she was born. Elizya was a close friend of Lycia's mother and took it upon herself to raise the young queen. All of Lycia's kindness, perseverance, wisdom, and outlook on life was taught to her by Elizya. Lycia was very fond of her and always clung to her like a small child needing to be nurtured.

"Twenty-five years later, and you're still the same little girl I raised," Eliza responded with a loving gleam in her crystal blue eyes. "If you insist, your majesty, call me what you like. Now, let's get you inside and well-fed."

After breakfast, Lycia entered the grand meeting hall, where battle preparation, tactics, and general important information were discussed by the highest-ranking individuals in the royal Lunian ranks. Lycia approached the table, and all stood from their seats as her presence was announced.

"Rise, for her majesty has arrived!" Elizya shouted sternly. As Lycia sat, the rest followed. Elizya remained standing to the right of the queen. A shorter middle-aged man stood and cleared his throat.

"My queen," he said with a bow. "I, General Rehcumber, have assumed the position of commander for all of your royal military." His emerald eyes quivered as he continued. "It is with much regret that I inform you of the passing of former General Corqulox." He bowed his head. "May the mother of mystery watch over him and guide him to his next life." Lycia's visible eye became misty, and tears slowly slid down the curve of her rosy cheeks. She bowed her head and said a prayer silently to herself for her fallen warrior. Lycia loved her people; that was common knowledge. But what most didn't know, apart from her council, was that she wept for each and every one of her fallen soldiers individually. She lifted her head, dried her eyes with her tail, and nodded to let the general know he could continue. "Your majesty, my scouts have discovered a disturbing piece of information on the situation within Sol's walls." Lycia's visible eye grew wide.

"Please continue, general, enlighten my council."

"We have reports that King Radric has developed a talisman that allows his marines..."

"Allows what general? Please cease with the suspenseful pause!"

"Of course, majesty, forgive me...He has developed a talisman that allows his marines to harness fire, as he does." Commotion erupted around the table, but Lycia remained calm, her gaze fixed on the stone model of Uçebar that lay on the table. After thirty seconds of chaotic arguing commenced, Lycia shouted sternly, bringing it to a halt.

"That's enough!" Her voice fell gentle. "My dear council members, look what's happening to you. You are allowing the evil of Sol to cause us to fight amongst ourselves." The council members wore shame on their faces. "Let's remember that our enemy is strong, and we are weak if we are divided." They nodded their heads. "This is a very serious matter, for if this has truly been done...Sol may have become much more dangerous than ever before! So, for that reason, during the next raid, I will be accompanying the marines on the battlefield."

"My queen, please, I know it has been a while since your axe has tasted the freshly slain flesh of a Solyan marine...but things are different now. No one may be able to strike you with their weapon, but if magic?" The general responded in a concerned tone.

"See here, my good general!" Lycia responded with energetic valor. "I am the queen of this kingdom; my people need me. And the love I have for my people is my strength. Nothing Sol can do will strike me down! Besides, accompanying me will not only be the finest military force in all the land but my young dire wolf Onceli."

"My queen, you mustn't!" Elizya shouted in protest, her eyes growing misty. "She's only a baby! She's your daughter!" Lycia closed her eyes and stood slowly from her seat, resting her hands against the table, her gaze on the floor.

"I love you, Mother, but never question me. Especially before my own council." Lycia responded gently yet sternly. Tears gently rolled down Elizya's cheeks.

"Forgive me, my lady, I was out of line." Lycia opened her eyes and wore a warm smile.

"Besides, I'll never allow anything to happen to my sweet little girl." Lycia spoke cheerfully and confidently. "She may only be a pup, but she is growing fast. She needs to learn how to be strong. Otherwise, she could lose her life. She won't do any fighting; I just need her to watch. I will make Sol pay for the pain it causes my people!" The council members all cheered, throwing their fists in the air. However, one member was not celebrating. Elizya stood quietly with her back now turned to the table.

"My lady, I hope you know what you are doing." She thought to herself in a state of worry. "Your heart breaks for every man and woman we lose on the battlefield, even for your own enemies. How much more can you take, and how will your heart handle the loss of your only daughter? I just...I cannot bear to see you in such pain."

"Alright, my council members, you are dismissed!" Lycia shouted in a chipper manner. "May the mother of mystery, the mother of the night, always watch over you." She remained smiling in front of her chair until the doors were closed behind the final member. As the doors shut, her silver eye began to water. She turned to her right, gazing upon her worried mother, whose eyes were still shut, lost in thought. Lycia embraced her tightly from behind, Elizya's long pink hair tangling up in the silver strands of her own. Upon feeling her embrace, Elizya's eyes opened wide. Her crystal spheres clouded with worry and glistened with unfallen tears.

"I know why it is that you stand stiff and lost in thought," Lycia spoke gently. "I'm sorry that I'm causing you this worrisome grief. But please understand, I have a reason for everything I do." She smiled, releasing her embrace, took hold of Elizya's wrist, and gently spun her around. She took both of Elizya's hands in hers and stared up into her eyes with a warm smile. Looking down, Elizya matched her gaze, and her worry seemed to fade at the sight of Lycia's smile. "It will be okay. Have some faith in me, Mother." Elizya smiled as Lycia playfully swayed their hands around.

"Yes, of course, my lady, you're right." She gently left Lycia's grasp and departed from the meeting hall after bidding her good day. Lycia's smile faded.

"Radric, you fool, what are you trying to prove here? How will this help bring about peace?" She thought to herself, becoming irritated.

"Always one-upping me at every turn, always one step ahead of me!" She shouted as her fury erupted. She threw out an arm across the table, knocking several pieces off the map with her forearm. Her face grew dark red, and her breathing became heavy. She ran to her chambers, drew her axe, and decapitated the first statue that came into her view. As the head rolled to the floor, her eyes widened, her teeth gritted, and she slid down onto her knees, dropping her axe to the floor. She exhaled deeply.

"Now look what you've done! I'm destroying my palace because of you." Her angered thoughts continued. Slowly, she calmed down. "What am I doing? This is exactly what I corrected my council for. I can't allow him to get to me. I must remain composed...you won't get to me, Radric of Sol." She dove into her bed and drifted away for a nap before continuing her day.

Karakus Wartox

The next morning, in Sol, Radric rose from his bed. He walked out on to the balcony and slammed his powerful hands together. He raised his arms, commanding the artificial sun to rise and slightly brighten the land. Radric jumped down from the balcony, cracking the ground beneath him as he landed. The two guards standing watch jumped slightly out of surprise. Recomposing themselves, they saluted the king.

"Good morrow, your high..." Radric was already walking away with his back turned to them.

"At ease, gentleman." He responded before grumbling to himself. "Freaken goofballs, what the hell kind of training are these soldiers receiving?"

"What was that, my lord? Did you require assistance?" One of the guards shouted out to him, having heard his grumbling.

"No, no, carry on!" Radric shouted back in a frustrated manner, waving his hand slightly as he continued away from them. Radric was not a glory hound of a king, nor did he expect his people to be stiff and serious as he walked by. They gave him their respect, and that was all he wanted. He would make regular trips to town and spend time with his subjects. As he made his way into town, a group of small children playing tag began to run around his feet. One hid behind one of his giant legs. He let out a booming laugh and gently patted them on the head. He stopped by a fish stall run by an elderly man to check on him and brighten his day. As they engaged in small talk, a mysterious figure stalked the king in the shadows.

"This time, you fool, you are..." The mysterious man thought to himself as he planned his next move.

"Mine!" He shouted as he sprung from the shadows with outstretched arms in an attempt to grapple the king. Just before he could make contact, Radric drifted slightly to one side, causing him to smash into the old man's stall. Fish flew into the air like leaves caught on rushing wind.

"By the name of Gi, my fish!" The poor old man cried. "I had just received them from trade with Aquaria. Now they are filthy and mangled!" He continued screaming incoherently at the mysterious man. Radric approached the mysterious man with an angered expression on his face. The man matched his gaze from the ground, and the tension grew. The old man fell silent, absorbed by the intense yet silent moment, and became too fearful to move. Radric offered his hand to the man, who reluctantly accepted his aid. After being lifted up like a child's toy, the staredown continued. Radric's stare intensified as his gaze burned in the brown pools of his confident opponent. The old man looked back and forth between the two large men, still unable to bring himself to move from the obvious skirmish that was about to take place. Suddenly, the mysterious man cried out in childlike admiration with a big, goofy smile on his face.

"Damn cousin, how the hell did you know I was coming?" The old man's expression became blank with disbelief. Radric chuckled and wrapped his cousin in a tight headlock with one arm.

"Come on, Karakus! You didn't think you'd get me with a

pathetic attack such as that, now, did you? Even when size favored you, you couldn't stop your little cousin." Radric continued to boast as Karakus's face began to turn blue. He began frantically tapping Radric's powerful arm, begging for release. Radric released him with a cheeky grin as he went crashing to the ground. He breathed in heavily as his face returned to a normal golden-brown color.

"I don't know, I thought I was pretty stealthy there," Karakus replied in a winded manner. They both laughed together as Karakus slowly came to his feet. Radric began to morph into his maniacal laughing posture and fell into a fit of cartoonish laughter. Karakus's face went blank, and the old man stared dumbfounded, as he surprisingly had never witnessed the king's signature ridiculous laugh.

"So there, big guy, still doing that weird laugh of yours, huh?" Karakus spoke mockingly. "I always thought it was just some teenage phase, yet here you stand, a grown man of twenty-three, ruler of this mighty kingdom, making a fool of yourself with that amateur actor's laugh." Radric came to an immediate halt. His flaming orange eyes locked on to Karakus, who began to back away nervously. "Now listen cuz...I was only joking." He began chuckling fearfully. "See, look, we're laughing." Radric's face remained serious and unamused. Karakus fell still as he awaited his cousin's move. Radric drilled his fist into Karakus's abdomen, causing him to hunch over. Radric grabbed his head, picking him up over his shoulders and smashing him to the ground. Karakus remained on his back, stunned in the dirt.

"Make fun of my laugh, will you? Well, how's that 'Lil Kracky'?" Karakus's eyes dilated, and his face became hot as flames. Rolling over on his hands, he tossed out his leg in a circular motion, knocking Radric off his feet. Radric crashed to the ground, and Karakus hurled himself into the air.

"How many times do I have to tell you? Never call me that

name!" He shouted as he landed on top of Radric, driving his intertwined fists into his chest. The frightened old man became frantic.

"This is insane, I can't tell if they are friends or enemies! I need to get out of here." He shouted as he gathered up his fish and scurried off. Radric burst into the air, sending small shards of rocks in all directions. He drove his heel into Karakus's head as he made his descent. Returning to his feet, Karakus hopped behind the king in an attempt to grapple him. Just before he could grab hold, Radric backflipped into the air. Karakus's eyes grew with disbelief as he witnessed his large cousin gracefully gliding on the breeze, staring down at him with a sinister grin. As Radric landed, he took Karakus's head and tossed him into the air. Radric hurled himself towards Karakus with his fist readied. Karakus responded with a kick before Radric could deliver. As their descent continued, they exchanged blows, seemingly equally matched. Soon, Radric caught Karakus off guard with a powerful shot to the gut, and while stunned, he smashed him to the ground. He put all his monstrous weight on Karakus's back, drilling his knees into him.

"Oh...kay...okay, you win. I submit!" He said weakly. "*Your highness.*" Radric grabbed him by his short purple hair and lifted him up to his face.

"What's with the sarcastic tone behind your voice, huh?" Radric said bluntly.

"What are you talking about?" Karakus replied playfully with a nervous grin. "I meant sincerely." A sweet-sounding feminine voice shouted from the distance, interrupting them.

"Lord Radric? Sire? Oh, there you are! My king, I must speak with you." A timid girl of average height scurried her way over to the king, who was still holding Karakus by his hair. She arrived out of breath and hunched over slightly, gasping for air. She leaned back, taking one final breath and releasing it slowly.

Resting in her hands was a gold-plated book. She was the king's handmaiden and scribe. Everything discussed in their grand council meetings was written in this book. A very important item, to say the least. She spoke timidly with her cheeks glowing. "Um, your majesty, we need to go. You have a council meeting to prepare for. We, uh...we must make our way to the council chambers." Radric stared into Karakus's nervous eyes with a mischievous smile.

"Saved by my cute little scribe, consider yourself lucky, cousin." He released his hold over him, and Karakus gently fell to his knees, letting out a deep sigh of relief. The young woman stood dazed from what she heard.

"Did...he just call...*me*, cute?" She thought.

"Well, alrighty then, Efyna, my fair maiden, shall we be going?" He held his arms out in the manner of "after you." She remained in a daze, her golden eyes staring blankly and lifelessly into the distance. Radric remained still for a second, then spoke again in a concerned manner. "Um Efyna?" He squatted down, resting his forearms on his knees so that he was at her eye level. He waved his hand in her face in an attempt to snap her out of her trance. When she didn't react, he gently poked her on the nose. She suddenly snapped back into reality and gasped. Surprised to see him so close to her, at eye level, and feeling his large finger still resting on her nose, she shouted out in embarrassment, tossing the golden-clad book into the sky. She hid her face behind her hands and released an embarrassed moan. Radric stood to his feet and snatched the book out of the air before it could drop.

"Oops, wouldn't want this hitting you on the head." He bent back down and held out the book to her. "Here you go, ma'lady." She lifted her head from her hands, looking into his calm eyes with awe. She reached out for the book, and when she touched it, her cheeks became bright pink. Her gaze was locked in his, and his gentle smile made her feel like she had not a care in the world.

"Well, this sure has been fun, cousin; we should do it again sometime." Karakus chuckled sarcastically, interrupting their moment. Radric let out an annoyed sigh and, releasing his hand from the book, stood to his feet. He glared at his cousin with unforgiving eyes. "What, what did I say?" Karakus asked impishly.

"Oh, never mind!" Radric replied bluntly as he rolled his eyes. "Come, my assistant, as you have said, we have much to get done today." She released a disappointed sigh and ran up by his side as he continued towards the palace. The king smiled sinisterly as he walked past his cousin. "By the way, Karakus...you're going to pay that old man 200 gold pieces for the damage you caused." Karakus's mouth dropped with disbelief, and Radric mockingly patted him on the shoulder as he continued by.

"Wait, wait!" Karakus pleaded as he snapped from his stunned silence. "Oh, come on, cuz! Are you serious? That's like a week's pay!" Radric continued without acknowledging him. "Come on! It was you who moved out of the way..." He began muttering to himself. "Wouldn't have hit the dang cart otherwise..." Radric bent over, scooping up a large rock. He quickly spun around and launched the rock towards Karakus's face. Karakus let out a fearful cry, but before he could react, the rock made contact with his face, knocking him to his back. Slowly coming to his feet with one hand holding his nose, he shouted nasally. "Hey! What was that for?" Radric continued to walk away but looked back slightly towards him with a grin.

"That'll teach you not to mumble under your breath about me."

"How the hell did he hear that?" Karakus's eyes grew wide as he thought to himself in disbelief.

Later, Radric and Efyna made their way into the grand hall,

where his council awaited their arrival. Efyna spastically tried to gain composure of herself to announce the arrival of the king.

"All ri...(Squeak)" As she attempted to shout, her voice cracked pathetically. "Rise for the..." Before she could finish, the council members erupted into thunderous laughter, slamming their hands on the table and slapping each other on the shoulder. Tears began to flow from Efyna's eyes; she only wanted to do her best for the king, but she was always so nervous. She slowly collapsed to her knees, resting the gilded book on her lap. Her face was a bright red, and the world around her seemed to be a dark void with muffled laughter engulfing her. There was, however, one individual who was not laughing.

"So, because of a slight crack in her voice, that makes it alright not to rise as I enter the room?" Radric's voice cut into the laughter with thunderous force. Immediately, the council members composed themselves and stood to their feet. Efyna's tears ceased, and she looked up to see Radric, yet again, crouched before her, holding out his hand with a warm smile. "Please, miss, allow me to help you up." Her cheeks began to glow a familiar dark pink as she reached for his hand. He brought her to her feet and beckoned her to head to her place by the right of his chair. The council looked on in annoyance as to why he was treating a commoner from an enemy kingdom in such a way. But as he sat down, they followed, and the meeting began. Before it could fully kick-off, however, at the left-hand corner of the table sat a miserable-looking, familiar fellow. His nose was bandaged and bloody. Major General Gorg looked over to him, chuckling slightly.

"What, see something you like, Gorg? You know what? You what your name sounds like? Like the sound of vomit!" Karakus shouted in an irritated manner making gagging sounds as he said Gorg's name. "Gah-org...see, that's what your name sounds like. It sounds like sour stomach from too much ale!" Gorg's expression fell serious.

"Ah, Karakus, mature as always, I see," Gorg responded plainly. A smile then road his face as he spoke in a manner of holding back laughter. "I was just wondering, what happened to your nose?" Unable to contain himself, Gorg fell into a fit of laughter.

"Yes, Karakus, how *did* that happen?" Radric cut in with a snide, sarcastic tone. The table erupted into laughter once more.

"Well, I'm just glad it wasn't me this time." Efyna thought to herself, hiding the amusement from her face gently behind the gilded book. She soon realized that Karakus was looking right at her as if he knew exactly what was going through her mind. She became embarrassed and began looking around frantically. "Oh gees, am I that transparent. Dear Mana!"

"Hey, hey, Karakus! Guess who's not invited to this year's reindeer games?" General Wasukah chimed in through the laughter. Everyone grew louder, and even Efyna was smirking slightly now. Radric slammed his giant fist repeatedly on the table, covering his eyes with the other. Soon, he tilted back and, throwing out his arms, fell into his trademark maniacal laugh. The room immediately fell silent, but Radric continued for a few seconds before he realized the quiet that had engulfed the room.

"Whoops, did I just ruin the moment?" Radric spoke in a slightly embarrassed manner. Everyone at the table wore similar embarrassed expressions on their faces as they stared blankly at him. Radric cleared his throat and composed himself professionally. "Well, let's begin then, shall we. Now, the fun must come to an end."

The King's Cunning

General Wasukah stood to his feet, and the council meeting truly began. Efyna was ready to scribe all that was discussed into the golden book.

"Well, as I'm sure most of us already know, the king has completed ten talismans of power. They have been embedded into rings to be worn by the marine commanders we deemed worthy. They are getting acquainted with harnessing the flames as we speak, and training is going swiftly. They shall be combat-ready by nightfall tomorrow."

"Excellent, general, this is great news," Radric exclaimed. "Oh, I do have some slight, last-minute changes to make to our plans, however."

"But sir...you, yourself, said our original plan was flawless. Why the sudden change?" Wasukah inquired with wide eyes.

"The plan was flawless, general," Radric said with a boastful chuckle. "However, recent developments have made it so that Luna may actually be aware of our Ignisque talismans already." The table erupted into murmuring out of sheer surprise.

"Highness, if this has truly happened..." Gorg said, hopping from his seat energetically. "Then a mole must have made its way past my watchful eye. As the intelligence commander, I take full responsibility for this failure." He fell to bended knee, lowered his head, and placed his right arm across his chest. "Please, ma' lord, behead me publicly. For I have failed!" The council members gasped with shock.

"No, no, don't say that," Efyna said quietly to herself with one hand covering her mouth. Radric began to laugh and grabbed Gorg by the signature red lizard skin armor of the Solyan military and brought him to his feet. Gorg looked to his king with confusion.

"My dear Gorg, you are but the biggest fool I have ever met if you truly believed I would behead such a man as yourself. Especially for something as insignificant as this." Radric responded with genuine ease. Gorg's eyes grew with shock.

"But, sir! Insignificant? How could it be insignificant? Luna knows of our weapon. We have lost the element of surprise. They will even be one step ahead of our plans!" He lowered his head, and his voice became weaker as he continued. "As head of recon...I should have caught this."

"Don't worry, general, we can use this to our advantage too," Radric replied confidently, placing his mighty hand in a comforting manner on Gorg's shoulder. Gorg's gaze returned to the king. "Now, please return to your seat." When Gorg returned to his position at the table, Radric cleared his throat. "Now, Queen Lycia is no fool. But then, neither am I. I realized we had a mole when you gave me the report from the marine recon team, Wasukah." The council members gasped with shock and confusion. "I didn't mention it before because I am not concerned by it. No matter what they know, I will always find a way to remain one step ahead."

"Your confidence is admirable, my king, but I still believe we should be worried about our tactics being brought to light of Luna," Wasukah responded. "However, that aside. If I may ask, how is it that you figured out about the mole based on the recon team's intel?"

"Is it not obvious, my dear general?" Radric said with a chuckle and playful smile. "The recon team reported that Lycia can only transform at night, under the silver moonlight." The council members looked on intently, awaiting his point. "Come now, my dear council. Most of you, if not all of you, were there... were you not? The day she gave me this." He traced his hand down the large claw-marked scar across his torso. "The day I first met Lycia on the battlefield and received my first and only battle scar. She had taken on her wolf form...in broad artificial daylight!" Multiple gasps of sheer disappointment erupted throughout the room. "So clearly, they were purposefully giving away misleading information. Which means they were aware the recon team would be skulking around their city limits." The council members remained in silence, miserably staring at the ground. They couldn't believe they had forgotten such a memorable battle and were so easily fooled. "Don't be disappointed in yourselves, comrades. Besides, I know the perfect counter to the fact that Luna knows of the Ignisque. All we need is for me to join the marines on the battlefield."

"But my king, not that we wouldn't be proud and honored to have you amongst our marines again...how is that a counter to their knowledge?" Wasukah responded with uncertainty.

"Well, if this hunch of mine is indeed true and they know of my talismans...then I can only imagine that Lycia herself will join the battlefield and take out the marines bearing them. She also may try to get ahold of one as well. But she is no match for me, I'll be happy to embarrass her out there as I always do! Well... except for the initial meet." He said boastfully with a chuckle. Everyone at the table shouted the signature battle cry of the Solyan military. Radric began laughing uncontrollably, falling into his usual fit. His intensity building and building with each breath. Efyna gently tapped him on the back of his arm from where she stood, bringing him to an immediate halt. He cleared his throat and recomposed himself. "Ah, right then. Well, that will do, you are dismissed."

As everyone was making their way from the grand hall, Radric called out to Efyna, halting her departure.

"Efyna, not you. Won't you please join me in my chambers on the balcony?" She let out a nervous moan and spun around. Her rosy cheeks aglow at the thought of alone time with the king, in his personal chambers no less. She anxiously joined him and stood beside the gentle giant as he gazed into the sky. He spoke in a soft voice. "Efyna, my dear young elf. Have you ever wondered what the sky was like?"

"Majesty, I don't understand what you are asking me." She said with a puzzled stare. He chuckled slightly, causing her to tense up and look away from him. Sensing her tension, he tried to ease her mind.

"Take it easy, it was a deep question. I understand if you don't quite follow where I'm going." She smiled and sighed softly as she returned her gaze to him. His gaze was still towards the smoggy sky. "What I mean is, what the sky was like before the fog. Before the hate...before we destroyed our planet with war." She gazed in awe at his words. "I think about it all the time. Wondering just how beautiful it must have been." A gentle smile formed on his face. "You know, they say the sky was blue. Not just any blue, but a light shade. A cool blue, a kind that, no matter what the peril...if you stared into it, your troubles would float away. Carried off by the gentle breeze." Her eyes began to glisten with unfallen tears. She had never experienced this side of the Radric before. He released a slight chuckle. "I come out here every night before I cause the sun to set." He gently outstretched his arms as if to catch the breeze he envisioned in his mind as his eyes gently shut. "And I imagine that I'm there. Where the crystal blue waters sparkle in the glorious, natural light of Father Gi himself. Where the breeze coming off the ocean of Aquaria is so clean and fresh, it fuels the very soul. I imagine animals frolicking in the fields, loving animals. Not these fell creatures that prowl our wastelands. I'm among them, just playing in the green grass. Yes, did you know that grass was once soft, and green? They say Gi's light gives color to the plants. Even the trees bore color of some kind, or so I hear." Efyna's tears gently rolled down the curve of her cheek. Radric shifted his gaze as he heard her sniffling slightly. "Are you alright?" He asked gently.

"Mhm." She softly uttered as she kept her gaze on him. "It's just...the way you talk about the planet is so beautiful. I never knew you could be so poetic, my king."

"I may be a giant, I may be a seasoned and skilled warrior, but you'll find my lady...I'm truly just a big softy at heart." He said with a slight chuckle. He suddenly felt Efyna wrap her tiny arms around his forearm and cuddle up to him, resting her cheek against his arm. He released a surprised, sharp "Hmm?" As his gaze fell over her, she suddenly realized what she was doing and quickly let go. Her face became red, and she did her best to hide her cheeks with her hands.

"My sincerest apologies, my king...I got a little caught up in the moment!" Radric chuckled softly and returned his gaze to the sky, and she followed in his example. Radric raised his hands and commanded the sun to set, allowing Mana's glorious light to penetrate through the gloomy sky. "Your majesty?" She inquired timidly.

"Hmm?" He replied, looking over to her.

"Why did you invite me out here tonight? Why are you telling me all this?" He chuckled again, this time slightly louder than usual, and placed his enormous hand on her tiny shoulder.

"What? Can a king not spend time with his faithful servant?"

He asked with a warm smile. Her cheeks lit up, and she moaned nervously.

"Well...I...yeah...of course." She stammered. He lifted his hand, and they both turned their gaze to the courtyard garden where a young violinist was practicing his music. Efyna became excited and ran to the edge of the balcony, closest to where the melody floated on the night air. She lifted herself slightly as she balanced on the rail. Her cheeks still aglow, her gaze fell on the young musician as her tension vanished. "Oh wow, how beautiful." She said sweetly.

"Ah yes, my late-night violinist, it has been a while since I last heard from you," Radric spoke gently. He walked over to her and bent his front knee, extending his arm out, and offered his hand to her. "My lady, tis a gorgeous night, and with such beautiful music, t'would be a shame to allow it to go to waste." He said playfully. "Might you do me the honor of a dance?" She blushed deeply before slowly extending her hand to his. He lifted her up and placed her feet on the railing, holding her hand tight and ensuring she didn't fall. They danced together along the sides of the balcony. They each worked together to maintain Efyna's balance. At each new segment, he would lift her slightly and twirl her over the protruding post. This was the first time Efyna felt at ease in a long while; the poor girl was always so high-strung. Trapped in a never-ending cycle of anxiety. Radric knew this, and despite what anyone would have thought had they witnessed the two atop the palace balcony...he wanted to do whatever he could to make her feel more relaxed. As the music faded, he lifted her up by her waist and placed her down on the balcony. She wrapped her arms around his abdomen and rested her cheek against him.

"Oh, my king, I apologize if this is out of line, but I must embrace you! It has been many years since I have felt so comfortable and so calm. I almost forgot how good it feels to have

my heartbeat at a normal pace. Thank you, my king, thank you."
Radric smiled and wrapped an arm gently around her as they
enjoyed the moment together. After a short while, Radric broke
the silence gently.

"Efyna, why is it you are so faithful to me? What have I done
to earn your loyalty?" She released him and backed away slowly.

"Sire, what do you mean?" She responded weakly.

"Well I did take you from Luna when I was a young teen.
Despite me taking you from your home, you serve me loyally
and without question. Why is that?"

"Majesty...I...I..." She felt guilt building in her anxious heart.

"Forgive me, I ruined the beautiful moment we were having."
He responded with a weak sigh. "Forget I asked. Please leave me
now." She walked towards the exit with misery clouding over
her. Before she could reach the door, he called out to her. "Oh,
and Efyna." She turned back to him with intrigue. "The way you
felt when we were dancing. That ease, serenity, and peace. I wish
for you to remain that way from now on." He said sincerely with
a smile. "Can you do that for me?" She bowed her head with a
warm smile.

"Of course, my king. I will." She responded softly. Feeling
more giddy, she turned and skipped from his chambers. As she
disappeared from sight, Radric's smile faded.

"Careful there, ol' boy, getting into some very taboo voo-
doo over here." He placed a thoughtful hand on his forehead as
he pondered. He shook his head. "No, it's not about that. She
needed this. How long could her small, frail body and fragile
heart have kept up with such a level of stress? I wish I had only
seen it sooner. I could have better helped the situation." He lifted
his arms to the sky and gazed toward the moon with his eyes
shut.

"Dear mother of mystery, I realize our kingdoms don't see
eye to eye, and there is a tension old as time between you and

Father Gi...But I ask this favor of you not for me but for her."
Suddenly, the moonlight fell upon him. His eyes opened with
shock. He could see nothing else around him but pale, glorious
luminescence and began to feel a feminine embrace as if the
same size as he. "Praise you, mother of the night, for hearing
me out! Please watch over and guide your daughter, Efyna. Forgive me for removing her from your kingdom. But I had to do
it. I'm sure you know. It was the only way the men would not
have killed her. She is a mystical race, fading with time, as did
my own. I know what it is like to be the last of my kind; I had to
help her. Besides, she was just a child! She didn't deserve such a
cruel punishment for the sins and hatred that she was innocent
of." Mana's embrace grew warmer and tighter as he spoke. The
feeling was like nothing he had ever experienced. "Dear Mother
Mana, this is my wish. Please protect her, keep her fragile heart
at ease, and her mind calm. Allow her to enjoy the life I am trying to give her." As he finished, the moon's light faded. Radric's
heart was joyful yet filled with sorrow at the same time. Battle
was upon them, and as much as he was good at it, he hated to
kill. He climbed into his bed, ready to get some sleep after a long
day.

The Grand Feast of Sol

The day before the raid was to take place, and after all preparations were made, Radric addressed the people from atop the palace balcony that overlooked the city square.

"My people!" He bellowed. "Tonight is a night of celebration. We will soon be attempting to establish a forward camp deep within the wastelands, close to Luna's territory. From there, we will build our strength and eventually pillage their kingdom. Their military will be slaughtered, for they can never be trusted. The civilians and children will be forced to be servants and builders. Sol will have dominance!" Radric said this to appease his people, but it was not his intension whatsoever. He was still trying to come up with a way to end the fighting with as little blood shed as possible. But he knew his people were not ready to accept such an idea, so he had to play his part. The crowd erupted into a thunderous roar of cheering. Radric raised his hand, and the crowd calmed. "Today, we feast. For tomorrow, at night fall...we march!" The cheering erupted again, and everyone made their way to the vast Solyan feasting grounds. Scattered throughout were thousands of tables, different fun things for the children, a large buffet table, and, most importantly, dozens of large casks of

Solyan Ale. There was enough food and drink to last the entire day, and that was exactly what the Solyans had in mind. Everyone was invited to these feasts. The marines gathered their families. Some were fearful they would never see their loved ones again, but they remained positive so as not to worry them for one last day of innocent fun. Well, some of it was innocent. Several large mugs of ale crashed together as the roar of drunken warriors filled the air. There was laughter throughout the tables, fools stumbling around, slurring their words. People danced, and small, playful fights broke out. But some were not so playful. A large kingdom guard approached a table where many of the marines without families were sitting. Behind him followed two other guards, all three wearing mischievous smiles. Silence fell over the table of marines as the stare-off began. Solyan marines were generally small and athletically built. Far better suited for long voyages through the wastes than their bulky, slow kingdom guard brethren. The leader of the mischievous group stumbled slightly as his drunken eyes rolled around in their sockets.

"Lookie here, boys! (Hick) Take a look at the scrawny children's dollies that we are sending out to the wastelands! (Hick) How much you wanna bet only half of them return." The leader disrespectfully teased, slurring terribly. What the kingdom guards were unaware of was at this very table was Colonel Axaiyan, who sprung from his seat at the table's edge in a blind fit of rage. His short black hair, just long enough to float on the rush of wind, fell to resting as he tackled the guard to the ground. Digging his forearm into the colossal man's neck, he pinned him in place with his thighs around his torso. The guard spoke nervously upon realizing there was a high-ranking officer among them. "Oh, uh, colonel. Didn't see you there, sir. (Hick)" Axaiyan brought his face close to the guard. His violet eyes pierced deeply though the guard, enveloped in anger. "Forgive me, colonel, I didn't mean any harm; it was a joke. I was waiting...(hick) for the right moment to drop the punchline."

"A joke!" Axaiyan roared an enraged response. "A freaken joke! What was there about what you said that was remotely a joke? Huh! Do you know what I've seen our there? Monsters! Hellacious beasts that not even your worst nightmares could possibly replicate. While you kingdom guard rats comfortably dwell within unbreachable walls, I have watched men die. Good men die! Gone limp in my very hands!" Tears poured from his eyes, but the flames of rage still burned, boiling the whites of his eyes. You think all that we have to worry about out there is Luna? You are sorely mistaken. With Luna, we at least engage in honorable combat. These monsters, they rip them limb from limb! Their families will never see them again, have no bodies to bury. Do you know what it's like, knowing you could have saved someone...had you just been a little stronger? Do you know what it's like when you fail to save someone and watch as the life fades from their eyes? Can you even comprehend how it feels to know that you are walking away alive...when the men you are supposed to support and guide aren't going to come home! No! You don't! You sit inside these walls like privileged, spoiled children. You have never seen a battle of any kind. You can hardly be considered soldiers!" He brought his face closer to the guard, almost to where their noses were touching. "Stay away from this table. I don't want to see your faces for the rest of the night. Get out!" He spoke in a stern whisper. The guard sprang to his feet as Axaiyan released him, and he and his comrades made a dash for their table. Axaiyan stormed over to a giant barrel of ale, scooping up his mug as he walked past. He filled his mug and began to aggressively chug his ale.

"Sir, don't you think it's best, not getting any more drunk?" A young marine grunt suggested respectfully. "I think we should bring you to your quarters, sir." Axaiyan looked at him with his teeth gritted and grinding them hard. Releasing an annoyed scoff, he drove his mug back into the flowing stream of ale without breaking his stare with a grunt. "Oh my, I wonder who could have possibly been dumb enough to suggest that? Definitely not me!" The young grunt looked around feigning innocence, chuckling nervously. The colonel stormed away, and the grunt released a sigh of relief. Suddenly, the grunt's vision faded, and immense pain began radiating from his face as it caved in from a mug that had been flung at great speeds. He fell to his back in a daze.

"There, I'm done. You happy grunt! Good night." Axaiyan shouted as he remained with his tossing hand out. Immediately following his sentence, he passed out cold, landing flat on his face.

"Hey, so, do you think we should carry him to his quarters?" An uninjured grunt suggested.

"Negative dumbass! I'm not risking him waking up and giving my face some reconstruction!" Another answered as he nervously looked down at the injured marine, who still had the mug imbedded in his face.

"I'll drink to that!" Another shouted as he raised his mug before chugging his ale.

At a separate table, a more civil rival encounter was taking place. A large kingdom guard stood towering over a small marine grunt in an aggressive stance.

"So marine, big day tomorrow, huh? Be careful, wouldn't want some Lunian bastard to strike you down before I get to." The large man said with a playful grin.

"Please, don't worry about me, guard. More so, worry about you." The marine responded with a mischievous glare. The guard's expression bore blank confusion. "Yes, I mean you really need to take care of yourself...wouldn't want you getting too fat while lounging around, defending the kingdom from nothing."

The marine teased. The guard let out a quick, angry grunt, then released a confident smile.

"Well then, marine, what would you say to..." He then projected his voice over the entire feasting grounds with great intensity. "A duel! Right here! Right now!" All the men, military and civilian alike, immediately stopped what they were doing. All went quiet.

"Duel!" An onlooker shouted from the distance. The guard and marine hopped into the air, landing in the center of the forming crowd. The women giggled to themselves at the typical male display. A random marine hopped between them, offering to preside over the right.

"Alright, listen up maggots! This will be a battle to knockout. Last man standing wins. No lethal contact is authorized. Clash your weapons together respectfully, and let the duel commence!" The guard and marine smiled deviously at each other with sickly amusement before clanging their weapons together and falling into battle-ready stance. "Fight!" The marine quickly readied two sharp hunting knives and began twirling them with impressive speed. The guard swung a large, heavy spear and whirled it around is body, his free hand beckoning the marine.

"Sure, grunt, you've got the speed, but speed won't knock me down!" The guard boasted confidently. They propelled towards each other. The guard flew through the air as he attempted to bring the blunt end of his spear down on the marine's head. A clang sounded as the marine caught the shaft of the spear with the blade in his left hand. With the blade in his right, he drove the blunt end into the face of the guard. The guard grunted in pain, covering his face and taking a few steps back. As his foot landed on the final step, the marine was upon him once more. Sliding to a halt behind the guard, the marine remained as he was. Blood sprayed from the guard's nose, and he began to fall to the ground in a daze. Before he could land, the marine whirled back into action. Kicking the guard in the back of the head, he forced him to crash down harder. Making a perfect landing, the marine twirled his blades, clanging them together in a taunting manner. The battle seemed won, for the massive guard remained motionless. The crowd grew silent in anticipation, awaiting the presiding officer's call. Suddenly, quiet murmurs began to break out in the crowd who could see the front of the guard. He was slowly and stealthily reaching for his spear. This battle was not yet finished. The marine realized the noise was picking up for that reason and readied his stance. The guard, now with spear in hand, lounged at his opponent. The marine narrowly evaded the attack and once again drove his handle into the guard's face. To his surprise, the guard didn't flinch this time, as if he was waiting for the hit. The guard took hold of the marine's wrist and tossed him to the ground. Using his superior fitness, the marine recovered quickly, dodging the heavy slam that was coming his way in the form of an enormous knee. He launched himself back towards the guard, but the guard slid from his attack and grabbed his leg, tossing him back to the ground. The guard attempted several punches as he had the marine pinned beneath him. Yet the marine still evaded his blows. Driving his handle into the guard's gut, the marine freed himself from the guard's grapple.

"Well, I think playtime is over now, guard. It's time to send you to lullaby land!" The guard chuckled, unconvinced, as they seemed evenly matched. He hurled his massive fist towards the marine, but he evaded him once more. Only this time, the marine unleashed a string of attacks that was nearly impossible for the eye to follow. Several to the face of the guard and one final deep blow to the gut. The guard remained in a daze, and the marine kicked his legs out from under him. The guard came to a crashing fall, face-first into the ground. The officer rushed in and, upon finding the guard out cold, declared the marine the victor. The marine clanged his blades together for a final taunt before driving them into their sheaths. Cheering erupted, but the marine made his way over to his sleeping foe. He dragged the guard with the help of his kingdom guard comrades and leaned him against a barrel of ale. He allowed the flow of ale to wash over the guard, who awoke immediately, shocked and disoriented. Coming back to his senses, he began to chuckle and shake his head.

"You cheeky bastard. If you could move that quickly, why'd you not take me out right away?" The marine smiled as he offered his hand to the guard.

"Oh, come on, and not give the audience a good show?" The marine boasted playfully as he held his arm to the guard. "Besides, what would be the sport in that?" The guard laughed as he took the marine's hand and was brought to his feet. As he regained his balance, they took each other in a hug.

"Jokes aside, be safe out there, little brother! Mother would never be able to handle the news if anything ever happened to you." The guard said tenderly. The marine smiled warmly, but their moment was interrupted by a thunderous shout.

"Now that is what I am talking about!" Radric boomed with unparalleled energy. "This is how you feast! Good food. Great ale. Unforgettable battles!" He raised his mug. "Here's to a glorious night! And an even more glorious morn! To victory!"

"To victory!" The rest of the Solyans shouted back. After a few seconds of motivated celebrating following the toast, everyone suddenly fell silent. General Wasukah stood before the king, sword drawn, holding the blade to the king's neck. He bore a sinister smile, and his eyes were clouded with fell intent.

"General, no! It can't be! Not you. You were the mole?" Major General Gorg exclaimed as he held his drawn sword to Wasukah's neck. The onlooking crowd gasped and began whispering amongst themselves.

"The mole?" An elderly woman said frightfully.

"What could this mean?" A young adult male said, looking at his friends.

"Gorg, you fool. Silence your indescribably unperceptive self and lower your weapon. Don't frighten the civilians with such nonsense!" Wasukah shouted as his vile and cruel gaze fell on Gorg. "Besides, you wouldn't want to get hurt, would you?"

"General, you have been like a father to me these many years. Pease cease this foolishness. I'd rather not, but if you don't, I will be forced to destroy you!" Wasukah laughed sinisterly as he returned his gaze to the king, disregarding Gorg's threats and the sword resting against his throat.

"So, you really think this is truly a grand feast, don't you, *sire?*" The king smiled confidently.

"Yeah...yeah, I do," Radric said calmly through his gritted teeth.

"Then let's have a duel, your majesty, and make it a truly memorable occasion!" Wasukah responded with a playful and sunny disposition. Everyone gasped with disbelief and confusion. All apart from Radric and Wasukah.

"What the hell is going on right now?" Gorg inquired, engulfed in confusion as he lowered his weapon. Wasukah began laughing uncontrollably and dropped his sword as Radric playfully punched him in the chest.

"You were right, Wasukah!" Radric said, laughing with equal intensity. "He did get all serious about it!"

"Oh, ow, ow!" Wasukah began to respond with his sides hurting from laughter. "I told you he'd jump to the conclusion that I was the mole."

"Huh?" Gorg released a depressed and weak sigh as he slumped with his arms dangling to the ground. "Wow, I can't believe you two would do this. Is something as serious as the mole really even a joking matter?" Wasukah playfully floated over to him.

"Aw, come on now, general tight ass. Loosen up a bit, huh?" Wasukah teased as he playfully elbowed Gorg in his side. "But hey, it's cool that you look to me as a father figure..." Wasukah's face began to cringe as he held back his laughter, but when Radric lost it, so did he. Gorg looked away in embarrassment, unamused by their antics. Radric and Wasukah finally calmed down.

"But seriously, Wasukah, that acting...it was really convincing," Radric said, placing his hand on Wasukah's shoulder. "For a second, I almost thought you came up with this whole plot to seriously come out as the mole."

"I just like to mess with Gorg." He said with a guilty chuckle. "That being said, I should probably get him a drink." They both laughed again briefly, and everyone went back to their business. The feast raged on for several hours, but soon, it was time for everyone to retire to their chambers.

Secret Love

In Luna

Lycia arose from a long and stressful slumber. In Lycia's unparalleled love for the Uçebian people, she has constant nightmares about all the individuals she has killed. Reliving the sight of the pain and worry for their families seen in their dying eyes. Lycia's wounded heart only held on because of her people and her wonderful daughter Onceli. She dried her eyes and gently fell from her bed to her feet. Not far from where she stood rested the black-furred wolf cub. Lycia walked over to Onceli and laid on her side beside her sleeping daughter. She smiled warmly and began to glow as she reached out and gently stroked Onceli's cheek with her index finger. Onceli's eyes slowly opened, sporting a unique complexion. Her left eye was silver and glorious like her mother's, but her right eye was a fire-orange as burning as the sun. She looked over to Lycia, and her tail began wagging with excitement. Although she was still young, she was already the size of a full-grown wolf. Lycia rolled over on to her back, and Onceli rested her head atop her stomach. Lycia massaged Onceli's head and scratched behind her ears.

"Dear daughter, I wait with much impatient anticipation for

your third birthday. Do you know why?" With her head still resting on Lycia's belly, Onceli shifted her gaze to Lycia. She tilted her head in confusion, not knowing what her mother was getting at. "At the rising of the moon on your third birthday, you will finally shift into your Uçebian form. Your true form! Mana has told me so." Onceli hopped up playfully excited. Although she couldn't speak in her current form, she still understood what Lycia was saying to her. She remained in a playful puppy stance, nibbling at Lycia's fluffy sweater. "Come back over here, silly, I'm not done cuddling with you yet!" Lycia said tenderly with a slight giggle. Onceli slid back over to Lycia, resting her head on her stomach and letting out quiet, joyful whimpers. "My sweet girl, we are fortunate the others understood. At first, they thought it was taboo. Accusing me of laying with the great dire wolf Silver Fang. How could they ever think that was true, yuck! Now they think you were a miracle from Mana. But no, my daughter, you were born of natural love; did you know that?" Onceli tilted her head and let out a slight woof-like, "Hmm?" "That's right, baby girl, your father was an Uçebian, a great Uçebian. Well, I say *was*, but he still is a truly noble man." She giggled slightly. "It's a shame he's not here to see you. He would be so proud!" Onceli let out several happy whimpers and tried to cuddle closer to her mother. "But soon, you will become the little Uçebian you were meant to be. Then we can finally be a real family. You, me...and maybe, one day...your father as well." Lycia's face filled with grief, her glow faded, and her visible eye became misty. She remained as she was for a short while before clearing her throat and hopping to her feet. "Well, my dear, there's no time for that now, is there? We must prepare for the wastelands." Onceli let out a majestic howl, and they both ran from the palace toward the armory and training grounds.

When Lycia and Onceli arrived, everyone fell to bended knee. Lycia gestured for them to rise, and Elizya emerged from the distance, her face painted with worry. Lycia hugged her tight, resting her face against Elizya's chest.

"Believe me, Mother, nothing will happen to my daughter. I won't allow it." Lycia spoke in a gentle whisper. Elizya smiled weakly and returned her embrace. Eventually, Lycia released her and skipped off in a bubbly manner towards General Rehcumber. Most of Luna's council no longer fought on the battlefield, as they had done their time. General Rehcumber, on the other hand, was one of the few who chose to remain active and participated in ninety percent of the raids. For this one, however, he was to remain in the city since Lycia would be on the front lines.

"Ah yes, good morrow majesty. We are nearly ready to deploy." He said with great excitement.

"Great! So that means the most important preparation will be made shortly then?" Lycia responded impishly. The look of great confusion encompassed the general's face.

"Well, highness, I, uh...would like to report that yes, it will..." He stammered with a nervous chuckle. "However, I'm not quite sure which preparation you are referring to."

"Ease up, dear general. I'm speaking of the grand feast for our warriors before they head out tomorrow night." She said with a giggle, her hands resting reassuringly on his shoulders.

"Oh yes...of course that's what you meant by "most important." He responded with a hint of disbelief. He exhaled deeply and regained his composure as he headed to check on the meal preparations. Lycia skipped around greeting all of her men. Following closely behind was Onceli, who would be greeted with pats on the head and ear scratches. Lycia began to giggle uncontrollably as she pranced over to the next victim of her, sometimes suffocating affection. Hearing her giggling growing closer, a young man, Colonel Boyox, began to quake with fear.

"No, no, please, my queen, wait!" He shouted frantically as he held his arms out in protest. However, Lycia was already airborne and diving towards him. He stared, paralyzed, await-ing his fate. As she was about to make contact with him, she squealed in a high pitch, schoolgirl voice.

"My little Kerny!" Her body reached his, and she wrapped her arms tightly around him. Her chest flew into his face, and his cheeks illuminated with steamy embarrassment. He fell to his back with her still resting on top of him. Her cheeks filled with strawberry pigment as she kicked her legs back and forth, remaining on top of him with her eyes gently shut. "Colonel Boyox, oh my adorable little Kerny! I just wanna pitch your cheeks and cuddle with you always!" The other men looked over in envy, as no other man received such a level of affection from their beautiful queen.

"Majesty, please, this is so embarrassing!" He pleaded, muf-fled under her body. She opened her eyes and wore a slightly embarrassed expression as she stood to her feet with a giggle. Boyox returned to his feet, rolling his shiny onyx eyes. He dusted himself off and fixed the mess that his long, spikey, green hair had fallen into. But before he could speak, Lycia embraced him tight, once again forcing his face into her chest. It was never intentional; Boyox just happened to be an incredibly short indi-vidual. Which was what Lycia found the most endearing about him, as not many adult individuals were shorter than her.

"Yes, yes, good morning, highness. I'm happy to see you, too." He said sarcastically and unenthused as he patted her back twice before quickly releasing her. He released an annoyed sigh. She released him and backed away slightly, falling into a cute pose.

"Aww, come on, Kerny. You could at least pretend to be happy to see me." He stared at the ground, grumbling to himself. Releasing a deep sigh he looked up at her.

"Eh, come on, your majesty, cease the wishy-washiness, please. You know I am happy to see you; I just have a strange way of expressing it." She began to glow brightly and waved goodbye as she skipped away. The envious onlookers remained fixed on him until he caught their gaze. "What the hell do you maggots think you're staring at, huh? Don't you have preparations to make?" They became nervous and scrambled back to what they were doing. He stomped away, drawing his axe, and massacred a training dummy as he walked by.

"Hey, you know, I heard he and the queen have some forbidden history." A watching grunt spoke to his comrade. The second grunt gasped loudly out of surprise. The first covered his partner's mouth, quickly shushing him. "Yeah, rumor has it, the colonel shared the queen's bed on more than one occasion." He continued, releasing his comrade from his clutches.

"Eh don't be a naïve fool." The second replied, brushing off the other's words. "People talk, comrade, but let's be real here. The Colonel cares for one thing. The heat of battle. He may be the only man in all of Luna who does not absolutely drool for the queen."

"I mean, true or not, you didn't have to go and ruin the fun." The first replied with disappointment. "Hey, wait, you say 'man.' Isn't he just a teenager?" The second grunt rolled his eyes.

"Dude, he's eighteen. That is a man in my eyes. Not to mention, he outranks us immeasurably; I think he's earned the right to be referred to as the man that he is. His deeds in battle are legendary."

"Quite a bit of admiration you got for the little guy, huh?" The first teased.

"Show some respect! I don't see him for his age. And I definitely don't see him for his height! I see him for his accomplishments and his impressive rank. Eh, forget it. I have things to do, and so do you, grunt!" They returned to their business.

Lycia was making her way to the medical tents next, now accompanied by Elizya, who joined shortly after Lycia's run-in with Boyox.

"Mother, do you think he hates me?" Lycia said with her visible eye heavy and staring towards the ground. Elizya flinched with surprise.

"But of course not, my dear queen," Elizya responded tenderly. "It's just...maybe sometimes you can be..."

"What? I can be what?" Lycia cut in frantically, looking at her with anxious intrigue.

"Well, maybe just a little too overbearing with him, my lady," Elizya responded with an embarrassed tone. Lycia slouched miserably for a brief second, quicky returning to her chipper self.

"I just can't help it though. He's so cute!" Elizya rolled her eyes, wearing a playful smile.

They reached the medical tents, and proper respects were rendered. The Lunian medics and their commanding officer, Captain Geeah, were all females.

"Greetings, mon capitaine!" Lycia greeted her, playfully rendering a salute.

"Good morrow, your majesty!" Geeah responded with a giggle as she curtsied.

"Are the finest ladies in all of Uçebar ready to kick some Solyan ass?!" Lycia shouted. The medics shouted heroically, yet wrapped in feminine allure, as they clanged their weapons together. "I expected nothing less from my deadly yet lifesaving and gorgeous medics!" She shouted as she hopped into the air. Landing gracefully, she spun around and skipped off.

The night grew dark as Radric set the sun, and Luna began a feast of their own. Lycia, of course, was in the midst of the celebration as usual. However, she noticed something was missing.

"I wonder where my little Kerny is." She thought to herself as she looked around. She caught a glimpse of his spikey hair making his way from the celebration hall and followed closely behind. He made his way outside to the courtyard garden, where a small woman stood near the brown bushes. Lycia hid behind a pillar nearby, but was too far for their eyes to detect. With her enhanced sense of sight and powerful wolf ears, she was able to fully see and hear everything they were discussing. Boyox placed his hands on either side of the small woman's waist tenderly. Lycia gasped with disbelief and watched on. "Hey, that is Uahka, isn't it? The last gnome in all of Uçebar. Are they a couple? (Her ears twitched) How cute! Her extreme tininess is perfect for him!"

"Why won't you tell anyone about us?" Uahka asked in an irritated manner. "We are to be married one day, are we not? How can we have a proper wedding if no one in the kingdom knows we are even together?" With his gentle hold still around her waist, he chuckled impishly through his teeth. She ripped herself away from him, raising her voice slightly. "So why is it, hmm? Are you embarrassed of me?" He closed his eyes and exhaled in an annoyed manner, only causing her rage to grow. "That's it, isn't it! You're ashamed to be with an outcast." She lowered her head as tears began to slowly roll down her rosy cheeks. "You're ashamed to be seen with a silly little gnome...the hermit that lives alone on the outskirts of town." Boyox opened his eyes and approached her slowly. He snatched up her tiny hands and held them to his chest level.

"See here, my darling Uahka." He spoke gently in a comforting manner. "Do you really think I care of your origins? Or about what anyone would think if they saw us together? Absolutely not! I love you...but I am the youngest and most respected colonel in the queen's marine force. The men must fear and respect me. I have a reputation to uphold, that the only thing on my mind is war. They must feel that I am the perfect warrior. Don't ever get to thinking that I am in any way embarrassed of you, my love." He gently nudged her chin with his fist as he released her hands. "You silly girls and your emotions." He teased impishly. Uahka became irritated and removed his axe from its holster, smashing him over the head with its handle. Her face became brick red, and her cheeks puffed out with anger.

"Don't make fun of me for worrying about how you feel about me!" She replied in an embarrassed manner. He slowly stabilized himself, grunting and wincing from the pain as he chuckled weakly. She became calm and dropped his axe. "I just really care about you. You are my moonlight in the darkness. You are all I have. I...I can never lose you...do you understand! You're not allowed to die until we have been able to live a long and normal life." She released a weak sigh. "I long for your service to this kingdom to end...for when we are finally married and have children." Her tears streamed down faster. "You come home to me, damn it! You hear me? I don't care how huge and important this specific raid is. You better come home to me." Boyox smiled warmly and cradled her face in one hand, playing with her flowing red hair in the other. His hands fell back to her waist and pulled her into his embrace.

"Don't you worry your pretty little head about it. Nothing, not even death, could keep me from you. But I shall never be struck down." He released her and stared lovingly into her ruby eyes. "Now, I should get back to the feast before I'm missed." She nodded her head and smiled weakly. He kissed her tenderly then began to make his leave.

"Be safe, my moonlight warrior. I will never forgive you if you die!" She shouted to him as he continued away. He looked over his shoulder with a smile and held his hand in a stationary wave goodbye as he pressed on.

Lycia, having heard everything, rested her head against the pillar, staring back towards the celebration hall, gently weeping.

"That is so beautiful!" She thought. "Ugh, I never knew Kerny had such a side to him. How adorable is he?" Boyox caught a glimpse of her as he was passing by.

"Hmm? Oh, my queen!" He said in a concerned tone. He fell

down on one knee and placed his hand on her shoulder. "Your majesty, is everything alright?" She looked up at him with a gleam in her revealed, luminous eye. With a gentle smile, she dried her tears with her tail.

"Yes, I'm fine. Don't worry about me." She responded softly. Boyox held out his hand and assisted her to her feet. He continued towards the celebration hall, Lycia following closely behind as she was lost in thought.

"That poor little gnome girl...I didn't know she felt that way about herself. Do people really see her as an outcast? After this raid, I'll be sure to address this matter myself. No one in my kingdom is going to be left out or feel that way. Not under my rule." She quietly continued to follow Boyox and returned to the feast.

The night rolled on, and the celebration soon came to an end. Reality began to settle in for the warriors as they prepared for sleep, knowing that tomorrow, they would be out on the battlefield.

To the Wastelands!

Part I

Back in Sol, the time for the raid approached. Radric stood atop his balcony, looking down upon his kingdom for one last daydream before the march to the wastelands commenced. He forced the sun to set, and the night was upon them. The marines were forming up in the city center, and thousands of civilians gathered to see them off. Radric stood at the head of the formation, riding atop a domesticated giant lizard. He drew his sword, and the rest followed. As he shouted into the air, the lizard took off. The marines shouted back and followed behind him on foot. The city gates began to open slowly as the men sprinted with Solyan fury. Upon exiting through the gates, the usual curses of the wastelands settled in. The gods protect their kingdoms from what the world's air was truly like. It was heavy and had far less oxygen than normal. It caused the lungs to constrict, and breathing became difficult. A foul odor sickened the senses. Most marines were ready for this and have had experience out in the wastelands, but the newer marines struggled a bit. That said, their training taught them to fight through the discomfort and carry on. Once they had fully left the city limits, the formation broke off into several squads. Each squad was led by a battlefield colonel, apart from the squad following Radric himself. The colonels had all been entrusted with a ring embedded with the Ignisque.

"Squads, disperse per guidelines of the forward scouting plan!" Radric shouted commandingly. The squads quickly dispersed throughout the wastelands. Some were tasked with hunting creatures, others to seek out Lunians. Radric's squad made haste for where their encampment was to be set up. Before they could arrive, Radric held up his hand, halting his squad.

"Make ready, marines, something comes! Be on your guard!" The sound of the ground cracking echoed all around them. "Come on then! Show yourself, fiend!" Radric roared. Suddenly, the ground they stood upon split into an enormous ravine, large enough to swallow Radric's entire squad. They began to plummet into the hellacious pit. Staring up at them from the bottom of the pit were incredibly large creatures. The monsters growled and gurgled, awaiting their meal to drop before them. "Quickly, cast your lines!" Radric commanded. The Solyans tossed their powerful spears into the canyon walls. Radric's lizard fell into the depths and was quickly devoured. The spears penetrated deep, and hanging from ropes secured to the shafts, most of the marines broke their fall with plenty of time to spare. A less seasoned marine failed to keep hold of his line. He cried out in fear at the thought of his impending doom.

"No!" Radric shouted as he looked down with concern. He quickly drew a second spear line and tossed it below the falling marine. "Grab the line as you pass by!" The marine took hold of it, but he had already built up too much momentum. His hand slid down the rope, causing severe burns, but he did not stop falling. Radric drew his sword and, harnessing the power of his flames, charged the blade, quickly making it red hot. He tossed it down at the beast with impressive strength. The monster was cleaved in two, releasing a foul flammable gas. Radric quickly channeled fire into the abyss, causing a great explosion that tossed the young marine from the ravine.

"My king, he was sent too high! When he hits the ground, all his bones will be ground to dust." His sergeant shouted. Radric let out a powerful battle cry as he jumped into the ravine and reignited the wafting gas with his flames, propelling himself toward the rapidly descending marine. He took hold of the boy in one arm and, with the other, channeled a powerful heat wave in an attempt to reduce their momentum. Radric crashed to the ground, taking the full force of the fall while protecting the young marine. The rest of the squad quickly emerged from the ravine and gathered around to ensure they were alright. The rescued marine stood to his feet, hyperventilating from the experience.

"My king. You saved me! Thank you, Your Majesty. You are the strongest in the land!" All the marines released a motivated battle cry. Radric chuckled victoriously, but upon trying to stand, he collapsed. He looked to his side to see a thick shard of rock deeply embedded between his ribs. The marines anxiously gathered around him.

"Sire, you are injured! We must desert the mission and carry you back!" The captain shouted.

"Nonsense! Press on forward." Radric responded sternly. He whistled a specific melody into the sky and instructed the marines to press on once more.

"At all costs, you must try to avoid Queen Lycia! Without me by your side, she will cut you all down. Be careful and be smart." The colonel assumed command, and they sprinted off. Radric grunted as he went to remove the shard. Pulling it free of his body, he utilized his flames to sear the wound. He surrounded himself with a wall of fire to fend off any monsters and waited patiently. Several minutes later, a majestic avian cry filled the sky. "My sweet little Octonia." He wore a weak smile as he watched her dive down in a spiraling manner towards him. She swooped back up before reaching the ground, and he grabbed hold of her neck, swinging himself to her back. Radric sat atop Octonia and let out a victorious laugh as they sailed through the sky. The marines looked back and noticed what looked to be a ball of fire in the sky.

"Look, it must be Octonia; the king is safe!" The captain shouted.

"Perfect! Now remain vigilant!" The colonel instructed as they continued.

One of the squads tasked to hunt creatures made its way to a dark forest of rotting trees. Something was not right, however, and more than usual. An abnormal silence loomed over them. The foul air suddenly became harsher, and the younger, less seasoned marines began gripping their throats as their breathing became significantly labored. Three new marines were present in this squad, and all began displaying the same symptoms. The medic rushed in to assess the situation, but other than their breathing, everything was fine.

"Colonel, never in my many raids have I encountered this condition." The medic explained. "Their vitals are all normal; it is as if they are stricken down by some fell force."

"Yes, there definitely seems to be an eerie presence among us. Be on your guard, men! Captain, take two scouts and sweep the perimeter. I will stay back with the medic and keep watch over the afflicted."

"Right away, sir!" As the captain and his scouts made their sweep, he quickly halted them and became concerned.

"Something is very wrong here, grunts." The captain exclaimed as he looked around frantically. "Get the hell out of here!" He commanded, drawing his sword. "Get back to the squad! Tell them to retreat immediately!" The sergeants were confused, for they saw nothing, yet the captain was swinging wildly and dodging as if engaging in battle with the air. He looked back to them as he defended. "Did you not hear me?" A clang sounded. "That's an order; get the hell out of here, now!" They did as they were told and sprinted to the colonel. As the rest of the squad came into their view, they shouted for the colonel. He looked over to them, and his eyes grew wide as his face bore a sickly fear. The sergeants suddenly vanished, swallowed in a thick shroud of darkness. The colonel could no longer see them nor the trees that once lay before his eyes. The medic looked over to the colonel and, upon seeing his facial expression, released a gasp.

"Sir? Are you feeling well? You look as if you have seen the devil himself!"

"Might as well have, doc!"

"Sir, please explain. You can't be serious!" The colonel, keeping his eyes fixed on the darkness that had consumed his troops, gripped tightly to his sword.

"Doc..." The colonel spoke ominously. "I have seen many a creature out in these accursed wastelands...I've seen them of all sizes, demented shapes, and with impressive strength. But never before have I encountered a creature...that seemingly has the ability of sorcery!" As he finished, the shadows closed in around them, and a foul growling and gnawing sound filled the dank air.

"Colonel...if this is to be where Gi has prepared our death...I want you to know it has been an honor and a privilege serving beneath you!"

"You do me honor, doc!" The colonel shouted as he readied his stance. "However, hush your insolent mouth with such nonsense! This is not the day we die! Get up and fight beside me, my friend; we cannot allow whatever it is to take out the young men!" The medic sprang to his feet, drawing his sword, and landed with his back against the colonel's. "Come, my comrade, it is time to show this creature the true might of Sol!" They each released a battle cry and made ready. Suddenly, the sound of torn flesh ripped through the air. The colonel and the medic's expressions fell blank and lifeless as their bodies were cleaved in two. Blood and organs splashed to the ground with a sickly sound. The younger marines cried out in horror with the little oxygen they had left. Before they could truly process the brutality that unfolded before their eyes, everything went dark.

In a separate area of the wastes, Colonel Axaiyan's squad, who was in charge of hunting Luna, found themselves facing monsters instead.

"Excellent work, marines. Despite this not being our task, necessarily, if they are in the way, then we must slay!" Axaiyan shouted with motivation as he mangled the final monster. The men joined in his battle cry, clanging their weapons together.

"Quite a kill count we've got right now, ay colonel. Too bad we haven't found any Lunians, though." A seasoned sergeant spoke boldly.

"Indeed," Axaiyan replied with a chuckle. "However, these monsters will do just fine as a replacement!" Suddenly, Axaiyan began to remember the words of the kingdom guard from the night of the feast. He gritted his teeth and shouted with motivation. "Stay strong, men! We shall return to our families. I shall make it my duty, to the death, to ensure you all get home!" They all shouted a battle cry and continued their hunt. Suddenly, the ground began to quake, and a massive stone golem sprang from the cracked, dusty ground. It hurled its fist at the colonel, catching him off guard. Its strike sent him with incredible force into a large rock and knocked him unconscious. The major took charge, and the squad formed up into a battle-ready stance. Two grunts ran in opposite directions to distract the sluggish beast. It looked back and forth, unsure of where to strike; by the time it did, the grunts had long since dodged out of the way. Due to its colossal size and slowness, it took a while for it to recover from each strike. As it was lifting its fists from the ground, two more grunts hopped on its back. It swung its arm to strike them, but they had already cleared its reach. It smashed itself in the back, forcing itself into the ground face first. The major launched into the air, drawing a massive spear. He hurled himself towards the beast, driving the spear deep into the golem's head. With a powerful battle cry, he pulled his spear down and to the left, sending a crack down the golem's body. He somersaulted from it as its body split in two. The men celebrated by pumping their weapons in the air and shouting with motivation. The medic was tending to the colonel, who was slowly returning to consciousness. He awoke in time to witness the celebration and smiled.

"You tough bastards. I guess you didn't need me after all." He thought quietly to himself. Of course, Axaiyan was one of the few individuals entrusted with the Ignisque and was ready to sacrifice it along with himself if he had to. He would do anything to see his men safely home. "I remember the first time I failed...I will never forget. I'll never allow that again."

Flashback to 2nd Lieutenant Axaiyan

"Ay, lieutenant!" An old salty marine master sergeant shouted to him as he ran to his side. Axaiyan looked to the sergeant with a polite grin. "Be safe out there, sir! Not many corporals get promoted to officers, forget at your age!" He placed a loving hand on Axaiyan's shoulder. "If your father were here, he would be very proud." Axaiyan smiled, and they began sprinting into the wastes side-by-side.

"Hey, Ox?" Axaiyan began warmly. The master sergeant looked at him. "Thanks for everything. For the life you gave me in place of my father. For all your wisdom and training. I

wouldn't be where I am today without you." Ox smiled and nodded slightly.

"Ay, lieutenant, just don't let us old dogs run circles around
ya. You got a reputation to uphold, yeah?"

"Not on your life, old man!" Their eyes squinted, and they
let out a thunderous roar as they continued into the desolate
scapes. Together with the rest of their squad, they were ravag-
ing the wastelands, destroying nearly every monster that crossed
their path. The rest they disabled to save time. Suddenly, things
changed; an eerie silence befell them, and the air became more
difficult to breathe. Axaiyan, being a young marine, could not
bear it and fell to his back, gasping for air.

"Doc! Get to the Lieutenant now!" Ox instructed with commanding authority. The rest of the squad readied their battle
stance, although they could see nothing. The captain stood firm
at the front of the formation. Soon, shadows had completely
engulfed the entire unit. The Solyans could no longer see a thing
apart from each other. Axaiyan's eyes filled with fear and desperation to help as he witnessed the captain's head falling from
his body in what seemed like slow motion for him. He tried to
scream, but nothing would come out, as if in a nightmare. The
medic was attempting to tell him something, but he could only
hear slight muffled gibberish. The medic's face soon went blank;
his eyes became still and lifeless. Blood sprayed from the medic's
throat, painting Axaiyan's face and armor. Axaiyan cried out in
remorseful agony, wishing there was something he could do to
help, but he just couldn't move. Body after body fell before his
eyes as his comrades were slaughtered like flies. Tears poured
from his eyes as he remained motionless, forced to do nothing
but watch. Soon, all that remained was Ox. With panic in his
eyes, he looked over to Axaiyan. Ox let out a motivated battle
cry and charged towards him.

"Oh no, you don't! Not this one!" Ox shouted as he scooped

up Axaiyan. He shouted louder as he prepared to toss Axaiyan from the fell shroud. "You shall not have this one!" Axaiyan tried to scream and plead for him to stop but was unable to say a word. Ox tossed him with all his might and whistled for Octonia. Axaiyan flew back out into the dim light of the artificial sun. Upon hitting the more normal air, he was released from the crippling effects of the shadows. He sprung to his feet and began to charge towards the foul orb of darkness that still contained Ox.

"Don't you dare, foolish boy!" Ox shouted in desperation. "Don't you dare come back into this horrid gloom!" Clanging sounded as Ox fended off the sinister creature. "You know you can't function in here. All you would accomplish by coming back is to die. (Clanging) Turn back now, get to where it is safe!"

"Not on your life, Ox!" Axaiyan replied with determination. "I will think of something; I will find a way. I can save you!"

"Don't be a fool, boy!" More clanging and shuffling sounded as Ox continued to fight. "You are not strong enough; get out of here!"

"That is a negative. You cannot give me orders! I'm an officer; I will make the decisions here."

"Stop!" Ox bellowed in further desperation. "Don't come back here! I am not speaking to you as your master sergeant!" Axaiyan came to a skidding halt, and his eyes flowed heavier with tears. "I speak to you now as the man who raised you in your father's stead. I speak to you as your mentor, as someone who loves you. Please...please get to safety, dear Axaiyan. Grant me this dying wish. I only wish for you to live!" Axaiyan fell to his knees, slamming his fists into the ground as he sobbed. He felt helpless; there was nothing he could do to save the closest thing he had to a father. "Go! Now!" Ox cried out one final time before he let out a choking, gurgle. A clang emitted as his weapon fell to the dusty ground, and Axaiyan felt as if his heart stopped. The sound of blood spray splattering on the ground echoed in his mind. He remained as he was, motionless; the world fell completely silent around him. The gloom began making its way towards him, but he remained. Suddenly, he heard a whisper in his head, a familiar voice...a loving voice. "Run, child...please do not let our sacrifice be in vain!" Axaiyan's eyes opened wide, and determination returned to him. Noticing the wall of shadows approaching him, he hopped to his feet and attempted to escape as he shouted into the heavens.

"I won't die! I will live for you, Ox! I'm so sorry I couldn't save you, father!" He looked back, and the gloom was gaining on him until a bright light illuminated the darkness as a torrent of flames ripped through it. A majestic avion caw filled the air, and Octonia spiraled down in a diving manner toward the shadow. Opening her powerful beak, she released an even greater heat wave, one that could have melted the rock itself. The shadow was blasted into oblivion and dispersed into the sky. Octonia lay beside Axaiyan so he could climb aboard her. With tears gracefully falling from his eyes, he looked up to the majestic bird.

"Please, oh great phoenix. Allow me to retrieve the body of my friend. He deserves a proper burial." She closed her eyes as she nodded her head in understanding. He ran and retrieved Ox's body. As he held the limp, lifeless corpse of his beloved mentor and stared at the gash in his neck, he shouted in pure anguish. He held him close to his chest as he wept. "You, who...or whatever you are! If you are still alive...I will make you pay! I will make you suffer!" He shouted into the empty wastelands. Suddenly, Octonia's caw filled the skies once more, only it was filled with urgency. Axaiyan's eyes quaked with anger as he began to witness the dispersed bits of shadow reforming together.

"Just try it...*boy*!" A foul demonic voice answered him sinisterly. The shadow dashed for him as Octonia flew forward and scooped him up in her claws. There was no time to waste; she only held on to Axaiyan. He watched as Ox's body fell back to the ground and was consumed in the darkness.

"No!" He shouted a long-sustained cry of agony as Octonia carried him off.

Present Day

"A job well done, marines!" Axaiyan exclaimed with pride. The men continued to celebrate when suddenly, the colonel's face bore a sickly fear like none other. His eyes were wide and trembling. But his fear was not for his own sake but for his men.

"Sir, are you feeling alright?" The medic inquired as the shadow began to close in. The junior marines fell to the ground, gasping in a familiar display.

"Get out! Get out now!" Axaiyan commanded desperately, "Major, get the juniors out of here and retreat! Doc, go with them. I need two senior sergeants to stay back with me; the rest of you, get out now! That is a freaken order; make it happen!" The major, carrying a young marine on his back, desperately struggled to escape the rapidly consuming shroud of darkness. He soon fell completely still, followed by the medic. Axaiyan's pupils dilated, and horror painted his face. The major and medic fell to the ground in mangled, bloody pieces. The two juniors they were carrying were still alive but could not move. Axaiyan roared with rage and sprinted with everything he had towards them. With sword in hand, he landed between the two and, whirling his weapon in a downward spiral, placed it directly in front of one of the grunt's neck. A clang erupted, the grunt was confused at first but soon realized the colonel had just saved his life.

"Remember your promise, *boy*?" A sinister voice spoke in a taunting whisper. "Will you be able to keep it?" Axaiyan returned his sword arm to a ready position. An odd presence began to invite itself into Axaiyan's heart. Clouding his mind with a desire for vengeance and warping his personality.

"You are nothing! You are weak!" Axaiyan exclaimed as he fell into a deranged state, laughing psychotically. "You are pathetic...to think...how, how did I let you defeat me back then? You are not invisible; you are no omnipotent being! You're just fast, and you cloak yourself in shadows." He swirled his sword in a taunting manner, his face further deranged. He opened his eyes as wide as he could as he shouted psychotically. "Well, guess what? I am fast, too!" Multiple clangs erupted as Axaiyan powered forward. A different sound emitted, and it seemed that Axaiyan had actually hit the creature. Suddenly, skidding across the darkened ground, the grunts saw a tiny black demon. The colonel stood over it with a frightening grin. Axaiyan drove the handle of his sword into the creature's abdomen. The whites of Axaiyan's eyes were slowly being consumed by blackness, and his pupils began to darken to a blood red that glowed with sinister light. He raised his sword and cleaved the demon's left hand off. It winced slightly but smiled deviously as it began to grow back instantly. Its sinister smile only grew as it noticed Axaiyan's amusement increasing. His face contorted, and he released a foul laugh. The darkness continued to grow in Axaiyan as his concern for his comrades was quickly replaced with blood lust.

"So, you regenerate? Perfect, now I can make you suffer over and over again!" Axaiyan shouted. "But you won't die! No! Not until I decide you die! I promised I'd make you suffer, and I will!" Axaiyan began foaming at the mouth as his body was further engulfed in the madness of hate. He swirled his sword in the pathway of an infinity sigh and slashed off all the demon's limbs. The creature may have been evil and a hellish monster, but from an outside perspective, it began to look more like Colonel Axaiyan was the true demon. Axaiyan rammed his sword into the demon's torso and swirled it around, scrambling the creature's insides. The demon's refusal to express any pain, apart from slight grimaces, was only fueling Axaiyan's lust. The demon was shaking uncontrollably with delight despite being completely outmatched. Suddenly, flames began to burn in Axaiyan's glowing red eyes as he lifted the tiny creature to his face.

"What's so funny, you putrid mess?" Axaiyan spoke in a demonic voice. "Shall I just kill you then, no need to waste any further time?"

"Look at you, boy, I'm so proud! You take to hate so openly! Submit, accept the power growing in you! *She* will soon own you! Soon, you will be just like me!"

"I will never be anything like you!" Axaiyan shouted as he tossed the little demon to the ground. He held his sword to the demon's throat. "It's time now, filth! I've decided you get to die early!"

"So boy, it looks like your promise may come to fruition after all." It responded in a sinister whisper. Its voice grew louder in the form of a demonic roar. "Too bad you couldn't save your comrades!" Axaiyan looked over with inconsolable dismay as one of the demon's dismembered hands hovered over one of the paralyzed marines, sword in hand. Axaiyan shouted out desperately as he sprinted towards the boy. But before he could get there, the floating limb cut the marine's throat. With everything his body had to offer, he rushed to the only living member of his squad remaining. The limb came down to slash the final marine's throat. Axaiyan dove to the ground, sliding with such force that he pushed the young marine free of the gloom. In turn, he took the demon's blade to his rib cage. He coughed out blood as he slowly tried to return to his feet. Failing to regain his balance, he collapsed to his knees. The demon stood before him, fully regenerated and seemingly uninjured.

"A valiant effort, but it only prolonged the inevitable. Once I'm through with you...it will be on to him. Had you only held to your values, you could have saved them both. But no, you gave into anger, just as I willed for you."

"You? Please! You've willed nothing!" Axaiyan responded.

"It matters not, boy! You will soon be converted. Then I will take your last subordinate!" It taunted. Axaiyan released a demented, psychotic laugh as he stood to his feet.

"That's what you think, monster! With him safely away, I can unleash the full depth of my power!" The Ignisque around his finger glowed brightly, and he let out a battle cry as flames poured from his hands. The creature was shocked and fell to the ground in an attempt to dodge. Axaiyan screamed louder as his flames intensified and consumed the darkness. The fell shroud dissipated, and the demon was exposed to the light of the artificial sun. It looked around, concerned, with nowhere left to hide. Axaiyan fell into a demonic fit of laughter as he showered the demon in a torrent of impressive flames. The demon released an ear-piercing shriek as it was burned to a soul-releasing crisp. Oddly enough, it was almost as if it were sounds of amusement.

"Get out of here now! Get back to safety!" Axaiyan shouted as he looked back to the marine. The grunt remained where he was, stunned by the sight of the demonic colonel who was staring at him. "That's an order; what are you waiting for!" The grunt felt reassured that despite his appearance, Axaiyan still seemed to be himself.

"But sir. You have defeated the creature; please, sir, come back with me."

"Don't be a fool to believe I defeated it that easily! This is no normal opponent!"

"Then, sir, that is all the more reason. Please retreat with me, then we can get the backup we need."

"No, now go!" Axaiyan shouted back in a demonic voice. Before he could act further, Axaiyan heard a familiar voice shout in his head. "Don't be a fool, boy! You are not strong enough;

get out of here! This creature is beyond you!" Axaiyan began to breathe heavily as he gripped his chest. His eyes filled with tears as the voice continued. "Don't lose sight of who you are; let go of the hate. Understand that I am happy and free of this wretched world. Look at yourself. Do you even recognize that face?" A ghostly mirror formed before his eyes, and his heart wept as he saw the reflection looking back at him. "You are becoming like it, one of those creatures...a lost soul...a demon! One who will forever plague the wastelands. For this creature was once like you. A tortured soul, agonized and vengeful. Only he gave in to it. As you are doing now! This creature is unphased by your attacks! It's merely trying to convert you! Soon you will not be able to distinguish friend from foe, and everyone around you will be a victim. Look at that young marine over there. Do you want him to bear the burden you do? Living his whole life out of revenge for his lost commander? Doomed to fall into a repeating cycle that will claim Solyan men, converting them to demons! You have lived with this pain for me in your heart for so long. But please, I wish for you to be free of it! I am happy where I am; I want you to be happy where you are. Spare this young marine the burden you have suffered for so many years, and leave. Leave now while the creature is recovering." Axaiyan closed his eyes, and he focused on the good memories he had and the thought of this poor boy suffering as he had suffered. His eyes opened, revealing a glorious pair of purple spheres resting in pearly white beds. His mind returned to a normal and rational state. A loud scream erupted as a black mist poured from Axaiyan's chest, materializing into the silhouette of a demon resembling the one he had just fought. It roared in his face as it dissolved into the air.

"Thank you, old friend, my soul is finally free!" With a cheerful look in his eye, Axaiyan sprinted over to the young grunt and picked him up as he passed by. The shadow began to reform and bolted towards them. "Marine, wrap your arms around my torso and hold on tight!" Axaiyan commanded the young man urgently. The grunt quickly did as he was told and braced himself. Axaiyan winced from the tightness against his wound but quickly turned, facing the demon cloud that was approaching him. He spoke calmly as he held out his hands. "You are fortunate, demon; I do possess the strength needed to kill you. However, the life of my marine is more important to me. So for now, you shall live to see another day." The Ignisque glowed brightly as Axaiyan used every ounce of his will to produce a torrent of flames from each hand, with enough force to propel them at impressive speed. Axaiyan kept channeling the fire as long as he could until his fatigue overwhelmed him, and he fell to the ground. His breathing was labored. The grunt hopped up to check on him. He smashed his fist into the ground as tears gently streamed from his eyes.

"I couldn't save them...why couldn't I save them? Why can I never save them? I promised...I promised them I would get them home to their families!" He drilled his fist deeper into the dusty ground. The grunt placed a compassionate hand on Axaiyan's shoulder.

"Sir, you cannot blame yourself. Gi had a plan for them, and they are happy now in a better place. Besides, sir, if not for you, I would have died. And my sickly mother would not be able to take care of herself. She would have no one. Colonel, thank you so much!" Axaiyan dried his eyes and looked up at his young marine.

"Think nothing of it, kid." He responded weakly as he lightly slapped the young marine's face twice. He hopped to his feet, and they began their journey home.

When Axaiyan and the grunt finally arrived at the kingdom, they were quickly escorted to the medical manor. Upon hearing of their arrival, the king rushed to the recovery chambers. As he walked in, Axaiyan attempted to stand to render him honors.

Radric quickly ran to his side, gently placing a hand on Axaiyan's chest, forcing him to stay in bed.

"Colonel...what the hell happened? Where are the rest of your men?" Radric inquired with much concern. Axaiyan explained everything that happened, including what he learned from the spirit of Ox. "Have you heard anything from the other squads?" The king asked. Axaiyan gently shook his head. Radric poked his head out of the window and whistled for Octonia. She promptly flew to him and listened closely as he instructed her sternly. "Listen, my dear Octonia, use your connection to the Ignisque's power to seek out their remaining holders. There are still nine of them out there." He wrote a message instructing them to return immediately. "Give this message to the commanders. Please hurry, my darling phoenix." Octonia cawed majestically and flew off with haste into the vast wastes. She soared through the sky, and after locating eight squads, she realized things were not looking good for Sol. Octonia shed a small tear as the eight squads she had located thus far were completely vanquished. Octonia located the final squad; they were in full retreat from what looked to be a wall of shadow. Her caws wrang through the skies as she rushed towards them.

"Look!" A marine corporal shouted as he pointed to the sky. "The king as sent the mighty Octonia to render us aid! Comrades, we are going to make it!" They all shouted a motivating chant and ceased their retreat as they turned to face the demon. The demon was angered to see Octonia and released a foul roar. It launched what appeared to be a shadowy spear towards her. She spiral-dove, dodging the projectile, and launched a massive wall of flames at the demon, engulfing it in a roaring inferno. Severely injured, the demon vanished into the mists to heal. Octonia let out a quick caw as if to encourage them men to return home. They proceeded towards Sol, Octonia hovered closely behind, evaporating any monsters that got too close.

Radric was on the North Gate watchtower, awaiting the return of Octonia. In the distance, he noticed a great fiery glow. Below her, the entire ninth squad, completely unharmed.

"Open the gate!" He shouted energetically. The men poured into the city and fell to their knees, cheering and gasping for air all at once. Radric dropped from the watch tower. "What happened? How were you able to get back so fast? Were you not able to make it to the halfway point?" The colonel approached the king and fell to bended knee. "Rise. Please enlighten me."

"Sire, it is very hard to explain. But we actually made it to the destination. We began setting up the encampment when we were suddenly engulfed in shadows. Then, we were attacked by a demon, which we could not manage to injure in any way. Sir, I have come to believe this creature may have taken out the other squads. None of them made it to the checkpoint, and we were the furthest behind." Radric clenched his fist and stared at it intensely.

"I should have been there!" He thought to himself, crippled with regret. "I should not have been so weak. I should not have been so carless to impale myself in a simple rescue attempt. The poor kid didn't even make it back! What was it all for? I could have saved them! No creature of this world or the next is powerful enough to defeat me. I should have been there, Argh!" Radric shouted in self-disappointment.

"Sir, it isn't your fault." The colonel replied empathetically, "The demon took advantage of your accident; it can't be helped."

"Get your men to the medical manor. You need your rest; we will put this raid off for a while to recover from this great loss." Radric said with a sigh. We need to let the families know and hold a grand ceremony in the honor and memory of all those who have fallen." The colonel nodded in understanding and did as he was told.

Radric returned to his chambers and stood on the balcony

as he always did. He began to think to himself in a sorrowful manner. "Why Luna? Why Sol? Why must we fight each other? Can we not have peace? Why is there still hate out there? Look what evil now prowls these lands. Demons, who would see us all destroyed! We should band together to fight against this great evil. Not each other. Father Gi, please, give me the wisdom to free my people and the people of Luna from this confounded nightmare." Finishing his prayer, he commanded the artificial sun to set on a long and miserable month.

To the Wastelands!

Part II

*One week after Sol departed for the wastes,
Luna made their own departure.*

Lycia and Elizya emerged from the palace. All the supportive citizens of Luna stood in the city streets. Lycia's entire
demeanor would change whenever she would take off on a raid.
Her usually peppy, chipper, smiley attitude would fade and be
masked by seriousness. Mainly because she knew she must do
the one thing she hates more than anything, killing. Colonel
Boyox and Captain Geeah knelt before the queen, rendering
proper honors.

"Stand and be ready, my battle commanders, assemble your
warriors." She spoke blankly and devoid of any emotion. They
quickly came to their feet, drawing their weapons, and signaled
to the awaiting military to march into the square. Small children
became excited to see their troops marching in the street. They
thought it was so cool to see them all decked out in their armor
and weapons. In their innocence, they didn't realize how serious
this was, but they ran up to their heroes energetically.

"Go kill those bad guys!" The warriors smiled and patted the children on the head. Captain Geeah approached a group of children and crouched down to their level. She smiled warmly and opened her arms wide. They all happily jumped into her arms and held tight as she embraced them back. A single tear fell from her eye as she felt the lovable children's warm embrace.

"Miss Captain, why are you crying?" A small child who took notice asked. She giggled as she came to her feet.

"Don't worry, young one. Your warriors fear nothing, and your captain won't cry." The children cheered as they ran off, talking about how cool the warriors were. She turned away, slamming her eyes shut as tears poured from them. Having spent her life becoming a doctor and then dedicating herself to the military, she was never able to find a husband of her own. She wanted nothing more than to raise children but answered a different calling. Holding those little ones brought her more joy than could be expressed, but it also filled her with immense sorrow. She was afraid she would never know the joys of being a mother as there was no certainty that she would even be coming back from this raid alive. Having witnessed the whole scenario, Boyox wrapped his arms around her from behind, resting his head against her. She wore a stunned look as her eyes opened wide. Gathering her bearings, she twirled around and rested her head against him, returning his embrace.

"You're still holding back, Geeah, just let it out." He spoke in a compassionate voice. "I know exactly what you are going through." Geeah squeezed him tighter and began sobbing loudly. He guided her away from the square with her still resting in his embrace. He knew she wouldn't want her troops to see her like this. They reached a quiet spot in an alley.

"One day, this war will end, hopefully in our lifetime." He continued with similar compassion. "I'm sick of all the fighting.

All I want now is to start a family of my own." Her sobbing came to a quick halt, and she opened her eyes.

"You too? So you really did know what was going on in my mind." She responded with intrigue. She squeezed him tighter to where he was having difficulty breathing. "Oh, thank you, colonel. I never realized you had this side to you. Now I see why the queen is so taken with you." He tapped her back lightly and tried to speak, but all that came out were muffled choking sounds. She released him as she realized what she was doing. Her face began to shine with a pink glow as she looked away, slightly embarrassed.

"Gees, what is with you women and all the intense squeezing!" He exclaimed in an irritated manner as he gasped for air. He continued to grumble to himself for a short moment but was interrupted when he suddenly felt her body against his face as she rested her head on top of his. Only this time, she held him tenderly. He received her embrace.

"Seriously, sir, thank you. I really needed this." They remained as they were for a few moments until Boyox realized just what part of her body was pressed up against his face. His entire face grew dark red, and he gently slipped away from her hold.

"Alright then, captain, glad I could cheer you up." He said in a slightly embarrassed manner as he cleared his throat. "Let's return to the ranks; it looks like Queen Lycia is about to address the kingdom."

Lycia stood at the base of the statue of Luna's founder. She held on to the stone spear with her left hand and leaned out with her right fist in the air.

"My beloved citizens, your safety is in the capable hands of Uçebar's finest military force!" The kingdom erupted into cheering. "Sol thinks herself superior!" The cheering shifted to booing and shouting insults. "Sol hides behind magic greater than our comprehension, but we need no supernatural projectiles to cut them down mercilessly!" The cheering returned. She raised her hand, and the crowd became silent. "My people, I will not lie to you; many of us may never return to you after this raid." She continued in a stern yet calm manner. Shock and nervous murmurs broke out throughout the crowd. Her voice became energetic again as she shouted. "However, I will risk my own life to ensure as many of us get back while sending as many Solyans to their graves as possible." Everyone cheered loudly except for Elizya, who stood not far from the statue beside Onceli. Lycia hopped down and ran up to her. For the first time this day, she allowed her emotions to soak into her expression. She smiled warmly and threw her arms around Elizya, resting her cheek against Elizya's chest.

"Don't worry, Mother, we will both return. That's a promise." She released her and made her way to the front of the formation. Drawing her axe and holding it in the air, she released a powerful battle cry. "Onward Lunians, to the wastelands! To victory!" She looked over to Onceli with a courageous smile. "Come, daughter, momma will show you how to be a skilled hunter!" Onceli howled, and the Lunians sprinted off through the kingdom gates. Onceli remained by Lycia's side as they charged into the dank gloom of the wastelands. Lycia, having the keen senses of a wolf, led the warriors towards the Solyan marines she could smell on the air. Unlike Sol, Luna stayed together in the wastelands. This would take them longer to sweep the perimeter, but Lycia knew it was the best chance she had to protect her troops.

Mana's light illuminated the sky, and the air was still. Lycia held up her fist, bringing the formation to a halt. Most of them placed their hands on their knees in an attempt to catch their breath. Lycia realized the impressive speeds she could maintain may be too much for them, and they needed rest.

"Set up camp here!" She shouted sternly, "Colonel Boyox, establish a watch and ensure you get some sleep yourself. Captain Geeah, gather your ladies and establish a medical watch as well; of course, don't forget to get some sleep yourself."

"Aye, majesty!" They shouted in unison, then set out to fulfill her orders. It didn't take the Lunians long to get the camp set up. At the furthest reach of the encampment, away from the rest, was Lycia's tent. Now able to fully express the emotions she kept at bay for the entire day, she snuggled up close to Onceli. Onceli let out sad whimpers of empathy.

"Onceli, my sweet girl. Forgive me for bringing you on this journey so early in your life. You're not ready for this; I know that. I just...I don't know how many times I'm going to be able to cheat death, and I have to make sure you are strong enough to defend yourself... in case..." Onceli began whimpering more frantically, gnawing at Lycia's arm and slightly growing at her. Lycia smiled warmly. "I'm sorry, I won't say things like that anymore. Just know that I love you, dear daughter. And although he is not with us, I'm sure your daddy loves you too. Hopefully, this can end soon, so we can be a real family together. Won't that be great?" Onceli's tail waged energetically back and forth as she licked Lycia's face. Lycia giggled wildly, begging her to stop, until they both slipped away into their dreams. One of the marines on watch heard the commotion but could not detect the playful emotion behind the queen's voice.

"Do you hear that?" He exclaimed. "It sounds like the queen is in trouble. We should go check it out." His partner shook his head and chuckled in a demeaning manner. "Hey, what's so funny?" He inquired defensively. "We are on watch; take this seriously." The second watchman exhaled heavily and placed his hand on his comrade's shoulder.

"The only one who will be in trouble is you if you go anywhere near that tent!" He responded playfully. "Trust me, the queen is fine. If she wasn't, I guarantee we would see a giant wolf burst from her tent. Remember, she has her daughter here with her. No loving mother would be caught alive cowering and begging for help while the safety of her offspring is at risk. Besides, this is the queen we are talking about...she doesn't need *our* help. And relax a little, won't you? If you are so tense, you will lose your composure when the time comes to actually fight." The first watchman looked down in an ashamed manner as he lightly kicked up dust with his foot repeatedly. "Eh, come on, kid, don't be such a stiff." The second watchman continued. "This very well could be our last night alive, right? So why spend it in constant worry or shame?" he lifted his hand from his partner's shoulder and lightly slapped his face.

"You're right. I must do my best to enjoy my last moments alive." His determination slowly faded as he began to slouch. "But how can I do that out here in the wastelands? I'm just so tense; I feel like the lives of all our comrades rests on our shoulders right now." The second watchman chuckled playfully.

"We are the current watch standers; everyone's lives *are* on our shoulders. This is your first time out here, huh?" He chuckled as he looked at the sky. "I remember the first time I was here. Listen, just think of something that you really like and use it to keep yourself calm."

"It's kinda hard to focus on things like that right now. Although, there is something that distracts my mind enough to forget about the wastelands."

"Great, well, let's hear it then." He responded with a proud grin.

"Uh, I'd rather not say." He looked away, and his face grew red.

"Oh, come on, what can't you tell a brother-in-arms?"

"Well, I guess you're right, again..." He reluctantly agreed as his face glowed a brighter red. "When I think of Queen Lycia, my problems seem to float away." The second watchman's face bore a blank expression.

"Now that...that is something I, myself, would have kept a secret..." He responded bluntly. The first watchman turned his head away in embarrassment until the second continued in a goofy manner. "And that is exactly what I have been doing!" The first watchman turned to his comrade and gasped with shock as he saw the wonder dancing in his partner's eyes. "Since you were able to admit it, I am now too." They bantered back and forth like love-drunk teenagers over Lycia and her mystique. Suddenly, they both were clubbed over the head with an axe handle. They spun around and became nervous to see Colonel Boyox standing before them.

"You Pathetic fools sound like a couple of ditsy schoolgirls ogling over the popular jock. Please keep in mind you are on watch; you may enjoy yourselves, of course. But stay vigilant and attentive as well. Besides, you wouldn't want the ladies over in the medical tents to think you are little girly-boys, do you?" The watchmen looked over to see three attractive medics in the distance, staring and giggling at them. Their eyes widened, and their faces painted with embarrassment. "Looks like it may be too late for that," Boyox said with a chuckle as he walked away. The watchmen quickly turned their backs to the medics and stood stiff, staring into the darkness. The first watchman, without breaking his intense gaze, slammed his foot on his partner's.

"What the hell was that for?" The second exclaimed, keeping his stare towards nothing as well.

"Think of something you like, huh? Great idea, idiot." They each shifted to where they were facing each other.

"Hey, I was only trying to help." The second responded defensively. They broke out into monotonous bickering, and Boyox laughed quietly to himself as he continued to walk away. He was sweeping the perimeter when he noticed Geeah in the distance, staring up at the moon. She was seated with her knees tucked into her chest, her legs cradled in her arms.

"Good evening, Geeah." He spoke calmly as he approached her from behind. She turned her head back and, upon realizing it was him, jumped to her feet and saluted him. He rendered back but chuckled playfully. "We are in the field, Geeah, and it's the dead of night. Don't worry yourself with intense formalities." He spoke gently. She smiled and returned to her seated position as her eyes returned to the moon. He sat beside her, and she looked over at him with surprise. She gasped as she noticed his expression. He was seated with his arms behind his back, and he wore a large smile on his face as he stared intently at the moon.

"This is so weird; I've never seen the colonel display such emotions before." She thought as she maintained her gaze. "Earlier today, when he held me...like he truly cared..." Her face grew red, and her thoughts became frantic. "Oh gees, what am I thinking? He's eighteen...And he's the battlefield colonel. I can't be having things like this run through my head!" He noticed her embarrassed, awe-struck face staring at him from the corner of his eye. As he looked at her, her eyes grew wide, and she looked away.

"What, what is it?" He asked gently. Her gaze fell to the ground as her cheeks pulsed with heat.

"It's nothing, sir, don't mind me." Boyox returned his gaze to the moon, and his smile returned to his face. She looked back over to him. "Sir, what is it that has you so at ease and causing that big smile to form on your face?"

"Geeah, do you ever wonder if our lives are already planned out?" He responded in an off-topic manner without turning his gaze from the moon. Her eyes grew wider, and she let out a slight gasp.

"Well, no sir...a topic like that has never crossed my mind." She responded quietly, looking to the ground and playing with some dirt. He fell silent, and she looked over to him once again. Another gasp escaped her mouth as she stared on. His gaze still fixed on Mana with a bright smile, tears began to flow from his eyes. Geeah couldn't believe what she was seeing.

"Forgive me, captain, I'm not feeling myself." He said with a slight crack in his voice. "Normally, I never would have burdened you with what lies deep within my heart. Usually, I'd be able to stow it away, but in the company of another commander...I trust you can keep this a secret."

"Mhm." She mumbled.

"When I look up at Mana, looking down upon us...I feel this warmth as if she herself were saying, 'Everything will be okay.' Like if she is insisting my life has more meaning than just war and killing. I will not allow myself to die. Not until I have seen the world in a state of peace. Where I can finally start a family and retire from my position as battlefield colonel." His smile soon faded, and his voice grew soft as he continued. "A world... where I can be with her..." Geeah gasped and turned her head from him.

"I thought he was only showing his emotions and sharing his thoughts with me because...well, maybe, he liked me?" She thought, slightly confused and disappointed." But he has some-one...someone he loves. Oh no! Why do I care? Why is this both-ering me? I'm nearly twice his age!" She let out an embarrassed moan. He turned to her, her head still facing away from him.

"Geeah, what's wrong? You've been acting rather strange around me ever since this morning." He spoke gently.

"Strange, what do you mean strange?" She said frantically as she turned to him. "I'm just being me." She forced a fake laugh nervously. "What, are you saying *I'm* strange?" She forced another unconvincing fake laugh. "Oh, gees." He placed his hand gently on top of hers. She looked over at him and gazed into his dark eyes.

"Ease your mind, Geeah." He said in a comforting manner with a warm smile. "You will find someone who will love you."

She gasped and shifted her gaze to the ground. "I believe we are all destined to find one special person. Mana has linked our destinies to the soul whom we are meant to be with forever. Some find their soul mate sooner than others. I can feel it in my heart, Geeah, this war will end during our lifetime. Somehow, when we finally find a way to quell all the fighting. Once that happens, before you know it...he will suddenly be there, and you will feel it deep within your soul as you meet him." She kept her gaze to the ground.

"How the hell does he always know what's going on in my head?" Her thoughts continued to race. "Ugh, what's with me. The way he is consoling me, you'd think he was the mature one, and I was the teen." She exhaled miserably causing his smile to fade as he looked to her with confusion.

"You still look like you are wallowing in misery. Gees and this is good stuff; I felt my own soul ignite during that little speech." He responded in a playful manner, lacking modesty. She giggled and looked at him with a warm smile.

"Thank you, colonel. Again, it seems like you always know just what to say." He smiled and hopped to his feet, offering his hand out to her.

"Come, captain, let me escort you to your tent; you should get some rest." She received his hand, and he guided her to her feet. They made their way to her tent, and she hugged him tenderly good night. He returned to find the two watchmen still bickering loudly. He rolled his eyes as he approached them. Standing behind them, he cleared his throat. They spun around nervously, and proper honors were rendered.

"Wake your relief and return to your tents; your watch is over." He said sternly with a blank expression. He made his way to the officer's tent and awoke the battlefield major. "Take charge of the post as a watch commander in my stead. Have the lieutenant take the last watch before morning." The second watch was manned, and the night rolled on.

It was halfway through the second watch's stand when Lycia's eyes burst open. She sprang from her tent urgently.

"Everyone on your feet! Something is very wrong!" The Lunians quickly emerged from their tents and gathered around her. Onceli peeked her head out from the tent. "Onceli, it's time; stay close to Mommy!" Colonel Boyox bowed before her.

"My queen, what is it? What has you so concerned?"

"Get this encampment packed up, pronto. We've got to move! I smell Uçebian blood on the air!" Everyone gasped and drew their weapons. "Blood that carries the dense foul odor of decay. These Uçebians...are dead! Judging from the potency, I'd estimate over forty deceased. Something was powerful enough to vanquish an entire Solyan platoon. Whatever it was, it is sure to still be out there. We must hunt it down and destroy it before it can destroy us. Move out!" The Lunians quickly packed up their camp and began to seek out the creature.

"Beast, whatever you are! Show yourself!" Lycia shouted as she and her troops sprinted deeper into the waste. "You may have slain my enemy, but you are still no friend of mine!" Suddenly, the entire Lunian platoon was engulfed in a shadowy gloom. Lycia looked around in shock, realizing they were surrounded by darkness.

"What is this?" Boyox exclaimed as he fell to one knee, struggling to breathe. "The air has become twice as heavy, and the foul odor seems to be burning inside my lungs." Several other young warriors fell to their backs, gasping and choking. Boyox fought through the discomfort and began making his way towards them. A clang sounded, attracting everyone's attention. Boyox had quickly drawn his axe and held it to his neck at the precise moment the demon was going to slit his throat. Those watching could not believe what they were seeing. Not only had they never seen a demon before, but they could not understand how the colonel even knew it was there. The demon wore an amused expression and slipped back into the shadows. Lycia remained by her daughter's side, prepared to give her life to protect her.

"Major, get over there quickly and get them out of the darkness," Boyox commanded. "Any medics who can function, assist in the evacuation of the afflicted." He began coughing as he continued to fight through the harshness of the gloom. The major began sprinting towards the fallen warriors but suddenly wore a blank expression, and his motion ceased. "Major, what are you doing? I'm not going to get there in time! Move your ass." Suddenly, the major's limbs flew into the air with intensity, and his head fell from his body. Lycia and Boyox stared in absolute horror. Geeah ran toward the fallen young warriors.

"No! Wait! Stop! Stay away from them; they are the bait!" Boyox shouted desperately.

"Colonel, I can do this, sir! I can save them. It's like you said; our destinies are set before us. I will not die today!"

"I know what I said, but be smart; this is not a normal opponent!" He shouted to her as he continued running towards her. The sound of torn flesh erupted in the air, and Boyox skidded to a halt. "Geeah!" He shouted with worry. She had quickly blocked a killing blow, but the blade still carved deep into her cheek. Boyox began to charge towards her once again.

"You crazy woman!" He thought frantically. "You better not die! I promised you a future, and I will not go back on that promise!" Lycia joined the fray as she launched forward, propelling out of her clothes, and morphed into her monstrous dire wolf form. She let out a mighty roar and pounced on the demon, pinning it to the ground. She bit down hard, crushing the demon in her giant, powerful jaws. She shook her head violently, dismembering and shredding its body as her fangs dug deeper into its flesh with each movement. She tossed the mangled remains to the ground and then looked towards Geeah.

"Are you alright?" Lycia asked.

"What a relief. I had a very bad feeling about this whole situation." Boyox thought, standing idly by with a gentle smile. Suddenly, his smile faded, and fear painted his face as his thoughts continued. "But how could something this weak destroy the Solyan military?" His eyes grew wide as his thoughts became more frantic. "Unless it isn't that easy! Because why would the shadowy gloom still be upon us?"

"My queen, captain, be careful! This isn't over!" He shouted. Still in her wolf form, Lycia sniffed the air and looked around. Onceli began whimpering loudly. Lycia looked over at her to see she was significantly distant, lying down, covering her face with her paws, too frightened to move.

"Onceli!" Lycia shouted with the concern of a thousand lifetimes. She dashed forward, but she was not going to get there in time.

"No, what have I done! I never should have brought her!" She thought frantically. "How could I have been so foolish! No! Onceli! No!" The sound of torn flesh and blood splatter erupted once more, filling the air. Lycia morphed back into her Uçebian form with a slight trip as she fell to her knees and screamed with every ounce of air she had in her lungs. But suddenly, the sound of a man grunting hit the air as well. She looked forward and saw that Onceli was fine, and Boyox was flying past her in a blocking manner. Geeah and Lycia looked over in horror as shreds of blue leather flew through the air, surrounded by drops of blood. A large gash formed on his body from his abdomen to his shoulder as he crashed to the ground. Lycia sprung forward, morphing back to her wolf form, and dashed towards Onceli. The demon was upon the fearful little cub once more. As it went to strike, Boyox chucked his Axe with a grimace, knocking the demon's sword from its hands. Lycia finally reached them and pinned the foul creature under her massive paw. It smiled sinisterly at her. She bit into its neck and tore off its head. Instantly, it regenerated before her very eyes and despair fell over her.

"Is there no way to stop this monster?" She thought, feeling defeated. She bit down hard once more and tossed the demon far from Onceli. She stood over her in an aggressive stance to protect her. Lycia looked over to Boyox and could see he was not mortally wounded, but there was no time to lose focus. Geeah took advantage of the break in the fray and continued towards the fallen. Boyox tried to shout but was not loud enough to reach her. The sickly sound of cracking bones and torn flesh erupted on the battlefield. Geeah's eyes grew wide with shock and Boyox felt his heart grow heavy as he watched on. Geeah looked down taking notice to the blurry image of a sword tip piercing through her stomach. Her hands were trembling as she attempted to retaliate, but she was losing strength rapidly.

"I said I would save them! So I am going to save them!" She shouted with determination. She slowly walked forward until the blade was free from her body, and gathering the last ounce of her strength, cut the demon's head from its body. Having bought herself some time, she continued to the four unconscious warriors. Boyox was struggling to get to his feet as Geeah began dragging the first warrior from the shadow. The demon regained consciousness and stood to its feet. Boyox continued to struggle crumbling to the ground.

"What the hell are the rest of you doing?" He shouted fiercely. "Do something! Help her! What did you join the military for? Was it not to defend your kingdom? To defend your families? To fight besides your brothers and sisters in arms? *Or to just cower and watch them die!* If this creature gets past us, there will be nothing in its way from getting to Luna!" They found their courage, motivated by Boyox's valor. They shouted as they charged the demon. It smiled sinisterly, and they all came to an immediate halt. Boyox's eyes trembled and filled with remorse as they fell in pieces, completely dismembered in a matter of seconds. Despair clouded his mind.

"No...it can't be...that speed...that power..." He thought weakly. "If it had this strength the whole time, why would...It's toying with us. We never had a chance to survive. It just didn't want it to be over too fast." He closed his eyes in a manner of defeat.

Geeah managed to get three of the warriors out of the gloom. She grabbed under the arms of the last marine when she felt the blade of the demon pierce her from behind once more. She screamed out in agony as she coughed up blood, and her vision began to fade further. Boyox opened his eyes and gazed upon the scene. He continued to think to himself in a frustrated manner. "What am I doing? I can't give up! Look at Geeah, giving everything she has to save the unconscious. Even giving her own life." He let out a powerful cry and forced himself to his feet. Geeah was not ready to give up, and with the last of her dying strength, she hurled the final marine from the darkness. Feeling good in her accomplishment, she fell to her back as the sword came free of her body. Boyox was suddenly upon them and quickly slashed the demon into mangled bits. With a whirling kick, he launched its torso far from them. Placing a hand under Geeah's head, he wrapped the other around her back, resting her on his leg.

"Geeah, damn you! Why wouldn't you listen to me! Don't you dare die! Somehow, we will get you out of this. Remember, you have a destiny to fulfill." He spoke in a broken manner. Tears streamed from his eyes as Geeah began coughing up more splashes of blood. Her vision began to improve, and it became clear once she saw Boyox's face.

"I love your optimism, colonel, but I think my destiny differs from the one you envision." She responded weakly. She began to think to herself as she struggled to cling to her life. "Look at the concern behind his eyes. I can't die now, not like this...I must know love. I must experience it." She looked deep into the red-stained pools of his onyx eyes as she spoke weakly. "Boyox?" He gasped upon hearing her call him by name. He began to cry harder, knowing that could only mean this was probably the last words she would be able to say.

"Yes, Geeah?" She began to smile brilliantly; He didn't understand why.

"I refuse to die, Boyox...I refuse to die until I've known love! Please, wipe the blood from my mouth for me, won't you?" He drew a cloth from his trousers and dabbed the blood from her mouth. Her big bright smile shined in the gloom, and her hazel eyes sparkled with unfallen tears. Her aura was so soothing that Boyox began to feel as if his heart was melting as he gazed into her glorious eyes. "Boyox, I can't die yet, not until you've kissed me." Boyox gasped, unsure of how to respond. "I know your heart belongs to another, but admit it. There is something between us, even if only a little...it's still something." His eyes trembled as his cheeks grew flush. "Please, I must experience love before I die. Boyox, I love you. Please, before I die, just kiss me once, as if you love me too. I want it to feel like it is real, even if only pretend."

"There's no need to pretend, I love you too, Geeah." He said weakly with a slight smile. Her heart skipped a few beats, and her vision faded in and out, but her joy kept her alive for the moment. As his lips met hers, she raised her trembling hands and gently took hold of his face. When their moment ended, Boyox slowly pulled back to stare into her eyes one final time.

"Thank you, Boyox." She said weakly and barely alive. "You always know just what to do to ease my pain." She closed her eyes as she wore a content smile, and her body went limp in his arms.

"Geeah?" He cried as he shook her lightly. "No, no! Geeah... Geeah!" He shouted in anguish into the shadowy sky. Boyox gently placed her down. "Shine bright in the darkness, moonlight warrior..." He uttered gently. With determination burning in his sorrowful eyes, he attacked the demon as it was regenerating. But it was to no avail; the demon had nearly regenerated to its functional form. Lycia felt as if the very fibers of her heart and soul were being torn to shreds upon witnessing all that was taking place. Still in her wolf form, standing over Onceli, she let out a planet-shaking howl filled with empathy and sadness. She couldn't accept that she wasn't able to do a single thing but watch as she remained with Onceli. She roared with anger and such intensity that the shadows encompassing them shattered like broken glass. The demon was now exposed, but its confident demeanor never faltered. Having fully regenerated, it walked over to Boyox slowly, smiling sinisterly. Boyox gritted his teeth in anger and slashed with all his might. The demon confidently held its arm out, allowing him to slice it off.

"You foul creature! You accursed demon!" Boyox shouted.

"Pathetic Lunians! What made you think you could accomplish what Sol could not?" It spoke in a demonic, taunting manner. As its arm regenerated, Boyox slashed it off once more, attracting the demon's attention.

"How dare you toy with us like this?" Boyox shouted in anger and anguish. He slashed the creature's other arm off as it remained firm, allowing it to happen. "Why, what's the point to all this? When you could..." Boyox's eyes grew wide as Mana's light relieved a strange sight. He noticed the shadow that the demon's body projected was displaying the regeneration before it began happening to its physical body.

"Its shadow?" Boyox's thoughts raced. "Even while in the gloom it arrived with, there was enough light to see, even if only a little. So even if I couldn't see it before, it must have been casting a shadow. And if this shadow regenerates before it physically does..."

"My queen!" He began shouting. "I have a hunch as to how we can defeat this monster! It's a long shot...but even so, we have to try. However, only you can make it happen!"

"Yes, anything, what is your plan?"

"Its shadow seems to be the source of its regenerative powers!" He shouted as he continued to defend himself. "I need you to implore Mana to abandon the skies just long enough for you to kill it. In the complete darkness, with your wolf sense, you will be the only one who can find it. Without the moon or the slight light from its shadow dome, I assume you'd be able to fully kill it."

"That's absolutely crazy, Boyox! But...kinda genius! Okay, I'll give it a try!" She bowed her head and pleaded with Mana to abandon her throne briefly. Suddenly, Mana's light vanished from Uçebar, and a complete darkness that had never been experienced before overcame their world. Lycia sprang forward, and the demon squealed with genuine fear. She scooped it up in her mouth and bit down hard. It let out a horrifying cry of agony that echoed through the wastelands. Lycia growled, thrashed, and mangled the creature as it screamed. It began to bleed out a dark miasma that contained the suffering and torment of all those it had killed and fed off. It began clouding Lycia's thoughts, and she began to lose herself in its suffering. As it screamed, she felt a sickly pleasure and began ensuring she only crushed down on non-vital areas.

"My queen, finish it!" Boyox shouted desperately. "It's too dangerous to keep that thing around any longer. Its suffering is not worth the amusement! We have won, please, my queen!" The miasma filling her senses had grown so potent she lost control of her enormous body. A loud, horrifying sound echoed in Boyox's mind as he was nearly positive of what he just heard. Lycia fainted causing her to morph back into her Uçebian form, as she fell to her back. Onceli ran to her, whimpering and nudging her with her snout. Soon, Mana returned to grace the skies, allowing Boyox to see once again. His cheeks grew bright at the sight of her naked body and turned away to collect her clothes. When he returned, he couldn't help but notice a dark purple, void-like fissure swirling over her heart. He became concerned and fell to his knees beside her to get a better look. Suddenly, her eyes opened, and Boyox's embarrassment couldn't be expressed in words as her visible eye met his gaze.

"My queen, believe me; this is absolutely not what it looks like!" He frantically explained.

"Kerny, if you wanted to see my chest, all you would have had to do is ask." She responded playfully.

"No, no, no! Really highness! Look at the left side, right above your heart!" His franticness grew as he pointed to the fissure. It faded away just before she looked over at it.

"Alright then, you perve, you had your little sneak peak, now give me my clothes." Boyox released an irritated sigh and turned away as he handed them to her. She got dressed, and Boyox helped her to her feet. Tears filled her luminous eye as she looked around at the carnage that lay across the battlefield. She tossed her arms around him, resting her head on his shoulder as she gently sobbed.

"What...what have I done? I led my people to their deaths! I should not have been so rash to think a creature that could defeat an entire Solyan platoon would be something we could have destroyed easily. I let my people down; we lost...so many! I even put my daughter's life in danger. What kind of queen am I?"

"Majesty, you cannot blame yourself for this," Boyox responded compassionately as he returned her embrace. "This creature was beyond our comprehension. An entity seemingly not of this world. There's no way we could have been prepared for something like this." He released a heavy sigh as he retracted from her. "That aside, highness, there are some that survived thanks to Geeah. They need us; let's go tend to them."

"You're right, let's go home." She said weakly with a frown. "This raid must come to an end if we are to keep the safety of our remaining marines." She sighed sharply. "None of my beautiful little medics survived!" She began to cry, and Boyox took her hand, tugging her along.

"My queen, we cannot linger here; there will be plenty of time to grieve when we return to Luna." She wept quietly as he guided her along. They reached the young marines, who were still unconscious but breathing normally. Boyox knelt by their side and attempted to wake them when Onceli suddenly took off into the mists, barking wildly.

"Onceli!" Lycia shouted in high-pitched concern. "Get back here, where are you going?" Lycia charged after her.

"Your majesty, wait!" Boyox called out.

"Protect them! Once they awake, head back, with or without me!"

"Be safe, Queen Lycia." He said quietly as he watched her disappear into the mists.

Onceli kept running despite all of Lycia's pleading. Lycia sprung from her clothes and morphed into her wolf form as she continued to make chase. She caught up effortlessly and picked up Onceli by the extra skin behind her neck. Onceli whimpered and flailed, desperately trying to get free. She began to howl and thrash. She scratched Lycia, causing her to be dropped, and she ran into a small ditch where the body of a dead Solyan lay. Lycia looked around in awe at the graveyard of slaughtered Solyans. Even though they were enemies, she felt sorrowful for them. As she approached Onceli, she noticed something different about this particular Solyan. He bore a strange ring that revealed itself with a glisten in Mana's light. Onceli bit down and removed it from his hand. Lycia realized that it must have been one of their talismans of fire.

"Well then, daughter, I guess you weren't misbehaving at all." She said with pride. "Now, quickly, we must get back." They took off in a full sprint. Lycia scooped up her clothes as they passed by. She remained in her wolf form to cover more ground, but it proved useful in other ways as well. She arrived to see Boyox still watching over the sleeping marines. She picked them up gently, with her powerful mouth, and placed them on her back. Boyox secured them and held on tight. It was a long trip, but thanks to Lycia, they returned in record time. Boyox removed the unconscious marines from her back, and she morphed into her Uçebian form, falling to the ground exhausted. Elizya remained at the main gate the entire time they were gone. When she saw them, she sprinted to their aid assisting Lycia with getting dressed. Lycia flew into Elizya's arms, resting her head against her chest as she sobbed.

"I was wrong! I will never bring Onceli out there again! If it weren't for Boyox...I would...I'd have lost her! I couldn't protect my own daughter's life; forget all my warriors who died out there!"

"My queen, you mustn't blame yourself," Elizya replied tenderly as she massaged Lycia's silver hair. "Let's get you to bed. You can grieve in your quarters; you need rest."

Lycia made her way to her chambers and flopped into her bed with her face buried in a pillow. She gestured to Onceli to join her by gently patting the bed by her side. Onceli hopped up, and Lycia rolled to her back, allowing Onceli to rest her head on her stomach. They lay in silence as Lycia played with Onceli's fur until she fell asleep.

A New Evil

A full month had passed since the devastation on both kingdoms took place. Radric was in his usual spot, staring into the sky, while Efyna stalked him from the shadows behind a slightly cracked door.

"I can't do this, what am I doing. He has been so good to me... but...I just...I just can't do this..." She spoke quietly to herself.

"Can't do what?" Radric replied in a powerful yet calm voice, his gaze still on the sky. She gasped with sheer embarrassment and shock as to how he heard her and took off running. When he turned back, she was gone. With a shrug, he made his way to the courtyard where Karakus was awaiting his arrival. His eyes squinted as he fell into deep focus. A devious grin formed across his face, and he burst into a full sprint.

"I've got you now, cousin! This time, there's no escape!" He shouted with determination. Karakus was forced to an immediate halt, his arms dangling miserably by his sides in defeat. Karakus's head was buried in the large hand of Radric, who all but held out his open palm, robbing him of his movement. Karakus flailed around like a small child, his arms desperately reaching outward as his feet dug into the ground.

"So, you done making a fool of yourself?" Radric said with an impish chuckle. Karakus immediately stopped and looked around slowly to see many civilians gathered in the streets, observing the commotion. He released a deep exhale and composed himself, wearing a cheeky smile.

"You know, you're lucky you're a giant," he said playfully. "I will catch you off guard one of these days, cousin." Radric fell into his signature fit of laughter as he reveled in his dominance. "Hey, cousin." Karakus gently slapped Radric's arm, snapping him into reality. "You're scaring the civilians." Radric looked around to see several stares of concern and heard the sound of a baby crying in the distance.

"Well, Lord Fraytor shall be arriving any minute now." He said with slight embarrassment as he cleared his throat. "Ensure the rest of my council is waiting around the table before we arrive." Karakus nodded his head and ran off. Suddenly, the front gates opened, and a blare of trumpets filled the air. The trumpeters entered first, followed closely behind by a tall, thin man with an odd skin complexion. His blue, scaly skin was attracting much attention from the onlooking crowd. On either side of the mysterious blue man walked two tall, well-built individuals. One male and one female. The trio wore intense expressions and remained quiet as they approached Radric. The blue man stared at him intensely while the others kept their gaze forward. Tension was building among the civilians. They recognized this man; he was the king of Aquaria, and the two strong warriors were his highest-ranking officers. General Natia and Lieutenant General Relic. As far as everyone knew, Aquaria was still close friends with Sol, yet the expression riding Fraytor's face was making everyone uneasy. Fraytor tossed his hand into the air, causing the crowd to gasp, and whispers broke up throughout. The two ferocious-looking commanders backed away, giving the kings room. Fraytor released a powerful battle cry, eliciting complete silence from the crowd. He sprang forward and coiled his arms around Radric's neck as he jumped forward, pulling Radric to the ground with a heavy thud. The civilians stared in horror, unsure of what to expect next. Radric hopped to his feet, wheeling around, and drove his enormous foot into Fraytor's face. To everyone's disbelief, he endured the hit and took hold of Radric's leg, tossing him back to the ground with ease. Radric let out a thunderous roar as he recovered and hurled himself at Fraytor with his fingers intertwined, preparing for an axe handle. Before he could land the strike, Fraytor stepped to the side and drove his knee into Radric's gut. Radric backed away with a slight grimace as he glared at Fraytor with his teeth gritted in frustration. The crowd was too nervous to move but also intrigued. They never witnessed their king being toyed with so easily. Radric held out his arm at a ninety-degree angle and produced a spinning ball of flames. With a loud battle cry, he poured immense power into it, increasing its size by nearly five times. Fraytor crossed his arms and chuckled as he shook his head in a snide manner.

"Come now, Radric!" His voice was deep and raspy. "This pitiful display is unbecoming. Besides, you don't truly think you can actually hit me with those flames, do you?" Radric jumped into the air, landing behind Fraytor, and hurled the giant, spinning ball at his back. Fraytor gracefully and effortlessly stepped to the side without turning to face it. The flame ball flew past him and headed straight for the watching civilians. Fear and chaos erupted in them as they glimpsed into the face of their doom. Radric clapped his hands together with impressive force, and the ball dissipated before it could cause any damage.

"Not to worry, subjects, I would never allow my flames to harm you." He said calmly with a conceited grin. Many civilians passed out from the ordeal; others were petrified to near motionlessness. A loud crash emitted as Fraytor's foot drove deep into Radric's face, once more tossing him into the dirt.

"You've lost your touch, ol' boy!" Fraytor boasted. "How, at such a young age, do you allow me to embarrass you so?" Radric let out a long-sustained battle cry as he completely engulfed himself in flames. "This again, hmm? When will you learn, boy!"

"I'm going to turn you into seared salmon, you little squid!"

"Well, which am I, Radric? A salmon or a squid?" Fraytor teased with a mocking laugh.

"You...you knew what I meant! Argh!" Radric roared into the sky, causing the ground to shake and his flames to grow brighter. Fraytor braced himself, ready to dodge as Radric launched his flames toward him. Fraytor hopped out of the way with a snide grin, but it soon faded as he noticed Radric's conniving smile. As he landed, he looked towards Radric, unsure of what to expect. Suddenly, the torrent of flames he just dodged separated into four streams and flew towards him. He let out a fearful gasp as the flames consumed him, forming an orb around his body. Radric propelled himself into the prison of fire and took hold of Fraytor by the head. He cocked back and drove Fraytor into the ground, crushing down on his face with his hand. Fraytor lay in a daze as Radric cocked back, preparing for a vicious finishing punch.

"No more, I yield! I yield ol' boy!" Fraytor said, snapping from his daze and laughing playfully. Radric smiled sinisterly as he pulled his fist back further, still preparing to deliver the punch. Then, he reached out with his opposite arm, offering it out to Fraytor. Fraytor received his hand, and Radric guided him to his feet. Soon, their stare-down returned, and the crowd waited anxiously as it seemed the battle was about to begin all over again. Fraytor's lips began to quiver, eventually bursting into laughter, resting his hand on Radric's arm. Radric joined in laughter, the onlooking crowd could not have been more confused. Many began to disperse by this point and began to return to their business. The kings eventually calmed down and greeted each other energetically as their hands collided.

"Ahh, Radric, my young yet enormous buddy, it has been far too long!" Fraytor said with a smile. Radric scooped him up and drove his knuckles across his head.

"Indeed it has, you scaly old fool!"

"Alright, alright, mind the fin there, kid!" Fraytor grumbled as he grunted in pain.

"Well then, shall we head to the grand hall? I've had a feast prepared in your honor." Fraytor rubbed his hands together and was overtaken with excitement. Radric shook his head with a grin and proceeded towards the palace. Fraytor remained in a daze of anticipation for a great meal. Relic and Natia walked up slowly behind him, each grabbing one of his arms and carrying him off to the palace.

They reached the grand hall, and everyone stood, rendering proper honors, then found their seats. Fraytor fell back into a state of childlike wonder as the royal kitchen crew emerged with the feast.

"So, old man, I see your animal instants still make it difficult for you to compose yourself when in the presence of a grand meal." Radric teased mockingly.

"Be that as it may, ol' boy, I am not the animal here, as you are the mythical creature...I merely just resemble one." Fraytor returned his banter. Radric's face grew blank with slight offense. Karakus was the only one to laugh at the joke, as everyone else was too afraid. Radric shifted his gaze to him with a snide smile.

"Well, what are you laughing at Karakus? You've tried to get the best of me every day for years. Yet Fraytor, an old floppy fish, shows up and makes it seem like child's play." The entire table, apart from Karakus, broke out into laughter. Wasukah, who was seated next to Karakus, punched him playfully in the shoulder.

"Oh man Karakus, I don't know why you ever bother to try

to take on the king anymore!" He said mockingly through his laughter. "You always end up looking like a great fool!" The laughter grew louder, and Karakus took Wasukah by the throat and shook him violently as he shouted incoherently.

"Alright, alright, cousin, that's enough. Let's just enjoy the company of a great ally for now, huh?"

"Yea, easy for you to say, you great oaf; you're not the one who's constantly the joke of the table," Karakus said under his breath in a miserable manner. He crossed his arms and sat like an angered toddler who didn't get his way. The feast carried on pleasantly.

"Radric, old friend, this meal is exquisite," Fraytor remarked with delight. "The people of Sol are truly gifted when it comes to preparing a grand feast!" Radric folded his arms and smiled with pride and slight conceit. "However, there is one thing your people could never do better than those of Aquaria." Radric looked on with anticipation as he awaited Fraytor's point. "Enter...tainment!" Radric began to smile like a child loose in a free candy store. "Oh yes, ol' boy, I brought, *him*, with me!" The doors to the grand hall opened, and a famous Aquarian jester entered the room. He provided grand entertainment and laughter to the feast as quiet conversations continued.

"By the way, old man, we have another shipment of crops for you in exchange for next week's rain. Seeing how you are here, would you mind having some of your people collect it for me?" Radric politely asked.

"But, of course, it would be nonsense to send out a caravan," Fraytor replied with a chuckle.

The feast finally came to an end, and everyone went about their business. Radric walked out onto the balcony, joined by Fraytor.

"Fraytor, you've been around close to three decades longer

than I..." Radric spoke softly with his usual gaze to the sky. "Have any of your ancestors ever mentioned how the fighting began?"

"My, my old friend. For all the time we've known each other, you've never asked me a question such as this." Fraytor responded with intrigue.

"Ah, I remember the day we first met. I was a young boy, barely accepted by my people. I felt like an outcast. No one trusted that I wouldn't turn out to be a monster. I felt like I'd never fit in. Then, you came along looking all weird and fish-like." Fraytor chuckled gently. "But that is what I thought was the coolest thing about you." Fraytor's amusement fell to a warm smile. "You were different from everyone else, yet everyone still treated you with respect. It made me happy. It gave me hope that maybe one day, my people would respect me too."

"You know, ol' boy, you've never gotten this soft on me." He replied warmly, placing his hand on Radric's arm compassionately. "So what's got your mind so weary." He said, becoming more serious. Radric's smile faded, and his gaze fell to Fraytor.

"I'm not sure if news had ever reached Aquaria of this, but I lost nearly an entire battle platoon last month to a strange creature in the wastelands." Fraytor gasped with shock, taking a few steps back.

"My dear Radric, no, I had not heard such upsetting news. But how? The wastelands have never produced such a creature with the strength to smite that many Solyans since the dawn of Sol herself!"

"This creature was not given birth through the wastelands... it was a lost Uçebian whose heart was consumed by darkness. Apparently, one that has been lying dormant since its creation. Up until now."

"But that means..." Fraytor began to reply with his eyes wide.

"Yes, it means that Umbra has begun to show an interest in the wastelands."

"It can't be. Why would she corrupt the heart of an Uçebian? Her people have never been involved in the war."

"I do not yet believe her intention was to join the war, but if that wasn't what she intended, her people have a lot of explaining to do. As I'm sure, the creature murdered countless Lunians as well. If her intention was not on the war, then their king must answer for this, as this action has cursed both our kingdoms."

"Then we must send a message requesting to speak with Lord Maytold right away!" Radric nodded his head in agreement as he commanded the sun to set. Radric and Fraytor said their goodnights and retired.

The next morning, Radric saw Fraytor off and summoned his council members to discuss the matter of Umbra. He explained the conclusion he came to on the demon, and his council fell in shock.

"How could we have not seen this?" Karakus exclaimed in a disappointed manner. "A creature of such darkness could have only been given rise by the dark goddess herself. I guess their kingdom's quietness and seemingly peaceful nature has left us complacent."

"This is a matter of great importance," Radric answered. "We must discover how deep this goes. Was this an act of Umbra alone, or was Maytold involved as well." He slammed his fist into the table. "Those sneaky bastards, we never should have trusted their strange silence."

"What of Luna, my lord?" Wasukah inquired calmly as he stood to his feet.

"What of them?" Radric replied with an eyebrow raised.

"If your assumption is correct, and the demon indeed slaughtered Lunians...we now have a common enemy. This could be a chance for us to form a treaty with Luna." The table erupted into complete disorder and chaos in response to his statement.

"Do you hear what you are suggesting, you old fool!" Karakus shouted as he flew to his feet, slamming his palms on the table.

"Don't forget your place, Lieutenant General! You will watch how you speak to me." Wasukah shouted angrily.

"With respect general, it may be time for you to step down if you think that course of action shall ever be acceptable." He slammed his palms on the table once more. "They are our sworn enemy since the dawn of their nation. How could you ever consider such a thing!"

"Yes, general, are you sure of such a decision? This could tear the kingdom apart." Radric replied bluntly. Although he wished he could openly agree with Wasukah, it was too dangerous to reveal his true intentions at the current time.

"My king, my dear council members..." Wasukah spoke calmly. "Do we even know where our hatred stems from? I am the eldest man present in this room, and even my great-ancestors know nothing about the cause of our hate. Apart from the war we have always waged. And despite this war, each side has always followed respectable rules of engagement. Never before has the loss of an entire platoon been seen due to the battle with Luna and in such a disgraceful manner. This creature, this menace of Umbra, it slaughtered everyone. Mutilated them! Luna would never have sunk so low as to kill young and incapacitated marines. If we work together to silence this great evil, our battle with Luna may finally come to an end." Radric sat silently, suppressing his emotion. He couldn't believe there was finally another Solyan amongst them who wished to see the fight with Luna end. One amongst the highest respects of his council, no less. He began to feel hope however, for if someone like Wasukah yearned for peace, there could surely be others. Silent whispers broke out throughout the table as different discussions of approval and disapproval were swapped back and forth.

"I move for the immediate resignation of General Wasukah!"

Karakus shouted furiously. "I will step up as commander of the Solyan military!" Everyone let out a gasp of shock, and Wasukah looked over to his comrade with sadness behind his eyes. "This display of weakness will destroy the kingdom! We cannot allow the attack of another nation to deter us from reason!"

"That's right!" A Brigadier General shouted as he stood. "Never before has an alliance been formed with Luna, even if temporary. They cannot be trusted! I vote, aye, for the termination of General Wasukah and the promotion of Lieutenant General Karakas!" Wasukah slowly took his seat, quietly, stunned by how quickly his comrades turned against him.

"This is madness!" Major General Gorg shouted. "Too quickly have you all jumped to this course of action! General Wasukah has led us through many victories. This is a disgrace to his accomplishments."

"You fool!" Karakus shouted as he pointed his finger towards Gorg. "In no way do I wish to discredit the general's prior accomplishments! However, I fear that, in his age and time away from the battlefield, he has grown soft! We cannot allow the Solyan military to harbor these weak emotions towards false peace, or we risk being destroyed."

"Good general, we thank you for all you have done for this kingdom...but I fear Lieutenant General makes a good point...so I must vote...Aye." A second Brigadier General calmly replied. Several discussions continued, and the vote now rested at eight "ayes" and two "nays." In the end, however, no matter how the votes piled up, the king had the final say. Radric stood to his feet slowly, gently resting his palms on the table.

"I agree with what was said earlier..." He spoke calmly. Wasukah began to feel tense but maintained his composure. "It is much too soon to come to a decision such as this. I move to discuss our next course of action further before we even consider relieving the general of his duty and title. We must remain united. We must remain calm and collected. If we jump to radical, rash action right away, we risk causing ourselves more harm than good." Karakus tossed himself to his seat aggressively with his teeth gritted together.

Karakus harbored a hate far stronger for Luna than most Solyans, for he experienced a true reason to despise them.

Flashback to Eight-Year-Old Karakus

"Come on, wake up, sleepy head!" Mayven spoke as he gently shook his son.

"Daddy, stop, it's too early!" Karakus cried.

"Hey, didn't you say you wanted to kill some monsters? Where's my brave little warrior at? Has anyone seen him? Maybe he's hiding behind this cowardly bed pillow pretending to be my son." Mayven teased.

"Okay, okay, don't be mean. I definitely want to go; I just didn't know you would take me this early! I thought mom said I had to wait until I was thirteen?"

"Well, your mother isn't with us anymore...is she?" Mayven responded with heavy remorse. "So this is my decision to make now, and I say, you're ready!" He continued as he quickly perked up.

"Awesome! Let's go!" Karakus shouted energetically.

They made their way out into the wastelands, but not too far from the kingdom to avoid further danger. Karakus began to struggle to breathe and felt the unforgiving weight of the wasteland air.

"Be strong, my little Kracky! You have it in you to fight the stifling air." Mayven encouraged. Karakus did his best to control his breathing as they stalked their prey. "Watch closely, son, then I'll have you take on a smaller one!" Mayven engaged a large, powerful lizard. It wasn't very intelligent and was easily dispatched by Mayven's well-honed skill. Karakus watched on with pride and admiration as his father made quick work of the beast.

"And that's how it's done, kiddo! Now let's find you a tiny one, yea?"

"Wow, Daddy, you're the coolest! No one can beat my dad!" Suddenly, they heard shouting coming from the distance. A Lunian marine was running towards them, desperately trying to escape the clutches of a fell hound. He seemed injured and exhausted, nearly about to collapse.

"Stay back, Kracky! I'm going to go save him!" Mayven said as he prepared to sprint off.

"What? Why? He is an enemy! Let's just go home!" Karakus begged as he tugged on his father's arm.

"He may be an enemy, but no one deserves to die at the hands of a beast, my son!" Mayven replied as he ripped himself from Karakus's hold. "Hold on, Lunian, don't give up!" The Lunian collapsed, and the beast was nearly upon him. Before it could strike, Mayven chopped its head off. He knelt by the injured Lunian.

"What happened? Where are your men? Are you alright?" Mayven inquired.

"We were ambushed by an entire hoard of these beasts. We were quickly overtaken, but we managed to get them down to the last one. I was out of strength; the rest of my men vanquished." Tears rolled from his exhausted eyes.

"You're safe now. I'll send for a medic to treat you, and we can get you back on your way," Mayven responded as Karakus approached and stood beside him.

"Ah, is this your boy?" The Lunian asked.

"Indeed, little champ was out here to learn to be a warrior with his old man," Mayven responded with pride as he rested his hand on Karakus's head.

"Strong-looking lad, he will make a great warrior one day for sure." The Lunian responded with a smile. "Thank you, I never thought a Solyan would come to my aid."

"No man deserves to—" Mayven began. "Gwuakk!" Mayven grimaced as a sword pierced through his heart, and Karakus's eyes filled with horror.

"And that is what makes you weak!" The Lunian spoke menacingly.

"Daddy! NO! Daddy! Why did you do this! He saved you!" Karakus shouted in dismay. The Lunian stood to his feet, full of energy. Karakus shook with fear as the man loomed over him.

"Your father was weak! Showing any form of compassion to the enemy is nothing more than foolishness!" The Lunian replied as he backhanded Karakus, knocking him to the ground. "Let that be a lesson to you as well, kid." He said, turning around to walk away from Karakus. "Now, be a good boy and go home! Killing a weak man is nothing beneath me but to kill a child? Even I wouldn't sink so low." Karakus shook with rage and picked up his father's sword. Without hesitation, he sprang forward and drove it into the Lunian's back. He fell, and Karakus jumped onto his torso, stabbing him repeatedly in blind fury. The Lunian chuckled weakly as his vision began to fade.

"And thus..th-the boy ha-has become—a man." He uttered as his life came to an end. Karakus ran to his father's side, weeping uncontrollably.

"I'll never forgive them! I'll never forgive Luna for this! I'll become a great warrior dad! I'll become the best! And I'll kill every last Lunian!"

Back to Present

"Have you forgotten, cousin?" Karakus spoke bluntly, looking at the table. "Luna has not always fought an honorable fight as the general suggests. Have you forgotten how your uncle died? How my father died!!!"

"Of course not! How dare you suggest such a thing!" Radric answered back with anger.

"Then that should be enough for you to side with me here. My father died because he was compassionate to a Lunian... because he was weak! The general dooms us all to our deaths if he harbors a similar weakness!"

"That's enough! I've made my decision, and it's final! We will discuss this later! Everyone is dismissed!" Everyone began to make their way out, but Radric took hold of Wasukah's wrist discretely, preventing him from leaving. When they were alone, Radric stepped out to the balcony.

"Wasukah, my good friend...I agree with you completely." Radric said softly.

"I figured you would, sire," Wasukah said, joining him on the balcony. "I was really hoping the men would come around... unfortunately, it doesn't seem that may ever happen. My king... do you think there will ever truly be peace?"

"There will be general! We'll see to that, one way or the next. Too long have we been fighting with no purpose behind our actions due to our ancestors...our ancestors' hate. There's no reason for Solyan blood, or even Lunian blood, to be shed any further. That being said, we will have to find a more delicate way to go about it." Wasukah nodded his head. Radric quietly gave him a gesture to go, and he made his leave. Radric sighed deeply and retreated to his chambers to think.

Treachery of Umbra

It was a late Lunian afternoon, but the queen had not yet emerged from her chambers. A few council members began to worry and attempted to check on her. Elizya was standing outside; however, knowing what was going on in the queen's mind, she advised them not to worry but to maintain their distance. Inside, Lycia remained in her bed with Onceli resting on her lap. No amount of time could heal such a deep wound as this, but today, Lycia was burdened more than normal by it. Her mind raced, reliving the moment of almost losing her precious child and watching her people die. Onceli's animal instincts could sense the devastation plaguing her mother's thoughts. She nuzzled Lycia's neck with her snout to break her concentration from the nightmare she wallowed in. Lycia giggled and finally felt a small sense of ease for a short period. It was enough to give her the push to get on her feet and start her day. She had Elizya gather her council, and the meeting commenced. General Rehcumber stood and began reporting any news he had to the queen. In the last month, things have been still and quiet due to the heavy losses.

"My queen, this isn't entirely pertinent, but we believe something of importance to have arisen around the occasion." He began to explain. "Lord Radric had a visit from Lord Fraytor of Aquaria. We are not sure what happened other than comradery and entertainment. However, after their feast, the two kings spoke in private and sounded very concerned."

"I wonder if they were discussing the creature that wiped out our armies," Lycia responded.

"Speaking of highness, I regret to report that none of our scientists have been able to figure out how such an entity came into existence."

"For now, let us put this creature out of our minds." She said calmly with a sigh. "I have destroyed it thanks to the superior mental fortitude of Colonel Boyox." Despite her now cheery demeanor, Boyox stood from his seat anxiously.

"With all due respect, my queen, I cannot put this creature out of my mind just yet." He spoke with unease. "I know what I heard out there...I heard you swallow the demon while in your wolf form. Then a sinister aura emitted from your heart." Elizya gasped and looked at Lycia with worry. "I'm concerned that the creature is living off you in a parasitic manner."

"Very well. I will pay a visit to the royal shaman and see what she has to say after she examines me." Lycia responded calmly.

"Very good majesty." He replied, taking his seat. Lycia removed a small object from her pocket and placed it between her thumb and index finger as she flicked it to the table. The council members looked with awe.

"My queen, is this one of Lord Radric's talismans?" Rehcumber inquired.

"Sure is! My darling little Onceli found it!" She said with a proud smile.

"Excellent. I say we have our top scientists examine it to try to learn its power! What do you think, highness?" Before she could respond, she felt a sharp pain in her head, and her luminous eye faded to a dull grey. Her genuine demeanor and cheerful aura all seemed to melt away in an instant.

"No, general, I think we should sell the talisman to Umbra." She responded with an ominous smile. Boyox's eyes widened, and his unease grew.

"What the hell? Why in Mana's name would she suggest something like that? Such a weapon is far too valuable to just... Sell!" He thought.

"My lady, that is a most unusual suggestion; please explain," Rehcumber replied.

"Well, my good general, think of it this way. Our kingdom has no use for the power of fire; we don't want to reduce ourselves to Sol's sorcery. We are warriors of the night; we require no fell magic. Besides, if we sell it to Umbra, they'd replicate it themselves and remanufacture it as a mere plaything. Then, even a small child could hold the power of the *great* Radric. His name would be tarnished, and his kingdom would split apart after having lost faith in their king."

"That kind of sinister thought process could not possibly belong to the queen we know and love! Lycia is a noble warrior; she would never utilize such underhanded tactics to win the war she had been fighting honorably for years!" Boyox thought frantically.

"Well, that is a fair point, my queen, although it seems like a strange course of action. Our honorable tactics have never resorted to this kind of dirty trickery before." Rehcumber responded with unease.

"Do you question me, dear general?" She replied with a sinister smile and ominous aura. He shook his head quietly and took his seat. Boyox was certain now that whoever was in control of her mind was not Lycia. It was too dangerous to do anything at the moment, for he had no idea what kind of supernatural power they may be dealing with. For the time being, he remained quiet and calm.

At the conclusion of the meeting, everyone was dismissed, and Boyox signaled to Elizya from a dark corner to come meet him.

"I know, colonel," Elizya announced before he could even get out a word. It was then that Boyox knew his worst fear had been realized. Tears formed in Eliza's eyes. "I'm afraid you may be right about the demon living inside Lycia. The way she was acting and the tactics she proposed were absolutely despicable. They were not her own ideas, and that was not her personality. It's strange; it was like at the mention of the talisman...she started to change."

"Lady Elizya, I knew you would be the best person to entrust on this matter. However, I don't know what to do. This demon is well beyond our understanding, but I feel we need to remain very watchful of the queen from now on." She nodded her head weakly and made her way back to Lycia. Lycia remained quiet without a single greeting.

"My queen, I'm a little concerned about what the colonel said...did you really swallow a demon?" Elizya spoke with loving concern.

"And what if I did?" Lycia snapped at her. Elizya was shocked to hear such a tone from Lycia. She knew it couldn't be her, but she was still in denial of the whole situation.

"Well, weren't you going to go see the shaman to ensure you were alright?" She continued lovingly.

"What is this all about? You checking up on me, peasant? Am I not the queen? Why should I answer to you?" Elizya quietly wept as she realized Lycia was truly gone. The creature had total control of her mind. Elizya bowed her head and apologized as she quickly made her way out of the chamber. She bumped into Rehcumber in the palace halls.

"Lady Eliza, I imagine I know what troubles you." He said compassionately.

"Please, general, tell me you didn't actually send the talisman out to Umbra, did you?" She responded frantically.

"I'm sorry, my lady, I didn't know what else to do. It is a great loss, but I'm not sure what we are dealing with here. I imagine she will be monitoring everything. So, I figured the safest bet is to play along for now. I will discuss what we should do with the other council members in private. Please join us when the time comes, my lady. For now, it is probably best we read this letter before delivering it to her to ensure we know what's going on in case the creature tries to hide anything from us." He held out a small envelope before her. "A Solyan messenger just dropped this off at the gate." Elizya gasped as her eyes fell on the large glob of wax, holding it shut.

"Is that...Lord Radric's official seal!" She exclaimed. "How could we ever look at this letter without her knowing we broke the seal?"

"The palace architect is quite the artist. Come, Lady Elizya, perhaps he can mimic the king's seal; we must know the contents of this letter." He responded urgently.

They reached the architect, and to their great relief, he was very confident he would be able to replicate the king's seal. After making a copied drawing of the seal, Rehcumber opened the letter and read it aloud.

"Council of Luna, we have an urgent matter that must be handled. We believe Umbra may be responsible for the mass slaughter of my people. A strange creature, whom I am sure must have taken the lives of many of your men as well, has destroyed an entire Solyan platoon. It has come to my attention that this creature was once a Solyan whose heart was corrupted by Umbra and made into a foul demon. I know we have had our differences in the past; my people may despise me for this, and my council may retaliate against me...however, I propose a treaty. We now face a danger far greater than two honorable warring nations. As I imagine you have witnessed, this creature is the embodiment of evil. It has no remorse or moral thought. Just a born killer. I know how this must sound, but we must put aside our hate for the good of our people and silence this great evil together. ~Radric Wartox."

"That is the king's official signature at the bottom!" Rehcumber exclaimed. "This was truly written by the King of Sol! I don't believe my eyes," Rehcumber said with disbelief.

"This is what the queen has hoped for for a long time!" Elizya exclaimed, filled with hope and joy.

"Is this so?" Rehcumber responded with slight surprise. "I thought she hated Sol?"

"She only fights them because she must. She hates the violence and killing far more than Sol. She longs for a peaceful Uçebar, where all Uçebians can live in harmony."

"I had no idea about this. I knew she hated to kill, but never did I realize that was her true thought process." He responded with a look of shock. "This could be the answer, Lady Elizya!" His expression brightened with excitement. "I, too, have grown tired of the hate and war. If we can only get the other council members and the citizens to release their hate somehow..." Elizya smiled warmly with a hint of surprise at his words. "But then, what are we to do about the queen? What if she does not wish to form the treaty?"

"Let's deliver the letter to her. Maybe seeing news like this will wake up the real queen inside of her!" She suggested with excitement.

"Great idea, my lady! Our queen must still be in there somewhere." He responded happily, feeling encouraged. The architect placed the letter in a fresh envelope. He allowed the hot wax to fall over the opening and expertly carved Radric's seal into it.

Elizya reported back to the queen who was standing out on the balcony as she always used to, staring into the sky.

"My queen, is that you?" Elizya explained. "Have you returned to..." Upon noticing the queen's facial expression and the look in her eye, she forced herself to be silent.

"Who else would it be, peasant? What is with you lately? What brings you to my chambers? Speak quickly!" The false Lycia demanded.

"My queen, a letter from Lord Radric." She replied formally.

"Fantastic, now begone servant girl! There is no reason for you to linger." Eliza walked out of the room but watched closely through a crack she left in the chamber doors. False Lycia read the letter with a blank expression, then promptly burned it over a candle.

"No...why! Not even news as joyous as this can break her from her captor? What do we do?" She thought to herself. Suddenly, fear struck her heart. "Onceli...Onceli! I've got to get her out of there! Eventually, she will go looking for her mother, and she will know right away that whatever that thing is, it is not Lycia. The monster will kill her once she finds out!" Elizya rushed back into the room.

"Peasant! Why do you intrude so often in my chambers?" False Lycia snapped with irritation.

"Oh, my queen, don't you remember?" She spoke confidently through her nervousness. "I am to give Onceli her bath. So, I have come to fetch her."

"Who needs a bath?"

"Why, your pet wolf, of course," Elizya responded with a gamble. She hoped that the creature wouldn't have access to Lycia's personal memories, and fortunately for her, she was right.

"Oh right, the little beast. Of course, take the grotesque furball and be quick." Elizya ran into Lycia's personal chambers and called out for Onceli. As they were walking past the false Lycia,

Onceli went to run up to her. She suddenly stopped and began to growl.

"Come Onceli, we must not bother the queen right now," Elizya called out. Onceli ceased her growling as she picked up on the nervousness behind Elizya's voice. They departed, and Elizya brought Onceli to her chambers. Onceli began whimpering and nudging her nose against Elizya's stomach. Elizya dropped to her knees and embraced Onceli tenderly.

"I'm so sorry, child; something is wrong with your mother right now. We are doing everything we can for her, but for now, you must stay here. Okay? Do not leave this room!" Elizya spoke sternly but with compassion. Onceli laid down, whimpering softly as she did what she was told.

Elizya frantically searched for General Rehcumber but couldn't find him. She ran to the training grounds and found Boyox.

"Colonel!" She shouted out to him as she made her way over. She explained what had transpired and about the king's letter.

"Come, Lady Elizya, we must have the private council meeting now! There's no time to waste. We can hold the meeting in the underground bunker. If you are looking for Rehcumber, he's in the medical manor right now. Go to him, have him help you collect everyone else. I will meet you there! There's just something I must do first."

Boyox ran to the outskirts of town, where his house resided. Uahka was outside scraping rot from the wood of their house when she heard him running towards her. Before she could react, he embraced her tenderly. She instinctively wrapped her arms around him.

"Honey...what's going on?" She asked with confusion.

"It's almost over, babe!" He shouted with excitement.

"Wha...what do you mean?" Her eyes widened with anticipation.

"Lord Radric sent the queen a letter asking for peace!" A huge smile painted his face.

"Are you serious!" She exclaimed.

"Yes, the war may finally be coming to an end!" He said happily as he picked her up and twirled her around.

"Wait...what do you mean, may?" Her smile faded as he placed her down. "Did the queen not accept this offering of peace? Cuz that doesn't sound like her at all!" Boyox's smile vanished as he explained what was happening.

"What!" She shouted with despair. "Of course, a once peaceful nation goes evil just as we are about to have peace!" She fell to her knees as tears gently rolled down her cheeks. "Curse Umbra... why...why can't we just all live together? Boyox...this seems much more complex than just Luna and Sol quelling the fight now. I fear I'll never get to have a normal life with you." Boyox fell to his knees and cradled her face in his hands compassionately. With a warm smile, he wiped her tears away with his thumbs.

"My dear Uahka. I promise I will do everything in my power to help this war come to a swift end. We are almost there, my love. Soon, we will finally be married, and I will be free of the military." With a smile, she embraced him as they slowly came to their feet.

"I'll hold you to that, my moonlight warrior. Now go, go save the queen!" Boyox made haste with a chipper pep in his step. He reached the secret meeting place and joined the others.

It Won't Be That Easy

General Rehcumber stood and addressed everyone. Apart from the obvious knowledge of the queen, the rest did not truly understand what to expect out of the gathering. Rehcumber informed them of Sol's call for peace and left it up to a vote to decide on what to do with Radric's proposal. It was unanimous; the highest-ranking Lunian officials were all on board for the idea of peace. Different members stood and expressed their excitement and approval. Moreover, they agreed that the true threat to Uçebian life was Umbra.

"Very good!" The general shouted energetically. "So it is settled then, we shall accept Lord Radric's proposal for peace." Cheering erupted, and many shed tears, especially Elizya. Boyox forced himself to suppress his emotions, but in his heart, he was weeping with joy.

"Finally, life can move on. Together, Sol and Luna will triumph over Umbra and silence the darkness and hate forever. Do you see what's happening, Geeah? Peace is finally coming our way...I only wish you could have been here to see it. Rest well, my dear friend." Boyox thought to himself. The moment of happiness was quickly broken as Rehcumber called for silence.

"Please, friends, I hate to ruin this beautiful moment, but there are a few things to consider. We are making this decision at a military level; the civilians will still need to be onboard with us, eventually. Also, all is not well. We now must decide whether or not to confide in Lord Radric with the news of our queen. If we send a letter accepting peace, but our queen remains compromised, she could rally the civilians against the idea. With that said, I believe one of us should deliver the message in person and potentially explain our situation to the king. What say you?" The council all agreed that it would be best to confide in Radric. "Wonderful, now then..."

"General, I shall go! Please allow me this privilege!" Boyox energetically cut into the general's conversation.

"Absolutely not!" He responded sternly.

"But, sir! Why?" Boyox inquired defensively.

"Because it shall be I who goes. Colonel, I admire your courage and dedication. However, you are so very young. I will not risk your life on this. I have lived my life to the fullest, if on the off chance I don't make it...At least you will still be able to live your life."

"I understand, sir." Boyox was reluctant, but grateful to the general for the consideration of his life.

"Elizya!" Rehcumber said, looking over to her. "At the next meeting with the false queen, when she asks about me, tell her I have fallen ill and will be bedridden for some time. That should hopefully cover my absence long enough to reach Sol."

After slight joyous banter and further planning, the gathering came to a conclusion. Rehcumber snuck out to the stables.

"Ah, Steele, the fastest and most reliable transport wolf. I am in need of your strength, old friend!" Rehcumber affectionally stroked between the massive wolf's ears as he mounted a saddle on his back. He slowly snuck around the city, reaching the underground passageways that led out in case of emergency.

When they were safely concealed underground, he hopped aboard.

"Off we go, Steele, time to save Luna!" Steele howled as he took off with impressive speed.

Several weeks had passed, and everyone did well to keep the possessed queen in the dark. Rehcumber was flying a white flag attached to his saddle as he was rapidly approaching the grand walls of Sol.

"Not much longer now, Steele! We are almost there! I can see the walls in the distance." Steele howled majestically, but their moment was quickly robbed of them. Shadows closed in all around and enveloped them in darkness. Several hooded figures began to emerge from the depths of the gloom. They bore the insignia of Umbra…it was as they feared; Umbra was on the offensive.

"No, it can't be, I was right there!" Rehcumber thought to himself.

"Well, well, what have we here?" The sinister leader spoke with an evil chuckle.

"Stand aside, minions of darkness; you will not deter me from my mission!" Rehcumber shouted valiantly, drawing his sword.

"Woah, woah, easy there, general, we are not your enemies."

"Is that a fact?" Rehcumber said in disbelief as he dismounted Steele. "So what brings you here then? Out for a stroll just outside the borders of Sol? Yes, very believable. Especially when a servant of your goddess controls our beloved queen's actions. And you show up with a cloak of shadows engulfing the area. Do you take me for a fool? Too long have we turned a blind eye to your deception. It ends here."

"So be it." The leader responded sternly as his smile faded. Rehcumber readied himself, but he didn't know what to expect. Not many interactions happened with Umbrians at all, forget seeing their military in action. The four sinister combatants sprinted off in different directions. Trails of thick black clouds lingered in their wake. Rehcumber looked around, disoriented by the trails, as they came at him from all directions. He fended off their attacks without much difficulty, but he couldn't manage to get in an offensive strike. He hopped out of the way of another attack but endured a kick as he did and came crashing to the ground. Quickly recovering, he took advantage of the break in their formation to lunge at the leader. A demonic smile painted the hooded fiend's face as he launched a wall of flames at Rehcumber. Caught off guard, he was unable to avoid the blast. He propelled away from them as the flames pushed him and burned his body severely. Rehcumber's momentum faded as the Umbrian ceased his channeling. Steam rose from Rehcumber's burning armor and roasted skin. He winced from the pain and groaned as he attempted to stand, but he no longer had the strength to move and collapsed. The hooded group surrounded him, with their leader at this front. The leader slowly removed his hood, and Rehcumber's eyes grew wide with disbelief.

"No...impossible!" Rehcumber shouted.

"That's right, fool, I told you I wasn't your enemy!" The Umbrian spoke sinisterly with a foul laugh.

"Lieutenant General Acosta? No...I refuse to believe it!" Rehcumber shook and winced from the pain as he replied. "All this time, all those years of service. You have been working for Umbra? But why, you were one of us, a brother!"

"Your nations are weak-minded. Sol...Luna, even Aquaria! You are all fools. Umbra is an intelligent goddess. Her plan has been in motion for countless generations to counter and attempts at peace.. We have been preparing and training for this for so long. Waiting for the final piece of the puzzle. That oaf, Radric, finally made her plan possible. With this!" He held out the hand that bore the Ignisque. "All of your pathetic kingdoms will fall, until all that remains, is darkness! You all have come too close to succeeding in ending the conflict between Sol and Luna. So now we put her plan into action."

"How could we have been so foolish? We should have kept the secret council smaller; what have I done?" His body shook as the pain overtook him. "But then again, I probably would have still invited you there anyway. I never could have expected my right hand to be a traitor!"

"It's too late for remorse!" Acosta laughed manically. "Say your final prayers to Mana; you will become our new wasteland ghoul." Rehcumber tried to move again, refusing to give up, but he couldn't manage to budge an inch.

"Steele! Go! Make for Sol!" Rehcumber shouted desperately as his body completely gave out, flopping to the ground. Acosta's smile faded as Steele howled with determination and sprinted off with haste.

"Curses! Why didn't we slay that foul beast! After it, you fools, it has the letter!" The sinister crew made chase as Acosta knelt down and lifted Rehcumber by his singed, messy hair. With his free hand, he drew a blade with a strange evil aura emitting from it. He held it to Rehcumber's gut, just enough to elicit pressure but not pierce through.

"This blade was cursed by Umbra to send a soul into utter torment and change it into a restless demon. A ghoul who will forever haunt the wastelands and slaughter the innocent."

"Umbra shall never have my soul. I will never harm the innocent." Rehcumber responded weakly.

"Fool, there is nothing you can do! No matter what your resolve, Rehcumber, this curse will awaken every depressing and foul thought in your mind! You do not possess the will of a god! So you will fall. You will become our new demon." He laughed sinisterly but was interrupted by a sharp cut of light through the darkness. Mana pierced through the shadows that enveloped them and cast over Rehcumber, illuminating him.

"Praise you, Mana, claim your servant's soul before this foul demon does!" Rehcumber shouted boldly into the heavens. Immediately, his body went limp, and his pupils faded completely as his soul was ripped from his body.

"No! It can't be!" Acosta shouted furiously. "Hmm...no matter, we shall never allow that letter to reach Sol." He thought to himself. "Even if it does...we may just have to see to the death of Radric sooner than planned...that will set things back, but we will still have the advantage." He took off to join his comrades in the hunt for the wolf.

Steele continued with great determination, his powerful body quickly creating distance from his fiendish pursuers.

"If this keeps up, we will lose the beast! I will handle this." Acosta shouted with a sinister grin. He drew power from the Ignisque and launched a torrent of flames towards the struggling wolf. Suddenly, a larger wave of flames deflected it as a majestic avian caw filled the skies. They were now within Sol's territory, and Octonia was ever watchful. Octonia let out an intimidating and aggressive caw as her eyes met the Umbrians. The sinister force knew they were no match for her and faded into the shadows. Octonia hovered closely over Steele as he continued to charge forward with a graceful stride. The guards atop the gate noticed the wolf and became concerned.

"Look, a Lunian wolf approaches flying a white flag...but it has no rider." The guard shouted. "Octonia is escorting it; open the gates!" Steele made it safely into the city and stood proudly as the guards approached him. "Send for a stable boy to tend to this creature; I'll search the satchel it bears." The guard found the letter and, seeing the seal of the general of Luna, took it upon himself to bring it to the king. "Comrade, cover me; this letter seems of high importance. I must bring it to the king."

The guard was making his way into the palace when he was intercepted by Karakus.

"You there, kingdom guard!" He shouted.

"Lieutenant General! Greetings, sir!" He responded as he saluted Karakus.

"What is that? Is that the seal of the general of Luna? Give it here, boy!" The guard handed the letter to him. "Where did you get this?" The guard explained everything, and Karakus dismissed him. He opened the letter and read it silently to himself.

"Lord Radric, we accept your terms for peace graciously and humbly. We feel the time to end the fighting is well overdue. However, events have unfolded within our walls that have left us compromised. I am hoping to deliver this to you personally to explain our situation. If I fail to do so, please know the council of the queen supports you. Our civilians have not yet been made aware, and we politely ask for your patience as we work to mend the issues within our kingdom. May the gods bless you. ~General Rehcumber."

Karakus became furious and tore the letter to shreds, burning the remains.

"So, cousin, you have gone behind our backs." He thought to himself. "This is treason, and I won't allow it! For now, I'll wait to see what transpires, but mark me Radric. I will discuss this with you at a more appropriate time." He gripped his fist tightly, but his anger soon washed away into sadness. "Why, cousin... why of all people would you be the one to forsake our nation this way. I hope it doesn't come to anything...please Father Gi, don't let it come to anything." He walked off slowly into a dark alley and smashed a stack of old barrels as he vanished into the darkness.

In Luna

Several weeks after Rehcumber's death, a council meeting was held, and everyone continued to play their role. However, Boyox could tell something was off. Lieutenant General Acosta sat in Rehcumber's chair, and the false Lycia didn't acknowledge it at all. In fact, she never acknowledged Rehcumber's absence to begin with. The council meeting was brief and came to a prompt conclusion.

"You are all dismissed; gather the citizens in two hours. I will be addressing the kingdom for an important announcement." The imposter queen commanded. Everyone gasped, and Boyox stood aggressively from his seat, his eyes filled with shock. "Is there an issue, colonel?"

"No, my queen." He played along. "I merely just wish to know what is going on, as you never mentioned anything to the council about what this is pertaining to...all due respect, highness."

"Hmph, am I, the queen, expected to divulge everything to this council?" She said with a scoff. "Am I not the ruler of this kingdom?" Boyox could no longer maintain his façade and began grinding his teeth as his eyes clouded with rage. "Oh? Something I say upset you, *colonel*?" She teased mockingly.

"No majesty, I dare not question the queen." He said bluntly.

"That's more like it." She scoffed. "Now do as I say, and all of you are dismissed." Boyox stormed out, kicking over a statue on his way out. The evil queen chuckled quietly to herself as he disappeared. Elizya ran to Boyox, placing a compassionate hand on his shoulder from behind. He quickly pulled away from her and continued on. She stood motionless with a sad expression as she watched him vanish in the distance.

As ordered, the others gathered the civilians in the square to await the "queen's" arrival. As she arrived, the look on her face left the civilians uneasy. They began whispering amongst themselves, wondering if something was wrong with her. She raised her hand, and the civilians fell silent.

"Citizens!" The imposter shouted. "A great travesty has taken place before us!" Whispers broke out throughout the crowd once more. Boyox watched close by as he remained hidden in a dark alley. The crowd went silent as Lycia lifted the dead, limp body of Rehcumber over her head.

"Look upon your loyal general!" She said, tossing him into the crowd. Boyox's eyes widened as his anger and rage grew. "Look what Sol has done! I sent our loyal general flying a white flag, wishing only to deliver a message to Lord Radric. How did these evil fiends respond? They cut down the good general with no honor, no tact!"

"No, it's not true!" Boyox shouted. However, the noise coming from the roaring crowd effortlessly masked him. The imposter's deception left them in enough blind rage to disregard the fact that she dishonored Rehcumber by tossing him into the crowd like a hunted game. Acosta made his presence known by stepping up beside the false queen.

"Sol dishonored the rules of engagement!" He shouted. "This is low even for them. We cannot allow them to get away with this. Too long have they looked down on us. We must attack them full force with every man we've got!" Many civilians shouted in approval, cheering him on, while others shook their heads in fear of the war worsening. Boyox's eyes trembled with concern; he knew things were about to take a turn for the worse. He disappeared into the shadows to think of a plan and calm his mind.

"Was Rehcumber not a good friend?" Acosta continued.

"Yeah!" Several men shouted back.

"Was he not a noble warrior?"

"Yeah!"

"Should Sol not pay?" Acosta shouted with greater intensity.

"Yeah!"

"My queen, with your approval, grant me the title of general and allow me to lead a full-scale attack on Sol and make them suffer for what they have done!"

"Come then, *general,* not only will I allow this course of action, but I will join you as well!" The false queen replied with a sinister grin. "Are you for us, citizens of the greatest kingdom on Uçebar?" The crowd erupted into cheering and shouts of approval. The council members still loyal to the true queen slowly disappeared and went into hiding, unsure of what to do.

"I have to get Onceli into the catacombs! We must hide!" Elizya thought frantically as she ran for her chambers to collect Onceli. When she arrived, Onceli was gone, but an unexpected guest waited for her, sitting in one of her chairs.

"Hey there, Elizya, I figured I'd find you here." An unpleasant voice greeted her.

"Why, general, what brings you to my humble quarters? Don't you have important preparations to make?"

"Don't you play coy with me, woman!" He responded menacingly with a foul chuckle. "I know you and the brat are scheming in the background." She gasped and took a step back. "Yes, and I cannot have you interfering or rallying the others so..." She turned to run, but he quickly took hold of her wrist and pulled her in. He lifted her up over his shoulder and carried her to the underground prison. She kicked and struggled but did not possess the strength to phase or hinder him. He tossed her into a dark cell and secured the door, locking her inside.

"Now be a good girl and stay put until we are done destroying not only Sol but your precious Luna as well." With a sinister look in his eye, he turned to leave.

"No, please! Why are you doing this?" Elizya shouted as tears began to fill her eyes. "You have been a loyal warrior of Luna for many years. You are of the highest respects of the royal council. The people...the queen...we all trusted you!"

"You pathetic Lunians are so trustworthy and foolish. I have been nothing but a loyal servant to Umbra." He responded in a raspy voice as he wore a demonic smile, staring over his shoulder.

He left her stunned in the dark gloom of the prison with a feeling of hopelessness washing over her. She laid on her side with her knees tucked into her chest and silently sobbed, overcome by a feeling of defeat.

The night was soon upon them, and the Lunians made their preparations. Several of the civilians rallied energetically in the city square, following the burial ceremony for Rehcumber, to see their military off. This crowd was significantly smaller than normal. Many civilians hid in their homes, concerned for the queen and for their nation as a whole. The sinister pair of false Lycia and Acosta began to lead the march towards Sol and proceeded from Luna's gates, followed by Luna's entire remaining marine force. Faces of doom road their faces as they marched to what they believed would be the end of Luna.

"We can't all go. This is madness." The leading master sergeant whispered to his platoon. "If we are defeated, or even many of us killed...Luna's strength will be significantly wounded. We will be open for attack. And who will train the new marines if we don't make it back?"

"That's the point, master sergeant..." A young sergeant replied. "This is the end...the final assault. Either we win...or Luna vanishes from the tale of time."

"This is foolish...what happened to the queen on that last raid? Something is very wrong! She would never gamble the entire kingdom like this."

"Silence in the ranks!" Acosta shouted from the front. "We must be vigilant." The marines marched on, consumed with uncertainty.

Other evil was festering throughout the plagued scapes of Uçebar. In Aquaria, all seemed peaceful. Though Aquaria never participated in the war, they worked hard to help clear the monsters from the wastelands. A group of Aquarian marines returned to the city in time to see a great blaze roaring in the sky. They rushed to the aid of the others who were desperately trying to put it out.

"By Onox's name! The fish storage!" A marine shouted desperately, trying to find a larger bucket. King Fraytor suddenly emerged and summoned his powers to create a heavy rainfall over the fire, quickly putting it out.

"My lord, these flames erupted seemingly out of nowhere. We are unsure how this happened." One of the first workers on the scene explained.

"I can think of only one way this could happen, but I refuse to believe it. What's the damage?" The king replied calmly.

"I'm afraid, sir, nothing is salvageable. We have lost several weeks' worth of fish." The king became lost in thought until a guard shouted for the gates to open. Civilians of Umbra burst into the city, one tripping and falling to his face. Fraytor ran to his side and placed a compassionate hand on his shoulder.

"Dear Umbrian, what's going on?"

"Your highness, thank Umbra, we made it here alive!" The man responded out of breath. "We were on our way to seek your guidance on a matter of great importance, but on the way, we witnessed a terrifying sight. The king of Sol hopped down from the walls of your kingdom with a sinister grin. He noticed us and attacked."

"It...that just can't be...why?" Fraytor responded feigning disbelief.

"I'm sorry, my lord, but it's the truth."

"Guard, fetch the innkeeper, order him to find this man and his comrades shelter, and tend to them as they need." The king stared blanketly to the ground as his men did as he ordered.

Later, Fraytor assembled his council and explained what had just transpired.

"My king, clearly you cannot believe such insanity?" Natia said, smashing her enormous fists into the table.

"My lord, a few facts leave punctured holes deep in this story." Relic began to speak calmly. "Why would men of Umbra report here at such a late hour. Not to mention, if they truly had urgent matters to discuss, why would they have only sent civilians. No one to protect them, and no one of high rank to entrust this information to. More importantly, if Lord Radric did indeed attack them, none of them would have survived. Especially these fragile, little civilians. Yet they arrive merely out of breath with a few scratches on them."

"My lord, did Lord Radric not create talismans that could conjure and manipulate the flames of the phoenix?" Natia chimed in. "It wouldn't be hard to believe that Umbra could have gotten their hands on a talisman and attacked us, trying to frame Sol for it."

"Yes, but why would Umbra do such a thing?" Relic responded calmly.

"More importantly, why would Sol, an ally of old, ever attack us...and in such a shameful manner. You just can't believe this is truly what happened, my lord." Natia responded urgently.

"Of course I don't my dear general. It is as we feared..." The king said with a deep sigh.

"Please, my king, enlighten us. What is it that you speak of?" Natia inquired. Fraytor took his seat, gesturing for the others to do the same.

"I have not disclosed a disturbing bit of information to you, my dear council, as I hoped it was nothing more than a false horror. That said, Lord Radric and I had a private conversation before we departed from Sol. He expressed a concern that Umbra may be discretely entering the war, only without following the rules of engagement. It would seem that he may have been correct, for I do not believe Radric would ever attack us, especially with such dishonorable cowardice. As you pointed out as well, Lieutenant General, if Radric wanted us dead, it would have been all to easy for him. He would not have merely torched our supplies; he would have crushed us all!"

"Why now, though, what could cause Umbra to turn on the rest of us? Could this be an act of Umbra as a whole or just a corrupt group?" Natia inquired.

"I fear it is far worse than just their kingdom's involvement, my dear general." The king replied.

"What are you saying, my lord?" Natia inquired with her eyes growing wide.

"Radric believes...that the dark goddess herself has openly corrupted an Uçebian heart." Shock and disorder erupted briefly before it was calmed by the king. "Radric has informed me that his men encountered a creature not born of natural wasteland magic. It was a demon who was once a Solyan marine. His heart corrupted by shadow." Louder rambling and disarray erupted around the table. "Silence! What's worse is this monster effortlessly destroyed an entire Solyan platoon of around forty men!"

"That is impossible. How could something with such evil and strength take physical form in this world?" Relic inquired calmly.

"Only through the actions of Umbra," Natia said weakly with disbelief.

"General Natia, Lieutenant General Relic! I am counting on you to keep our people safe! Those fiends of Umbra are residing within our walls as we speak. Get to the inn now and play it casual. Summon them to my chambers to discuss this "urgent matter" of theirs. We must interrogate them and get the truth. We must remain one step ahead, or we risk our own part to play in this growing war.

Umbra's Weapon: A Tortured Heart

As they made their way through the wastelands, Acosta whispered with the imposter queen.

"My queen, what shall we do about the missing council members?"

"Pay them no mind." She said with a foul chuckle. "They are far too fearful and most likely have gone into hiding. We have the entire kingdom at our side. They dare not stand against all of Luna."

"But what of Boyox? Fear does not reside in any bone of that boy's body." He responded in a serious manner.

"What can one so young do to stop an evil as old as our great goddess?" She scoffed.

"Of course, master, forgive me!" He said, releasing a satisfied chuckle.

However confident the sinister pair may have been, Boyox, the noble warrior he is, was not ready to give up. With haste, he sprinted to his home at the edge of the kingdom.

"Uahka, get inside the house now!" He shouted as she came into view. Startled, she spun around to see him charging towards her. Before she could react, he scooped her up in his arms and barreled through the door.

"Boyox, what's wrong?" She inquired in a nervous, weak voice. He gently placed her down and, without so much as a response, began checking the cobblestones of the floor. "Please say something!" Still disregarding her, he wore a smile as he lifted a loose stone, followed by many others. He began unearthing a hidden door and held out his arm to her.

"Come, my love, please don't question me; there is no time to explain!" An urgent expression road his face. She reluctantly took his hand, and he guided her down a ladder formed of stone protrusions on the wall. He sealed the door, and they continued down in darkness.

"Boyox, where are you? What is this place?"

"Hush your voice, babe, please." He said from a slight distance away. The sound of two stones striking against each other echoed in the darkness. Slight sparks began to fly, and soon, a bright flame ignited in a large torch. Utilizing it, he lit the rest of the torches on the wall, illuminating the room. Uahka looked around in awe at shelves upon shelves of provisions and storages of clean drinking water. After Boyox lit the final torch, he ran to her and embraced her tight.

"Please...tell me...will this be the last time I see you?" She whispered weakly. He pulled away gently, taking hold of both of her tiny hands. He wore a tender smile as his dark eyes rested in the ruby pools of her own.

"Don't be silly, Uahka." He playfully responded. "I promised you, didn't I? When this war ends, we will be a real family."

"And you better keep that promise then." She replied with a weak smile.

"That being said, stay here." He said urgently as his smile faded. "Please, do not leave for any reason. You have plenty of food and water here for a while. I promise, I will come back for you, okay? I love you, Uahka!" Their lips gently met as he kissed her tenderly. He released her slowly and ran for the stone-like latter.

"I love you too." She said quietly as she watched him disappear. "Mana protect him, I implore you!"

Back in the dungeon, Elizya had all but given up hope and helplessly lay on the cold, damp ground in the fetal position. She was sobbing weakly and shivering from the sheer cold. Suddenly, she heard the dungeon door open with a loud slam against the wall. She pulled her legs in tighter to her chest as she let out a slight fearful moan.

"Elizya, are you down there, my lady?" A soothing voice called out to her from the top of the stairs. She immediately released her hold on herself and glanced at the light piecing through the darkness from the doorway.

"Yes, I'm here!" She called out in excitement. "Bless you for knowing to find me here, Boyox!" The sound of boots tapping the damp stones broke the dank quietness as he made his way to her. He swung his axe with impressive force, crushing the lock on the cell. As he opened the door, she flew into his arms. She clung tightly to him as she sobbed. "What are we going to do, colonel? Lycia is all but overtaken by a demon, and I've lost Onceli. I'm so afraid. Is there no hope?"

"Don't worry, Elizya, I have a plan. We cannot surrender our kingdom or our will to darkness or despair. That is how Umbra will grab hold of our hearts as well." She pulled away slightly, meeting his gaze with intrigue. He wore a confident smile, and it was as if his eyes were emitting a hopeful ray of light. She couldn't help but feel inspired by him and calmed by his genuine aura. "There's not much time, but the military could not have gotten too far. We can catch them before the queen reaches Sol."

"But what then? What can we do against the entire military?" She responded weakly.

"I can be of no help there, I'm afraid." He said confidently, without the smile ever escaping his face.

"What are you saying, colonel?"

"Yes, there is nothing I can do...but *you* can Elizya!"

"What...what could you possibly mean?" She responded with her eyes wide.

"Don't you get it, Elizya? You are the only one who can release Queen Lycia from the demon that plagues her mind, soul, and heart."

"But what could I do?" She said weakly, looking to the ground.

"Don't be a fool, Elizya!" He shouted sternly, his face now a serious frown. She looked over to his intense eyes. "There's no time to doubt yourself. You know what I mean, deep in your heart...I know you do. Who else has such an intimate history with the queen? Who else is emotionally woven tighter to her heart? You raised her. You have been by her side her entire life. She looks to you as if you were her own true mother. And I feel in my heart that you look at her in the same way. Maternal love is far stronger than any poison of some fell creature of Umbra. Only you can free Lycia. Then, I will be there to kill Acosta. The military will not interfere once they realize the queen has been possessed. I'm sure they already have suspicions that something is wrong, and they will rise up behind us. We will win! But I need you to believe in yourself. I first need you to free the queen's heart!" Elizya was stunned to experience this side of Boyox. He wasn't just some muscle head teen; he was a truly noble and wise man.

"You're right, colonel; forgive my weakness." A bright smile now riding her face. "Let's go save the kingdom, let's go save the queen!" They mounted a wolf together and made haste for the gates.

"Listen, my lady, this is going to be very uncomfortable for you. The dank, foul air of the wastelands is not easy to breathe.

Just remain strong and remember what it is we are fighting for, and you will be just fine." She nodded with determination behind her smile, and they hurried towards Sol.

Back in Aquaria, General Natia and Lieutenant General Relic frantically made their way back to the king's chambers. They fell to bended knee, rendering proper honors.

"My king, the citizens of Umbra are gone!" Natia reported quickly.

"Then it is truly as we feared. Umbra has betrayed us all. Sound the battle drums, relieve them of the dust of peace that has ever loomed over them for centuries...since the very dawn of our kingdom. Tonight, we march for Sol. I shall inform Radric of what has happened, and we can plan our next move together. Go, we are well prepared, now Uçebar shall finally witness the true might of Aquaria!" Natia and Relic nodded their heads and left the throne room. They made their way to a pair of very large drums that rested in a dark, funnel-like alley. Relic and Natia looked at each other with a determined nod and began smashing the drums in a rhythmic manner with their fists. The sounds of the drums echoed through the alley and filled the city. The civilians began to panic as the war drums blared through the air. The military rallied to the city square. The marines quickly formed ranks to await orders while the kingdom guards dispersed through the kingdom to calm and organize the frantic civilians. Fraytor stood in the city square, clad in battle armor for the first time.

"My people!" He shouted with intensity. "The dark goddess Umbra has betrayed us all! She burned our food storage and attempted to frame our greatest ally. She tried to divide us, deceive us, and take us for fools. I know our founding father made a vow from the very beginning never to engage in the war. However, we are left with no choice. If we are to remain an active chapter in the story books of Uçebar...Umbra must be destroyed!" The civilians looked on in horror, but the marines shouted with motivation and excitement.

"Finally, my blade may taste living flesh! No more wasting my talents on pathetic wasteland creatures." A marine grunt shouted.

"I'll say, it's about time we saw some real action. I never thought I'd live to see this day." The rash, overconfident shouts continued until a powerful voice interrupted.

"Fools!" The king shouted with rage. "Do not take this for some game! We should never celebrate in the killing of fellow Uçebians." They calmed themselves, feeling slight shame. "However, keep that pride. Just keep your mind sound. Remember that we do this for our people and for our brothers in Sol. Today, Uçebar will experience the power that is the Aquarian military!" The marines shouted energetically, and the king led the charge out of the gates. It would be a long journey back to Sol, but they made haste with great determination.

Back in Sol

Several weeks after Luna departed for battle, Radric stood in his usual position under the night sky. Efyna knocked on his chamber doors and walked in slowly. She stood by his side and looked to the sky as well.

"So, I was looking through the golden book earlier and didn't see any mention of when we discussed the mole." He spoke in a slightly interrogating manner as his gaze remained unchanged. Fear filled her eyes as she stared up at him guiltily. "Why is it that everything we have ever discussed is in your book, but that?" Suddenly, she rammed a large knife into his side. He looked down at her with shock as tears streamed down her sad little face.

"Efyna, what are you doing?" He said with a painful grimace.

"It was me! I was the spy for Luna." She shouted, applying greater pressure to the knife.

"So what then? Are you meaning to kill me?" He flinched slightly.

"I have to!"

"No, Efyna, you don't. Please stop this, I will forgive you. I will pardon you. We can pretend this never happened; no one needs to know. You are my friend. We've had such good times together. Why would you do this?" He responded urgently in a raised voice.

"It...it just has to be done." She responded weakly as her weeping calmed down.

"I don't understand Efyna, why? It really isn't a big deal, all that you have told to Luna...Never caused me any trouble. Just don't do it anymore, and all can be forgotten." He responded calmly.

"You just don't get it, Radric!" She twisted the knife around, pressing harder, causing him to fall to one knee.

"Efyna...please stop this...I really don't want to hurt you. No, I cannot hurt you. Please don't make me have to hurt you!"

"Hurt me? You couldn't possibly hurt me more than you already have!" His eyes grew with confusion. "You have always been so perfect...so kind to me. Why? Why are you like that? Why are you so sweet? You are a king. A king of an evil nation. A nation that steals children from their families. Yet you treated me as your own. Defending me when no one else would. Even after I've stabbed you...you are still willing to forgive me? I love you, Radric...don't you get it! I love you so much. There is no one I'd rather be with...than you. But it can never be. You are a king. I am a commoner. A commoner from an enemy kingdom. Don't you see? I have to kill you. If I can't have you...Nobody can!" She pulled the knife free and attempted to slit his throat, but she was no fighter, and her emotional state left her coordination compromised. He took hold of her hand, effortlessly preventing her strike.

"Please, don't make this harder than it has to be." She began weeping harder as she drove the knife into his gripping hand.

"Efyna..." He said weakly with a wince.

"Why is it, Radric, why do you treat me like I'm special? Is it just because I may be the last elf on Uçebar? Am I merely a trophy to you?"

"How dare you!" He shouted with sadness in his voice. "Efyna, you want to know why I've treated you so well?" He continued gently. "Why I've always protected you? It's because of the guilt that I have from taking you from your family. But I had to, don't you get that? When we raided your small village outside the kingdom...my men would have killed you! You were just a child; you didn't deserve to be a victim of an adult war! I just wanted you to be happy. I wanted to atone for my sins. And you really are special to me, Efyna. I am the last of my kind...the only living giant. I relate to you for that reason, being the last of yours." Radric noticed something off about her as he kept his gaze. Her once majestic golden eyes were faded and lacking in all splendor.

"What is this?" He thought. "Odd behavior aside, she even appears physically different...No...it can't be...why her? Umbra, you shall not have this heart!"

"Wait, Efyna, this isn't you!" He spoke with desperation. "You're not yourself, wake up. You're being corrupted by the darkness of Umbra. She must be tugging on your heart. Don't give in to her, don't let her take you. The sweet, gentle girl I know and love would never do this." She gasped slightly, and her tension began to ease.

"You...you love me?" She responded softly with her knife still embedded in his hand. He gently took hold of the knife with his free hand. He slowly removed it from the other and embraced her tenderly. Her hands remained by her side, one still gripping tightly to the knife.

"Of course I do. You are a good and loyal friend; you would never hurt me. Now deny Umbra your heart and come back to me." Her eyes narrowed with frustration.

"A friend?" She responded bluntly. "Is that all I am...yes...and that is all I can ever be!" Radric's eyes opened with disappointment. "It isn't fair! No! It isn't good enough!" She began to struggle, and his embrace grew loose. She broke free and stood in a combative stance.

"You must stop this, Efyna." He wore a frown as he responded sternly. "This is your last warning, I swear! Please don't make me have to hurt you!" He shouted with desperation. Thunder sounded as a flash of lightning struck the ground, and rain poured from the sky.

She screamed out in agony, lunging toward him, aiming for his gut. With both of his massive hands, he picked her up by her head. She frantically stabbed his hands repeatedly, trying to get him to drop her.

"What is this?" He thought to himself. "An unscheduled rain fall? And what are these blares of sound? That crackling spear of light? Are the gods angry at me...does this mean I truly failed to save her? What am I left to do...she won't let up." He closed his eyes as they began to fill with tears. "Mother Mana, forgive me... Father Gi, forgive me. I could not protect her as I promised!" He closed his eyes tighter as he jerked her head to the right and even harder and faster to the left. A sickly sound emitted as her fragile little neck snapped and her body went limp. He held her close to his chest and let out a horrendous scream of agony. The tighter he held her, the harder reality set in and the louder his agonizing cries became. The thunder and lightning became so frequent that his screams seemed to blend in with them. However, two guards heard the commotion and rushed into his chambers.

Shock painted their faces to witness the king on his knees in the rain as he sobbed with Efyna's dead little body cradled in his arms. One of the guards remained at the entrance, too stunned by the sight of the king crying to even move. The second rushed to his side.

"My lord, what in Gi's name has happened?"

"Umbra must pay; this time, she has gone too far!" Radric replied without opening his eyes. The guard released a gasp, but before he could respond, Radric roared into the sky. "Curse Umbra! And all those treacherous fiends who reside in her dank and foul walls!" The guard was overcome by Radric's intensity, despair, and the hate burning in his now-opened eyes. "Loyal guard, sound the battle horn of Sol! The rules of engagement have changed! I vow...every last Uçebian claiming loyalty to Umbra...shall die!" Both guards let out sharp gasps. "Did you not hear me? Sound the battle horn; rally my commanders! We march!"

"Yes sir!" he responded as he ran from the king's chambers.

"You there, by the door," Radric called out calmly to the guard still remaining in the doorway. "Come, we must provide her with a proper burial. She has no family, so it is now our responsibility." The guard nodded and followed the king to the graveyard.

The rain had ceased, and the guard stood watch as the king himself began digging a hole. Eventually the guard realized the blood dripping from Radric's side and hands was his own.

"My king, you are injured! Please allow me to dig the hole, and we should tend to your wounds."

"Silence, guard!" He shouted intensely. Radric released a deep sigh as he calmed himself. "Forgive me, soldier...I just...I must be the one to dig this hole." The guard nodded quietly and continued to stand by idly. Radric placed Efyna in the hole as his tears began to flow once more.

"Rest in peace, fair maiden. May you find the happiness in the next life that was denied you in this. Forgive me...I was unable to protect you. Unable to make you happy. Please allow your soul to rest; don't linger here in this horrid dimension of hate and misery." He filled the hole and carved her name into a stone. Then turning to the guard, instructed him to back away. He seared his wounds with the power of his flames as the mighty horn of Sol sounded through the kingdom. The marines gathered with urgency, and the civilians joined to show their support to the military. Radric emerged from the shadows; his facial expression and remnants of his tears left the Solyans in shock.

"People of Sol, a great travesty has befallen us this night!" He shouted with unmeasurable intensity. "The dark goddess Umbra has betrayed us! She has claimed the hearts of the tortured and forced them to harm the ones they love! Umbra is not the innocent kingdom we once believed. It has become apparent that they have been plotting in the shadows for many years! Waiting for the right moment to attack us where it hurts the most. Where we are most vulnerable. Our hearts! We have always been at war, yes. But never before has it not been an honorable war, with the rules of engagement well intact. Luna may be our sworn enemy, but she has always been noble. Today, we will march for Umbra and attack relentlessly as she has done to us! None in her walls shall survive!" The crowd was stunned into silence. Most began to think this was too sudden and seemed rash. "The forty good men we lost to the wastelands were not by the hands of Luna... but by the hands of a former Solyan marine!" Chaos erupted, and shouts of disbelief emitted from the crowd.

"But my king, why would a Solyan attack his own brothers?" A civilian inquired. "And what kind of warrior, other than yourself, could ever possess the power to destroy an entire army?"

"The marine was long since deceased, but he did not die by physical means. He had pain in his heart. A mortal wound for the loss of his brothers. Weak and lost in the wastelands, Umbra's shadows engulfed him. Tortured his mind and soul until his being deteriorated. She turned him into a demon, formed from hatred itself. She corrupted his heart and, despite how his pain came to be...forced him to kill his own brothers, to once again, watch them all die. Only this time...by his own hand. Put yourself in this man's shoes. His heart broke to pieces as he lost his comrades. In his broken state, he was taken advantage of and corrupted. Imagine if you had to witness the deaths of those you loved by your own hand! Umbra must pay!" The crowd shouted in support. "Marines, march with me! We will avenge our fallen and put to rest this great evil!" The Solyans quickly departed and began their journey towards Umbra.

Elizya's Maternal Love

Deep in the wastelands, the Lunians pressed on until false Lycia halted the troops.

"We've been followed, Acosta...I'm actually quite surprised." She said as they both chucked with amusement. They turned to see Boyox and Elizya approaching them cautiously. "Look here, marines, Colonel Boyox has betrayed us all!" Whispers of disbelief and shock broke out amongst them. Boyox maintained his stare towards the sinister pair as he and Elizya remained at a significant distance.

"I know you are not the queen!" Elizya shouted, eliciting louder gasps from the marines. She hopped down from the wolf and began making her way towards Lycia. "But I have an interesting proposal for you regarding my new-found loyalty to you!"

"What?" Boyox shouted, looking at her in horror as he hopped from the wolf. Elizya ignored him and continued moving slowly towards the imposter queen.

"Please hear me out, no weapons, just come talk with me." She said, coming to a halt, leaving a large gap between them.

"Well, isn't this an interesting turn of events!" She said with an amused, evil laugh as she tossed her weapon to the ground.

She slowly began moving towards Elizya. "Poor little Boyox. You rescued her, didn't you? Now she comes to join my side. How does that make you feel?" Boyox remained quiet, clenching his fists tightly. False Lycia reached her and raised a curious eyebrow. "Out with it then, why should I trust you?" Without saying a word, Elizya embraced false Lycia in her arms tightly as she wore a warm, loving smile. She shifted her head slightly, kissing Lycia's forehead. False Lycia stood completely paralyzed. Pulling Lycia closer, she rested her head on top of the little queen's, whose face now rested against her chest.

"My dear, sweet daughter." Lycia's body began to quiver as her eye flickered back and forth from its true color to the demon's. Tears streamed from Elizya's eyes as her smile faded. "You would never do this to your people. You would never do this to me! This is not like you, dear daughter. Please, come home with me. Banish that spirit from your heart...come back to me!" Elizya gently played with Lycia's silver hair as she continued to hold her. Lycia's cheeks lit up a bright red, and her silver eye regained its splendor. A cheerful smile painted her face as her skin began to glow with glorious luminescence.

"Mother...you've never referred to me as daughter before!" She responded tenderly, wrapping her arms gently around Elizya.

"Praise Mana, you're back, my dear daughter!" Elizya's tears poured harder, and Lycia giggled upon hearing herself referred to as daughter once more. She shut her visible eye and remained cuddled in Elizya's embrace.

"No! This cannot be possible!" Acosta shouted angrily.

"Oh, but it can!" Boyox responded boastfully as he slapped the wolf's rear. "Return home, loyal mount; your work here is done." He commanded with a smile before returning his attention to Acosta. "You overconfident fiends fell so easily into our little act." He chuckled. "I knew Elizya could free the queen!"

"Sir, what in Mana's name is going on here? We knew some-

thing was up with the queen, but what do you mean by free her?"
The battlefield major saluted Boyox as he inquired.

"That man, that fiend standing before you, pretending to be
your loyal general...He is a servant of Umbra. Umbra, who has
sent a demon into the heart of our beloved queen." The marines
gasped and turned angrily to Acosta. "I wouldn't be surprised if
it was he, himself, who killed our beloved General Rehcumber."

"Let's kill him! Colonel, please give the order." The major
responded in a combative stance.

"No," Boyox said calmly.

"But why, sir, he is evil. He must die!"

"Because I, alone, will be the one who kills him!"

"Listen, boy, don't delude yourself into thinking you can
defeat me! I've been killing for a long time now." Acosta said,
crossing his arms and laughing evilly.

"That may be, you spawn of hell, but you have been killing with no purpose other than to cause despair. I kill for my
people...and for the woman I love!" The marines gasped at his
words, but the fight was on. Clanging erupted as their weapons
made contact, and Acosta tossed Boyox to the side with a mighty
parry. Boyox hit the ground hard, carving a deep skid before his
momentum ceased.

"Sir, please allow us to help; he is too powerful." A sergeant
spoke with concern.

"No, stay back! I will not have any of my men harmed in my
presence...not again...and definitely not by the hand of Umbra!
If I cannot defeat him, then I deserve to die! But I will not die!
This is where I put an end to your evil Acosta!" He burst back
into action, but Acosta dodged him without much effort, driving
the handle of his sword into Boyox's gut. He coughed hard as
the wind was knocked out of him. The marines had never seen
Boyox so helpless before, and once aid tried to aid him.

"Get back! I won't tell you again! I will defeat him!" He commanded, coughing slightly.

"Pathetic child!" Acosta laughed. "This is why the military should never have allowed such a young and immature little brat to hold such a high rank and responsibility in the marines."

"This isn't over, demon! I will be the one who destroys you!" Acosta flew towards him, smashing Boyox's face with his skull. Boyox was tossed to the ground once more, and Acosta stood over him with a confident smile.

"Come on now! Are you not the mighty Colonel Boyox? This can't be all you've got! You are pathetic and unworthy of your title."

"You are a fool to believe I would have this much difficulty fighting you!" Boyox spoke calmly from where he lay.

"You dare speak in such a way as you lay there helpless? Fine then, show me your skill, boy! Prove you are really a warrior!"

"A pathetic warrior relies solely on his strength. A true warrior relies on both strength and cunning." Boyox replied, remaining on the ground. Acosta raised an eyebrow as he awaited Boyox's next move. "You once again have fallen for my act; your lack of mental fortitude is amusing!" Boyox shouted as he hopped to his feet energetically. "You have fought alongside me many times. Have you not been paying attention? Have you learned nothing of my true skill?" Boyox pulled a spear from its resting place on his back and drove it into a deep crack that lay in front of Acosta's feet. He jerked the spear violently, causing multiple new cracks to form erratically. Acosta attempted to jump, but it was too late. The ground beneath his feet gave way as he put his weight on it. As he fell, he grabbed on to the ledge of the rapidly forming ravine and propelled himself into the air.

"Did you think it would be that easy, Colon..." Acosta began to taunt but was quickly cut off as Boyox burst forward and drove his spear through Acosta's gut.

"You left yourself completely vulnerable to an attack. You are the one who is truly pathetic!" Boyox shouted with valor.

"No, it can't be!" Acosta thought as he coughed up blood. "I never should have toyed with him...I truly was a fool...forgive me, Umbra. I have failed." Boyox kicked Acosta, freeing his spear and sending him into the newly formed ravine for death to claim him. The marines shouted a victorious battle cry as they ran to the colonel. They punched him playfully and praised him in admiration. Elizya and Lycia remained deeply in each other's embrace, lost in their love. Still remaining in Elizya's embrace, Lycia's smile and glow slowly faded as she began to cry.

"What have I done? I've filled my people with even more hate. I've allowed evil to take hold of me. I almost led many of us to our deaths, yet again!" She spoke, consumed with shame.

"My queen, it's no time for you to worry about this. We must get back to the kingdom." Elizya spoke calmly.

"That's right, it's not safe, your majesty. Please, let's make our way back to Luna." Boyox said as he held her axe out to her." With a weak smile and a nod, she took her axe from him.

"What is this?" A familiar, powerful voice suddenly cut through the gloom of the wastelands. The Lunians looked over in shock to see Radric and his entire marine force formed up behind him. "Lycia, what are you all doing here?" Before she could answer, both sides were shrouded in darkness. Octonia was close by as they were within the territory of Sol. She became concerned for the king as she recognized the heinous shadow. She dove down majestically in an attempt to render aid. The demon inside Lycia, having been defeated, was slowly dying as it could no longer feed off her life force. In a last-ditch effort to fulfill Umbra's evil plan before it died, it took control of Lycia's arm and forced her to hurl her axe into the sky. The shadows dissipated in time for Radric to witness Lycia chuck the axe. At first, he was confused as to why she would toss her axe into the air until his eyes followed its trajectory.

"What? Octonia, no!" He shouted with concern. Lycia covered her mouth with both hands and fell to her knees as the sound of torn flesh and a horrible shriek echoed in the skies. The majestic bird curled into a crescent as she began to plummet to the ground. Radric shouted her name as he ran towards where she was falling. Octonia fell into his arms, and he pulled the axe from her body, aggressively chucking it to the ground. She cooed weakly as she looked up at him with disappointment in her dying eyes.

"Don't you dare!" He spoke sternly yet tenderly, stroking her burning feathers. "Don't you dare feel like you failed! My dear, sweet Octonia. Be at peace, my beloved phoenix. You have served and protected our kingdom for countless generations. It is time your soul finally came to rest. We love you, and we are proud of all you have done for this kingdom and its people. Be at peace!" Octonia rested her head under his chin and, with her little heart at ease, faded from existence. She burst into flames, leaving behind a cold ash that was eventually blown away in a gust of wind. Radric remained staring at his hands with his eyes wide and quivering.

"You...you devil woman! How could you sink so low?" He shouted without looking away from where Octonia once lay. Lycia shook her head frantically as he looked over to her. "How could you do such a thing?" He began walking towards her, and the Lunian marines formed up in front of her to prevent his passage. He had not yet reached their striking zone and came to a halt. "Do not hide behind your pawns. Own up to your evil! Face me! Speak woman! Why would you betray the rules of engagement? And right before my very eyes! We do not kill each other's kingdom creatures!"

"Stand aside, my dear marines," Lycia said weakly. They

parted, allowing her through. When she reached Radric, he struck her with the back of his hand, sending her to the ground. The marines began to draw near to retaliate, but she held out her hand, gesturing them to stop.

"I asked for peace! No...I offered you peace! I warned you of the true evil that we both face now. You would betray my kindness for a nation that is an enemy to all of Uçebar?"

"Radric I..." She began weakly.

"Do not refer to me so informally, devil woman!" He interrupted.

"That's enough, you giant buffoon!" She shouted angrily as she came to her feet. "How dare you speak to me as if I'm some common warrior! I'm a queen. You speak to me as if *I* should be talking to *you* in any certain way? And all the while insulting me in front of my own people with your misinterpreted understanding of what happened!"

"What did I misinterpret? I watched you toss your axe!" Lycia hopped up, slapping him across the face. As she landed, she maintained her intense stare with her piercing luminescent eye.

"How big of a fool are you?" She said with disappointment. "As you say, you were the one who warned me of the evil of Umbra, yet you stand here acting as if you have forgotten the whole thing? Did you not happen to take any notice of the darkness that enveloped us suddenly before Octonia was killed? How daft are you? You know me, Radric! You know me well!" Everyone from both Sol and Luna released a shocked gasp. "Better than any of our people are aware of. Is that not true?"

"This is not the time, woman!" He shouted angrily.

"Not the time for what? I am quite intrigued to know what's going on here!" Karakus cut in sternly.

"Hold your tongue, Lieutenant General, and learn your place!" Radric snapped.

"With respect, my king, but no." Axaiyan calmly yet sternly

interjected. "We deserve to know what's going on. What is this about peace that you just said?" Radric gasped and looked around at his men.

"You didn't tell your own people?" Lycia asked weakly. Suddenly, a howl cut through the air.

"No, why now...why is she here?" Lycia thought as she felt her heart grow heavy with worry.

"Don't worry, my loyal subjects, I would never deceive you," Radric shouted with valor. "I will prove my loyalty to you by slaying the beast of the treacherous Luna, as they have slain ours!" The Solyan marines shouted in approval.

"No, please! Are you insane? You know I didn't kill your precious bird!" Lycia pleaded as Onceli ran right up to Radric in a playful stance.

"Hush your mouth, foul traitor! You have stolen my loving little pet from me. Now...I'll steal yours from you!"

"She's not just some pet Radric! She's my daughter!" She pleaded further as she took hold of Radric's arm, but he tossed her aside.

"I care not of the beast's origins, woman, nor what it is to you!" Lycia was drained of her energy from the parasitic demon and didn't have the strength to stop him or even morph into her wolf form. Radric surrounded himself and Onceli in a circle of fire, preventing anyone from interfering. Onceli became paralyzed with fear and whined nervously as she sensed his anger. Radric drew his sword and readied his arm. The Solyans cheered loudly as the Lunians watched in despair.

"Radric, stop!" Lycia shouted from where she lay. "She's your daughter!" Radric gasped as he dropped his sword, and the entire battlefield went silent. Everyone was stunned into wide-eyed paralysis.

"That...that isn't possible. It's...a wolf." He responded in disbelief, forcing his flames to dissipate.

"For now!" More gasps of shock erupted. "She will change into her Uçebian form at the rising of the moon on her third birthday!"

"It's lies! Hush your deceitful tongue, woman; this creature cannot be my daughter!" He retrieved his sword and prepared to strike.

"Is it that hard to believe, you fool! Look into her eyes! She has one eye, silver and glorious as Mother Mana herself. The other...intense...like a raging flame...and orange as Father Gi." Radric began to lower his sword and gasped at the sight of Once-li's gaze. "She has both of our eyes!"

"I've heard enough, cousin. Kill it. Make Luna feel the pain it has caused us!" Karakus shouted as he gripped his fists tightly. Suddenly, Onceli's body began to glow, and started to morph.

"What did you do? Stop!" Lycia shouted frantically.

"I did nothing, I swear!" Suddenly, where the large wolf once resided, a tiny toddler sat in its place. Her skin was pale white on the side that bore Lycia's eye and red on the side that bore Radric's. Poking through her flowing black hair was a pair of sharp. black horns. A thin red tail with a sharp edge coiled around her little torso. Radric stared in disbelief, stunned into silence. The little girl tried to stand for the first time with her Uçebian feet. Her legs wobbled, and she tripped over her tail, failing to maintain balance. Rolling to a seating position, she held out her arms to Radric as if to ask to be picked up and giggled softly. A tear welled in Lycia's revealed eye as she witnessed her daughter's true form. Without a word, Radric turned from Onceli and began to walk away. Sadness began to fill her tiny heart and she tried to stand again. She fell to her little bottom, unable to master her new legs.

"Daddy, come back!" She shouted desperately. He stopped in his tracks, and his face bore shock and sadness simultaneously as he remained with his back to her. "We can be a real family now, Daddy! Mommy said once I changed, we can be together! So here I am."

"Look at her, you jerk!" Lycia cried out. "What's wrong with you! Don't you see? This can end our fighting. She can unite our people. The first child born of Solyan and Lunian blood!" Without turning to them, Radric continued to walk away. Onceli called out again and again, but he never turned back. Major General Gorg placed his hand on the king's arm compassionately as he was walking by.

"My lord..." He spoke softly, but Radric pulled away and kept walking.

"Return to Sol, all of you! We leave now!" Radric commanded sternly.

"No! That monster must be destroyed; it's an abomination!" Karakus shouted angrily. Gorg cocked back his fist and punched Karakus to the ground. He fell to one knee and pulled Karakus's face close to his. "Release me!" Karakus demanded.

"What is wrong with you?" Gorg shouted. "Can you even imagine what is going on in the king's mind right now? This is not the time, general!" Karakus pushed Gorg off him and jumped to his feet, standing in a combative stance.

"What's going on in *his* mind? What about what's going on in yours? He has laid with the enemy, yet you would still follow him?"

"Not—now!" Gorg shouted sternly.

"I won't repeat myself," Radric said calmly as he continued towards the kingdom. Lycia's visible eye filled with sadness, but she was at a loss for words as the Solyans vanished into the distance. Elizya ran to Onceli as Boyox rushed to Lycia's side. Elizya scooped up Onceli, who hid her face in Elizya's chest as she sobbed. Elizya wrapped a cloth around her little body and held her tenderly. Lycia looked over, heartbroken, and gently asked Boyox to help her to her feet. She made her way over to Elizya with the aid of Boyox. Tears streamed from her luminescence eye as she held out her arms, receiving Onceli.

"Mommy...does Daddy hate me?" Onceli struggled to ask through her sobbing.

"No, my sweet girl, he doesn't hate you. He is just surprised. Daddy loves you, Onceli!"

"Come, my queen, we should go." Elizya encouraged as she placed a compassionate hand on her shoulder. With that, the Lunians quietly began their journey home.

A Ray of Hope

In Sol, the morning after everyone had returned, the much-an-ticipated council meeting was held. At first, everyone remained in silence, unsure of what to say.

"Well, fine, I guess I'll start things off!" Karakus shouted as he jumped to his feet. "Are we all just going to act as if our *loyal* king has not only slept with the enemy but produced an offspring? This is the greatest treason of our history!"

"With respect...Calm yourself, general. As the king's cousin, you of all people should understand the delicacy of this satia-tion...not to mention, that girl is your blood now, too." Major General Gorg spoke calmly yet sternly.

"Do you even hear yourself, Gorg? That child was born of the enemy." Karakus snapped.

"But she has royal Solyan blood." Gorg rebutted.

"You cannot be serious! Brothers, help me out here!" Karakus shouted as he looked around.

"My friends, I know you were not on my side before on the matter, but this changes things, does it not?" Wasukah cut in calmly, standing to his feet. "Why must we fight with Luna any further...Do any of us even know why our nations hate each other?" This time, the idea was received without a chaotic uproar.

"I don't know how I feel about this after watching good men die at the hands of Luna," Axaiyan said calmly.

"At last, we hear a sensible notion!" Karakus shouted.

"That being said, I cannot deny the fact that the child has royal Solyan blood coursing through her veins. No matter how she came to be, she is now a part of the noble line." Axaiyan continued. "It's true, I've witnessed many men die at the hands of Luna, but many Lunians die by our hands as well. Perhaps it is time to let bygones be bygones, or we risk the loss of more comrades."

"Not to mention, it is clear who the real enemy is now." Wasukah chimed in. "Especially after all the deception and the loss of our beloved Octonia."

"What is wrong with all of you!" Karakus shouted, slamming his first into the table.

"What is wrong with *you* cousin?" Radric shouted. "We have a chance for peace with an enemy since the dawn of time...We have a chance to never lose another brother...or father ever again." Karakus exhaled angrily. "Is your hate so boundless that you would put our people in danger to continue a fight that could end today? We have bigger problems now, an enemy that does not fight honorably. If we continue our fight with Luna, Umbra shall see both our kingdoms destroyed." Karakus stormed from the grand hall, slamming the door behind him.

"So what shall it be then, my king?" Wasukah asked calmly.

"This decision is far too great for this council to make for the kingdom. We must bring everything to the attention of the people, and we will allow them to decide."

"I agree with his motion," Axaiyan responded calmly, followed by many others.

"It's settled then; gather the kingdom to the square in the

next three hours, and we shall address them. Dismissed." Radric walked out to the balcony and looked to the sky. A small smile formed on his face as the image of the baby Onceli popped into his mind.

"She did have my eye! Ha, and my skin too." He thought to himself, but his smile slowly faded as he recalled her sadness as he left her. His gaze fell to the ground as he continued to ponder the horrific things that he said to the woman he loves.

After a few hours lost in thought, Radric hopped from the balcony and made his way to where he buried Efyna. He fell to one knee, placing his hand on her tombstone.

"Well, my dear Efyna, it seems the fighting may soon come to an end...I'm sorry you couldn't be here for it." He spoke softly. He heard commotion building in the city square and began to make his way. Radric stood at the center and was prepared to address his people when trumpets sounded, and the gates of Sol began to open. Radric was stunned to see not only Fraytor and his council but the entire Aquarian military in full battle gear.

"Fraytor, what brings you back to our humble kingdom?" He said with a slight bow. Fraytor explained what had transpired in Aquaria and how they had decided to enter the battle against Umbra as well. The Aquarian military was offered the Solyan barracks to rest after their long journey, and the kings retreated to Radric's chambers to continue their conversation as Radric brought Fraytor up to speed.

"I'm sorry, old friend...Octonia will be sorely missed. So what now? Will you and Luna finally cease your fighting?"

"I sure hope so, my friend. I am leaving it up to the decision of the people."

"A wise and noble gesture, ol' boy." Fraytor placed a compassionate hand on Radric's arm.

Later, Radric approached the city square, accompanied by

Fraytor. The entire kingdom gathered, including several Aquarians who were not willing to sleep.

"My people, I have betrayed you!" Radric shouted. Shock loomed over the council members, as this was not the way they expected him to go about it. "In secret, I have been fraternizing with the Queen of Luna...and shared her bed. But it didn't end there. I fell for her, heart and soul. Unbeknownst to me, a child was born." Chaos erupted in the crowd, but Radric gently held up his hand. "My people, I do not expect you to forgive me. All I ask is for you to hear me out and remember how it was that I came to be. My father laid with a giant. It was considered taboo then; many of you wished to revolt against him. But when he spoke of his love for her and the pride he had for me when I was born. He touched your hearts. I only ask that you remember you once despised me. You once thought *I* was the abomination. But you came to accept me; could you not do the same for my daughter? I love her mother, the Queen of Luna, with all my heart!" The crowd gasped. "Don't you see this could quell the fighting; this could end the 800-year conflict. A child born of royal Solyan and royal Lunian blood. This could unify our nations. This could be our chance for peace! But I won't make this decision for you, my people. What say you? Do we hold on to hate in our hearts that we don't understand for the rest of our lives? Do we keep fighting a battle that truly seems to have no origin and witness the constant death of our loved ones? Or...do we let go of the past that our ancestors created and move forward to preserve our nation? To preserve our world! The real enemy still loams over us in the form of darkness and deceit. An enemy who, unlike Luna, fights with no honor, attacking our very hearts. I fear we cannot survive a war against two great kingdoms. If we come together and fight alongside Luna and Aquaria, we can silence hate and violence forever! What say you, my beloved people?"

"Come now, brothers and sisters!" Karakus shouted, fueled

with hate and anger. "Look at your king! He has forsaken you! Talking of peace with a nation who has taken many men from you, the ones you love!" A few voices started shouting in approval as he spoke. "Shall we just forget the memory of those stolen from us and forgive an evil nation for their crimes?"

"My people, ending the hate is not forgetting the loved ones that we have lost!" Radric cut in. "They will always remain in our hearts and live on in spirit. But we must think of the ones we still have with us. Should this war continue, how many more lives would be claimed?"

"How do we know we can trust them, my king?" A civilian shouted.

"We don't, dear citizen, but it is a risk I feel is worth making to prevent further Solyan death."

"What happens if you are wrong!" Karakus shouted to him.

"Then you were right, Karakus! Would that make you happy? This way, we can at least have a hope for positive change. With continued hate, the war will inevitably continue, and more shall die. But with peace, we have a chance to end all this senseless violence."

"I vote peace!" A middle-aged man energetically hopped onto a large rock as he shouted. "Too long have we lived in fear of not seeing our sons return home! Too long have we buried the ones we love. If there is even a small chance for the fighting to end...I support it. I support King Radric!" The few who were rallied around Karakus slowly became swayed by the king and the man's words, feeling encouraged by their hopeful auras. Amid further shouts of approval, the decision was unanimously reached.

"That settles it then! We move for peace!" Radric shouted. I shall march to Luna myself and speak with the queen on this matter. If Luna is in agreeance, we shall sign a declaration of unity into a large stone tablet. Two identical stones shall be signed by myself and the queen, promising an end to this war, once and for all. They shall be mounted in the center of the kingdoms as a constant reminder that our great nations will thrive!" Loud cheering and applause erupted but was soon interrupted by an angry shout.

"Seems you've got this all planned out very quickly, cousin!" Karakus shouted. "Are we to believe you weren't plotting this from the beginning?"

"Plotting what Karakus? A solution to the war? Of course, I've always wanted that! Who wouldn't! But no, I didn't plan on having a child with Lycia, and I most certainly didn't plan on falling in love with her. Don't be ridiculous!"

"Cousin, if you do this, I will forever leave Sol! You will be my enemy."

"You fool, you would turn your back on the kingdom that raised you over meaningless hate?"

"Meaningless? They took my father from me!"

"Stop playing the victim!" Radric shouted with ground-shaking might. "How many fathers do you think you have taken from their sons?" Karakus's eyes widened, and Radric's voice grew softer as he continued. "On the battlefield they may be our enemies...but they are still Uçebians who have lost love ones too. Uçebians just fighting for their people, just as we are. Yet, they may be able to forgive us and move on. Why can't you?"

"You are weak! All of you! May Gi curse you all! I make my leave; those wishing may join me." A small few began to collect behind Karakus.

"Wait, cousin, please...don't do this; it doesn't have to be this way." Radric pleaded.

"Yes, it does, cousin, you have betrayed me," Karakus responded weakly.

"Where will you go then?! You cannot survive out there in the wastelands." Radric shouted desperately.

"Watch me!" Karakus shouted as he vanished from the city with his few followers, and the crowd remained silent as the grave.

"My people, today I set out," Radric spoke after a short stare of silence towards the gates. "I would like for some of you to join me. This will put the Lunians at ease to see other civilians coming to support the idea of peace. It would further help if we could bring the children along with us; however, I would not risk their safety for this. I would warn you; the wastelands are not safe. The air is foul, and the creatures, ravenous! I cannot promise that those who venture with us will all survive. I will not force you to come, but I humbly implore any of those willing to join us. The military and myself will protect you with all we have. But we must show Luna that we are serious about ending this war at all costs." Many civilians began to collect around the military with excitement mixed with anxiety at the thought of braving the treacherous wastes. But felt at ease upon seeing their valiant warriors with confident and warm smiles.

"Listen, ol' boy, this is a momentous occasion," Fraytor said with excitement. "Would you allow my military and I the honor of accompanying you to witness this great happening?"

"It would be *my* honor, my friend," Radric said with a nod. "Not to mention, with two grand armies, I can be sure of the safety of my civilians." With that, Aquaria and Sol made their final preparations and headed out into the dank wilderness for a long journey.

In Luna

When the Lunians finally made it home, the gates slowly opened. Lycia placed Onceli down and told her to remain with Elizya. Lycia walked into the city center as the people gathered. Sadness painted her face as she collapsed to her knees before them. Realizing she had returned to her normal self, the crowd rushed in with concern to support her.

"Forgive me, my people." She spoke weakly. "I have allowed a demon to corrupt my heart and control my actions. The Lycia who stood before you, encouraging your hate...was not me. But I am to blame. I am to blame for being too weak to take control of my own heart."

"My queen, no, you cannot blame yourself for this." A supportive citizen spoke softly.

"Yes, we knew something was wrong; many of us didn't wish to see this action against Sol through." Another joined. Several more spoke lovingly in the queen's defense, and her visible eye grew misty.

"My beloved people, you all make me so happy!" But her smile soon faded as she stood to her feet. "The real issue now...is Umbra is the nation that corrupted me. They are the nation that killed our beloved General Rehcumber. It was their demon that decimated our force from the previous raid. They are trying to trick us into never letting go of our hate. But my dear subjects, I ask you...do you truly believe we should let this fighting continue? My heart cannot bear the loss of any more of you." Whispers broke out throughout the crowd until an elderly woman stepped forward.

"I have been around for many years." She spoke gently. "Yet I do not know the cause of the hate between Luna and Sol. In fact, neither did either of my parents. Maybe this is the sentiment of my old age, but I have grown weary of this war. Tired of seeing our young men and women die. I would love to see a day of peace."

"She is right; we have no reason to quarrel with Sol any longer!" An energetic young man joined in. "Each side has suffered loss, but now...perhaps we can see the dawn of a new Uçebar! An Uçebar where we no longer live in fear, and we can thrive!"

The deliberations began, and slight arguments broke out, but Boyox was sure the outcome was inevitable. He made haste to his manor and smashed through the door. Uahka became fearful upon hearing the noise and hid in the corner of the dark bunker as she extinguished all the torches. Boyox hopped down from the latter and called out to her, but before he had a chance to fully make himself known...a stone wok smashed him in the face.

"Why the hell would you smash through like that?!" She shouted, realizing it was him as she dropped the wok. She started slightly pounding his chest with her balled-up fists. "You scared me half to death, you jerk!" Fighting through the pain, he embraced her tight, and her flailing ceased.

"I'm sorry, love, I'm just excited!" He spoke tenderly.

"Oh, why is that? What has happened?" She inquired, returning his embrace.

"Because today..." He began as he squeezed her tighter. "Today is the day that I introduce you to the kingdom as my girl!"

"Your *girl* huh?" She said sarcastically, unenthused as she backed away, her eyes narrow.

"Come on, Uahka, this is a grand day!" Without another word, he took hold of her hand and began charging up the stone ladder.

Back in the city square, the final decision was made. Lycia hopped with joy as Luna called for peace. Her people were overjoyed to see her chipper, playful demeanor restored.

"My queen, I'm excited about our decision, but what if Sol does not agree?" A civilian spoke in a manner of concern.

"My people, I'm sorry I hid this from you, but..." She responded calmly as she beckoned Elizya, who walked over holding Onceli. Many gasps emitted from the crowd at the sight of the unique-looking child. Elizya placed her down, and she happily waved into the crowd.

"Hi everyone! It's me...Onceli!" She shouted in her adorable toddler voice. The crowd erupted into shock, and Onceli nervously hid behind Lycia's leg as her little tail coiled around her body timidly.

"Onceli was not born of mystical conception as you all once thought." Lycia began to explain. "Her father is the king of Sol! Again, I'm so sorry I hid this from you, I figured it wasn't safe to reveal her. But this is how we will convince Sol to end the fighting! She is a living representation of the union between our two kingdoms." Some whispers of disapproval began to ride across the air until an adorable voice cut into the tension.

"Soon, when the fighting is done, I can finally be with Daddy, and we can all live happily together!" The crowd was instantly overtaken by Onceli's genuine aura and by how much of her mother's personality shined in her little heart. A young, large battle lieutenant walked up to her as she cheerfully held out her hands. He picked her up with a warm smile and placed her on his shoulder.

"Could a child so pure be born of evil blood?" He shouted into the crowd. "Let us support Queen Lycia and do what we can to make this union a reality!" He bounced Onceli playfully as he looked at her with a smile. "And let us support our adorable princess!" The crowd cheered wildly in approval, but their moment was interrupted by a shout from the gate guard.

"My queen! Lord Radric, accompanied by many military members, Solyans civilians, and the Aquarian military, accompanied by their king, are at our gates! They are flying white flags and request entry.

"Let them in!" Lycia shouted with anticipation. As the gates opened, Radric made his way into the kingdom alone, wearing a friendly smile.

"Greetings, Luna! I have..." Before he could continue speaking, Lycia's foot drilled deeply into his face, knocking him to the ground. The crowd looked on in shock and disbelief. Radric slowly stood to his feet, rubbing his cheek, as his smile remained. "Yes, I guess I deserved that." Lycia ran to him, screaming incoherent nonsense, pointing at him and then towards Onceli. Disregarding her shouts, he fell to one knee and embraced her tight. "Oh, how my heart has longed to hold you again, Lycia." Her rage quickly calmed, and she returned his embrace as a warm smile road her face.

"Daddy, you came back!" Onceli shouted as she squirmed in the marine's hold. He gently placed her down, and she mustered all the strength her tiny little body had in order to master the use of her new Uçebian legs. She began wobbling over to him. When he saw her struggling her way over, he gently released Lycia and ran to her, scooping her up.

"My darling little girl!" Tears filled his eyes as his tiny daughter's body rested in his arms. "Please forgive Daddy for being so rude when he first met you! Daddy loves you, my little one." The spectating crowd erupted into affectionate sighs. Onceli snuggled up under his strong chin as her multi-colored eyes streamed with tears of joy.

"I'm so happy, Daddy; we can be a real family now. Just like Mommy said!" Lycia joined the embrace as her skin began to glow brightly. Radric placed Onceli down and walked into the center of the Lunian civilians.

"Dear citizens of Luna, I come begging you for peace; we all do! Our nations have suffered for far too long because of the hate of our ancestors. But it can finally end." He fell to bended knee and lowered his head. "I kneel before you humbly begging your forgiveness on behalf of all of Sol. I implore you, please accept our offering of peace!" The kingdom erupted in cheers, and two small children ran up to him as he remained on his knees.

"Wow! Look how big he is! Lord king, are you a giant?"

"Woah, I didn't think they were real!"

Radric chuckled with delight and patted them on the head. "I am indeed child, the last of my kind."

"Wow, so cool!" They were called back over to their parents, and Radric looked over to the gates.

"Now come, my friends, and join your new comrades!" Everyone engaged in friendly relations, many falling into spells of joyous tears. The kings, the queen, and the battle commanders smiled as they watched with great joy, knowing peace was truly on the horizon. Suddenly, the world began to brighten, and the Uçebians looked to the sky with amazement as it opened up around the entire kingdom, cutting through the shadowy gloom and filling Luna with natural light. Everyone shielded their eyes as they looked upon a sight they never thought possible. The sun, the true sun, Father Gi, was shining majestically upon them as he rested in a glorious blue blanket. Many fell to their knees and sobbed at the mystical presence of their long hiding deity overtaken by the beauty of his radiance and the true sky. Radric could not believe his tear-soaked eyes as they met with the beautiful sight he had always dreamt to see. The unbelievable warmth of Father Gi fell upon them as a spiritual embrace, and the Uçebians felt true happiness. Lycia's eyes quivered as a new sight graced the baby blue sky. Mana appeared before them, floating beside Gi. Mana's light merged with Gi's and graced the sky with a splendor that could not be explained. Golden beams of sunlight gently cradled the pale luminescence and sparkled more brilliantly than the rarest gemstone. Even before the gloom, never before had both Gi and Mana shared the skies in such harmony. Lycia began weeping as she gently fell to her knees.

"Is this really happening? Oh, please don't let this be a dream!" She spoke weakly. Radric knelt down and placed his massive hand on her back.

"Believe it, love, we have done it!" He said warmly, with his gaze still towards the sky. "We have realized a dream that never seemed possible, and even the gods have joined in our cause." Lycia smiled brightly and rested her head against his powerful body. A concentrated beam of combined light cast on them as if in a spotlight, filling them with the paternal warmth of both deities. The crowd then fell to their knees in veneration to the rulers who made this all possible, as they were being directly acknowledged by the gods.

"This is a glorious day, my friends. May the gods bless us all!" Fraytor shouted with his hands in the air.

"Hey!" A voice shouted from the distance. Everyone looked over to see Boyox running towards them, pulling along a tiny woman. Boyox reached the crowd but was quickly overtaken by the sight of the baby blue sky as Mana and Gi shared it harmoniously. For a moment, he was far too entranced by the mystical sight of Gi, finally gracing the heavens and Mana by his side. "No better time than now; this is perfect!" He thought to himself.

"Luna, Sol, and Aquaria!" He shouted. "This is a wonderous day that I could never have dreamed would take place in my lifetime! We finally have peace, and the natural beauty of Uçebar is slowly being restored! I would like to announce my resignation from the military, but more importantly..." He fell on one knee before Uahka and took one of her tiny hands in both of his. Her cheeks began to glow as her heart quickly skipped a beat. "Uahka, my love. Would you do me the lifetime honor before all our friends, new and old...and before the gods, of being my wife?"

"Of course, my love." She responded sweetly with a warm smile as she began to cry. The entire crowd erupted into cheers and applause. Uahka looked around in shock.

"They aren't shunning me. They support us...perhaps, it was always just in my head. I was never truly an outcast; I just never gave anyone the chance to know me." She thought to herself but was interrupted as Boyox stood to his feet and merged their lips together. Lycia ran over and embraced them both tightly as her skin began to glow brighter.

"Oh, I'm so happy for you, Uahka!" Lycia shouted as she pushed Boyox aside. She took hold of Uahka's tiny hands and began hopping up and down. "Oh please, please let me help you plan the wedding!" Uahka blushed and nodded gently as Boyox began laughing.

The three kingdoms celebrated together for the remainder of the day in perfect harmony. Soon, the night was upon them, and Gi proceeded to sleep. Mana remained casting glorious pale beams upon the world. But the people became entranced by a new sight through the hole in the sky. Beautiful, twinkling diamonds of light danced throughout the darkened sky. Radric picked Onceli up, placing her on his shoulders as he pointed to them.

"Look, little one, those are called stars! I can't believe I am finally seeing them for myself and basking in their glorious splendor." Lycia looked at the sky in awe.

"Stars? Wow...so beautiful. These weren't in my mural!" She said softly.

"And they don't have to be. They are a part of our life now." Radric said warmly. "Everything...everything I ever could have hoped for..." He looked up at Onceli. "And more have now become a reality. Never in a hundred years could I have ever imagined this day would come during my lifetime. And it's all thanks to you, my dear daughter." She giggled as he placed her down. He looked over to Lycia, taking her hand. "And, of course, thanks to you, my love." Lycia smiled warmly and began tugging Radric as she started walking towards the palace.

"Come, there is something I want you to see!" Radric began to follow her and scooped up Onceli in his free hand. They made their way to Lycia's chambers, and in the corner of the room, there was a large easel covered in a white drape. Lycia released his hand and ran over to it. She grasped the cloth and looked over to him with her cheeks a bright pink.

"My dear Radric, there is another mural in my possession that no one else knows about." His eyes grew wide as he waited in anticipation. Maintaining her smiling gaze, she ripped the cloth away. Radric slowly made his way to the mural. His eyes shined with pride and happiness.

"Did...did you make this?" He asked softly as he placed his free hand lovingly on the mural. She nodded with pride. The mural depicted Lycia and Radric standing together under the light of both Gi and Mana, staring deeply into each other's eyes. Onceli, still in her wolf form, stood in a playful stance by their feet.

Radric put Onceli down and took Lycia by the waist, pulling her in close and gently crouching down. Their eyes met in a deep gaze, and he leaned down to kiss her.

"I've missed you so much...you big stupid oaf!" She said with a playful giggle. He chuckled softly as he traced the curvature of her face with his index finger. Suddenly, he felt Onceli's little arms wrap around his leg. He picked her back up and cradled her in one arm.

"We are finally a real family...I am truly happy, but it is too soon for celebration." He said sternly. Lycia nodded. "We must first deal with Umbra, then we can have true peace. I promise not to allow anything to happen to either of you until that dream is realized."

"I promise the same!" She responded warmly.

"I don't want you to join the battle against Umbra." He said sternly as his smile faded. Her ever-lasting glow finally faded, and she slowly stepped away from him.

"Excuse me, don't think you can waltz over to my kingdom and start ordering me around, *Lord* Radric!" She responded in an angered tone.

"That isn't what I am doing." He responded calmly.

"Then what is it you're doing, hmm? Asking me not to fight for my kingdom? That is just unacceptable. I must be there. You may be strong, Radric, but I am a warrior too. One who has never been injured in battle, unlike you."

"There's no need to be snide, Lycia. I'm only looking out for you."

"I don't need your protection, Radric! This is my war, too, so let me help you. How do you think I would feel if you failed...and I wasn't there to protect you!"

"Mommy, Daddy, please don't fight! It makes me sad." Onceli pleaded softly. Radric chuckled as he rubbed his nose against hers.

"Don't worry, my little Onceli; Mommy and Daddy aren't fighting." He said playfully as he put her back down and placed his hand on Lycia's face. She placed her hands on his and rested her cheek against him. "Lycia, I just can't bear the thought of losing you now that we are finally together. I may be strong, but I'm not that strong."

"And you won't!" She responded warmly as she clung tighter to his hand. "Don't you remember how we met?" She asked as she tenderly traced the scar across his body.

"Of course I do; how could I ever forget?" He responded with a smile.

Their First Encounter

Six Years Ago

Sol and Luna met in the wastelands as a dramatic stare-down between the two leaders began. Radric had just taken over the kingdom and was meeting Lycia for the first time. Even with the anticipation of the inevitable battle, he could not help but fall for her alluring beauty. Her silver hair floated majestically in the wind, and her piecing silver eye cast angry judgement upon him.

"I wonder how things would be under different circumstances." He thought to himself as his stern expression fell soft.

"What's the matter, young king? Losing your edge before the battle can even start?" She mocked. Radric threw out his hands and released his signature, over exaggerative laugh. She took two steps back with an embarrassed look on her face.

"Cousin, stop making a fool of us!" Karakus shouted from the formation. He became serious and drew his weapon.

"To the death then, Queen Lycia?" He said with a slight smile.

"Die minion of evil!" She shouted as she lunged towards him. The marines on both sides watched in awe as their leaders fought with almost choreographed elegance. The battle was intense, causing gravel and dust to burst all around, yet they each seemed so calm and sure of themselves. The marines were overtaken by the brilliance of their monarchs and could not help but feel pride, no matter what the conclusion. Lycia swung her ax as Radric dodged. He Lunged his sword towards her gut, and she flipped out of the way.

"For one so large, you move with great speed." She spoke in a mocking manner.

"Are you calling me fat, queen?" He responded with a chuckle. She laughed in an oddly playful and amused manner before dodging and catching his blade in the edges of her axe.

"I merely call what I see!" She said in a confident and victorious manner. Then, spinning her axe, tossed his sword from his hands. She hopped up, swinging her axe at his neck. He flipped away from her strike and held out his arm, channeling a torrent of fire. Knowing she couldn't evade the attack like this, she jumped out of her clothes in a spiraling motion, morphing into the great beast of her family's lineage. In this form, she was even larger than him, and his eyes grew with shock. He had never witnessed the act of shape-shifting before and was temporarily stunned motionless. She came at him with a massive claw. He was able to move just enough to avoid being cut to shreds. He received a deep slash from his shoulder to his waist, resulting in his signature battle scar. Blood splashes flew as droplets throughout the sky. The Solyans gasped with concern as the Lunians shouted victoriously. Recovering quickly, she went to lunge at him with her jaws open, to deliver the killing blow. As her powerful legs went to push off from the ground, a large crack opened up, creating an immense ravine that split the battlefield in half. Lycia fell in and, without her hands, began to plummet fast. She morphed back into her Uçebian body, quickly taking hold of the side. She slowly climbed to the top, and Major General Rehcumber ran to assist her. He pulled her up with slight redness in his cheeks as her naked body emerged from the crevasse. He looked away as he handed her clothes over to her. She quickly clothed herself and looked over to the opposite side of the massive divide. It was far too wide to jump across and too long to walk around; for now, they were at an impasse.

"Consider yourself lucky, young king. I don't usually let my enemies leave alive!" She shouted with a stern frown.

"Me? Woman, this battle was far from over." He shouted back mockingly. "Let us just thank the gods that they decided it was too soon for either of our passing." He finished with a chuckle. She scoffed as she began to walk away, followed by her troops. "Wow, what a woman!" He thought as he continued to watch her. "Why is it we must be enemies?" As she finally disappeared from his view, he slowly turned and proceeded to return to Sol.

A few weeks passed, and Radric decided he would pay a visit to Luna. He informed his council that he was taking a leave of absence and that the general would stand in as king regent. They were confused, but he claimed that he wanted to visit the remains of the old giant's territory. He climbed aboard Octonia and secretly flew towards Luna. He had her land where the Lunians wouldn't see her, and he continued on foot to await the cover of darkness. When the time came, he forced the sun to set. He effortlessly scaled the walls and snuck to the courtyard below the palace balcony. He hid behind some boulders to look upon Lycia as she stood on her balcony. She was looking up towards the moon in a dream-like state.

"But soft, what light beyond yonder window breaks!" (Just kidding)

He watched on as she began to speak to her goddess in a manner of sadness.

"Dear Mana, why must we fight? What are we fighting for? All those faces, Uçebian faces, with the life vanishing from them. They haunt my dreams, my thoughts, my heart. We are enemies, yes, but they are still Uçebians."

"She...feels the same way I do. She doesn't revel in the killing of her enemies; she feels for them. Quite a convincing façade she wore during our battle." In his thoughts, he slightly lost his hold of the boulder he hid behind. A massive thud emitted as his enormous body crashed to the ground. He remained still for a brief moment, then leaned back up, casting his gaze to the empty balcony. "That's odd, she's already gone?" He thought. Suddenly, he felt the sharp tip of a dagger dig shallowly in the side of his neck and a tiny body clinging to his to hold itself up.

"What the hell are you doing here?" A feminine voice spoke in a stern whisper. He chuckled as he held up his hands. "Well, don't just give up now! Somehow, your oversized, oaf-like self snuck into my kingdom undetected! Surely you didn't come here without a plan?"

"No, my queen, you're right. I did have a plan, but it's not as you think; I have already achieved what I came for." He responded warmly. She raised a curious eyebrow and slightly eased up the tension of the dagger.

"Explain yourself. What are you talking about?" She demanded calmly. He slowly stood to his feet, forcing her to slowly slide to the ground. She backed away slightly as he turned to face her. Her radiant skin reflected the moonlight beams, and her body was illuminated by their splendor. Radric couldn't help but smile as he soaked in her mystique. "What are you smiling at?" She continued with a frown. "Have you only come here to mock my kindness for leaving you alive? Don't take me for a merciful fool; I will kill you right here, King Radric!"

"But it won't bring you joy to do so." He continued to smile. She gasped and took a slight step back. "I heard how you spoke of those you killed."

"Do not mock me..." She said weakly as her frown began to bear sadness more than anger.

"You misunderstand me, my lady, I too feel as you do. I don't revel in victory, for to me, there is no victory in taking life. I only do so because I must protect my people." Her visible eye trembled as she stared up in awe. He began to draw closer to her, and she hopped back.

"Not another step, I'm warning you." She said weakly, holding out her dagger.

"I'm sorry, but I cannot do that. You see, this is why I have come here. If we are destined to eventually kill each other, I must look upon your face and hear your voice a little longer before that day comes." Her cheeks began to glow bright red, but she covered them with her hands and looked away. He continued towards her. "How I wish things were different. What would be if this meeting took place under different circumstances." She looked towards him with an angry glare as she held her dagger out.

"And what makes you think I feel as you? You are talking as if I have the same infatuation with you!" She responded nervously as her cheeks flared brighter.

"Well, if you truly don't, you have a strange way of expressing yourself, my lady." He teased. With her free hand, she covered one of her glowing cheeks.

"Shut up! Don't confuse yourself. You are just scaring me is all, you creep." Her dagger-bearing hand began to tremble as he continued towards her. He gently placed his hand on hers.

"Please, we are not on the battlefield right now. Can't we just enjoy a moment of peace together as Uçebian people?" He gently lowered her hand, and she slowly dropped the dagger.

"Very well, but let me lay down one very important ground rule." She responded sternly as she looked away from him, ripping her hand from his.

"Sure, what is it?" He asked as she jumped into the air and kicked his face with impressive force, sending him to the ground.

"Never touch me again!" She shouted angrily.

These secret meetings would happen from time-to-time. Getting less and less frequent with the passing years. Their bond only grew greater with each visit, no matter how long the time between.

An End to Hatred

Present Day

Radric's hand still resting on Lycia's cheek, he chuckled as he reminisced on their early years together.

"I'm grateful to Mana and Gi that you were such a persistent oaf!" She said playfully.

"Let's get some rest; we have a lot of planning to do in the morning." He said softly, placing a tender kiss on her forehead. She nodded gently, and they both proceeded to put Onceli to bed. They tucked her in, and each kissed her goodnight, then made their way to Lycia's chambers. Lycia laid down, and Radric kissed her cheek before turning to leave.

"You aren't coming to bed?" She asked softly as she took hold of his arm.

"I must send a messenger home to inform my people of the good news and rally the men towards a midpoint near Umbra." He replied without turning around. "We have no time to waste, and the messenger will need a long head start to make it to Sol before we are ready to move. We must prepare quickly. With word of our union, I'm sure Umbra will mount an attack soon."

"Okay, but don't be long. I'll wait up for you." She responded

sweetly. He chuckled softly as her grip loosened, and he proceeded out of the palace. He reached where his men were camped
and gave his orders to a messenger. A Lunian guided the messenger to the stable. The messenger made haste from the city, riding
atop a Lunian wolf. As Radric was making his way back to the
palace, Fraytor called out to him from behind.

"Alright then, ol' boy, what's the attack plan!" He said in a
chipper manner.

"What?" Radric responded with a confused expression.

"Aquaria is as much involved in this battle as Luna and Sol."
He said sternly as his smile faded. "We are all affected by Umbra's
evil. We must work together to bring her down!"

"Thank you, old friend," Radric responded with a smile as he
placed his hand on Fraytor's shoulder. "We will plan tomorrow,
after we are well rested." Fraytor nodded, and they went their
separate ways for the night. Radric continued into the palace and
returned to Lycia's chambers.

"You kept me waiting awhile, my king, how rude...but so like
you." She said in a playful whisper. He chuckled as he slid into
bed with her. Finally able to enjoy each other's warm embrace,
they drifted off into a pleasant sleep. A carefree sleep, which neither ruler had been able to experience in many years.

The next morning, the three rulers and their council sat in
Lycia's meeting hall. To Lycia's surprise, Boyox was present.

"Boyox, what are you doing here? You formally resigned!"
She spoke with concern.

"Yes, my queen, but it was preemptive. I have every intention
to resign once I know Luna is safe."

"Absolutely not!" She said sternly, jumping to her feet. "You
are finally able to be with the one you love. I cannot allow you
to risk losing that!"

"With all possible respect, my queen, is that not what you are
risking yourself?" He responded boldly.

"That is slightly out of place, colonel." She said calmly.

"Forgiveness, my queen. I only wish to fight for the protection of the ones I love." Lycia reluctantly nodded her head and slowly took her seat.

"Comrades, this may be the most dangerous challenge, any of us have ever or will ever face," Radric said, getting things started. "The enemy is unlike any other. They do not have love in their hearts as we do. They do not fight honorably. It is tough for me to say this, but..." He released a deep sigh. "For that reason, I feel they must all die! Even their innocent."

"You can't be serious!" Lycia shouted as she jumped back to her feet.

"I agree with Lord Radric," Boyox replied. "Though the thought pains me, we have all witnessed the true evil of Umbra. Especially you, my queen. There is no good in the hearts of the Umbra; they must be removed as a whole."

"Let's think about this for a minute," Fraytor said calmly. "We don't know what goes on behind those walls. The people could be forced under a harsh dictatorship that they do not wish to be a part of. We have no way of knowing the true intensions of the Umbrian civilians."

"Indeed. Besides, you can't be suggesting we slaughter children?" Lieutenant General Relic replied calmly.

"I'm sorry, good general, but that is indeed what I am suggesting," Radric spoke weakly as his gaze fell to the floor.

"Do you hear yourself!" Lycia shouted as she slammed her fist into the table. "Imagine it was the other way around. Imagine we were under the watch of an evil goddess, and another nation came to the conclusion that there was no good in our hearts... imagine they decided Onceli must die for the actions of our goddess!" Radric's eyes widened as he looked at her. "There is always good in people. No one thought our two nations could ever get along. Yet here we sit, united. Who are we to pass judgment on those who may be suffering, wishing for liberation from behind Umbra's walls!" Silence fell amongst the entire council for a brief moment as Lycia kept her stern stare at Radric.

"With respect, my king, I agree with Queen Lycia." Major General Gorg responded calmly. "We should use caution and seek out only those who would do us harm. We may be able to save many lives."

"Forgive me, everyone," Radric said softly. "In my selfishness, I was only thinking of my family and no one else. If we are in agreeance, then I suggest we do our best to save the Umbrian citizens. Any objection, Colonel Boyox?" Boyox reclined slightly in his chair, resting his head on his hands.

"No, my lord, Queen Lycia has moved me with her speech." He said warmly with a smile. Lycia looked over in awe to see how different Boyox was now that he could finally be himself.

"Good. By the time we reach the midpoint, Radric's forces should already be there." Fraytor began as he pointed to their anticipated location on the stone model. "They should be safe at this distance, granted Umbra doesn't make the first move. Which is why it is of upmost importance that we make ready immediately to aid them. If we send out the van guard a few days early, they should be able to provide backup to Radric's forces if need be. Then our main force won't have to worry about rushing in."

"Well, well, old man, for a ruler of a previously non-combatant nation, you seem to have quite an understanding of battle strategy." Radric teased.

"Well, as you pointed out, ol' boy, I am old, and with my age comes wisdom!" They both began laughing together. The other council members felt at ease as two of the most powerful beings on Uçebar were so relaxed while in such a predicament.

The complete strategy was discussed, and everyone began to ready themselves. Elizya walked over to Lycia, holding Onceli, who held her arms out. Lycia received her and cradled her in her arms. She began to tickle under Onceli's neck, making her giggle wildly. Lycia stopped and stared deep into the multi-colored eyes of her beautiful daughter.

"Be safe, Mommy, and don't let Daddy get hurt," Onceli commanded playfully.

"Oh, you know I won't. Mommy is strong!" Lycia responded with a giggle.

"So, you think Daddy needs protection, huh?" Radric replied playfully. Onceli became excited and slowly slid from Lycia's arms and began wobbling over to him. He picked her up and held her close. "Sweet little Onceli, both Mommy and Daddy will come home, we promise." Lycia placed her hand on his arm and nodded with a gentle smile. Radric walked off with Onceli still in his arms to inspire the troops. He figured her playful innocence would help ease the tension and bring them joy. Lycia watched as he was walking away, when Elizya embraced her from behind. Lycia rested her head against Elizya and gently shut her eyes. Her body produced its luminescent splendor as her cheeks grew flush.

"My dear Lycia...I thought I lost you once." Elizya spoke in a broken manner through her gentle tears. "My heart couldn't bear it if I ever truly did. Please be safe!"

"I will be. Don't worry, Mother." She responded as she remained in her snuggled position. "But I need you to do something for me." She said, removing herself from Elizya's embrace and turning to look upon her crystal eyes.

"Anything!" She responded warmly. Lycia embraced her, resting her head against her chest as she always had.

"Please refer to me as you did that day. Just one more time... in case..."

"Stop!" Elizya cut her off desperately. "Not another word, dear daughter!" Tears of joy flowed from Lycia's tightly shut eyes as her glow intensified. "Don't you dare finish that sentence. You will come back, you hear me!" Lycia giggled as her tears slowly ceased.

"I love how commanding you just were, Mother! Let's see more of that side of you when I get back!" She released her embrace and skipped off to where the marines were preparing.

As she had always done in the past, she made her rounds greeting the marines. She eventually made her way to the medical tent. As she arrived, her smile and bright glow faded as she was reminded that Geeah was gone. The new medical commander reported to her and took notice of her sad expression.

"Your majesty, are you alright?" She asked in a concerned manner.

"Be safe, my dear Lieutenant," Lycia responded softly as she cradled the lieutenant's face in her hands and held their foreheads together. "My heart cannot bear the loss of any more of my beautiful ladies. Watch out for them and for yourself." The lieutenant returned her embrace with a warm smile.

"Don't worry, my queen, your ladies are strong! We will not fail you." Lycia released her with a smile and happily skipped off to greet the other warriors, only now things were different. She had more stops to make. She made her way over to the Solyan marines. Gorg was the first to see her and fell to bended knee.

"Greetings, mighty warriors of Sol!" She said with a happy giggle. "It makes me giddy to have you all here in my city; it's kinda fun!" They all smiled warmly, and she skipped off. Gorg couldn't help but notice Axaiyan as he stood as if petrified in an invisible lining of stone. Gorg walked over to Axaiyan and waved his hand in his face, but there was no response.

"Colonel, snap out of it! You alright?" He asked.

"Did you see how her ears twitched as she smiled?" Axaiyan replied in entrancement as his body remained still. "It never really sunk in until I looked to her as an ally, but the queen's beauty is truly beyond compare!" Gorg smashed him over the head, finally breaking him from his trance.

"Come on, Axaiyan, we all have to control the emotions she creates in us so as not to lose our heads," Gorg responded in slight embarrassment.

"So you too, huh?" Axaiyan replied in a whisper.

"Yes, so shut up! It's harder to ignore it when others give into it." Axaiyan nodded with a cheeky smile, and they went about their preparations.

Lycia made her way to the Aquarians and immediately honed in on a specific warrior. Her visible eye filled with mischievous excitement as she sprinted over.

"Oh wow! Look at you! So big and strong!" Lycia spoke in the manner of an entranced schoolgirl. She grasped the big muscular arm of Natia and began massaging it sensually.

"My queen, what are you doing?" Natia responded with embarrassment, her entire face a dark red.

"You're the biggest woman I've ever seen! It's so intimidatingly intriguing!" Natia stood with stiff embarrassment, only making her muscles seem harder. Lycia giggled with admiration as she continued to massage her arm. Natia's embarrassment grew as Lycia couched down and squeezed her powerful quads.

"Please, my queen...this is incredibly undignified!" Natia pleaded. Disregarding her, Lycia hopped on to her shoulders and began playing with her trap muscles. She finally hopped down, facing her protruding abdominal muscles.

"It's almost like you were carved out of unbreakable stone!" Lycia said as she traced her fingers between Natia's mighty abdominal indentations. Having witnessed the entire thing, Radric failed to hold back his laughter. Natia looked over with horrified embarrassment to see Radric.

"Well, now, Lycia, why have you never done that to me?" He inquired playfully.

"Because you're a man, your body should be strong!" She began to speak with slight seduction behind her voice as she continued to trace Natia's abs. "But when an elegant and beautiful woman is so densely clad in muscle, that is something to marvel over." Radric drew closer, laughing uncontrollably at poor Natia's distress. He never witnessed her seem so vulnerable. Still carrying Onceli in one arm, he picked Lycia up with the other. His arm wrapped around her stomach, she dangled like a hunted game, still lost in her trance.

"Forgive her, Natia. Lycia, will be Lycia!" He said playfully as he began to walk away, still chuckling. Eventually, Lycia snapped from her trance, and a bored expression painted her face as she dangled in Radric's hold.

"Now, why did you have to go and ruin the fun?" She said as she released an irritated sigh. Without a word, he let out a slight chuckle and lightly put her down. She walked beside him with her arms crossed like an upset toddler.

"Mommy is funny, right, Daddy?" Onceli said with a playful giggle. Radric laughed, and Lycia couldn't help but crack a slight smirk.

A few days after the vanguard was deployed to the wastes, the main force finished up its preparations. Onceli remained with Elizya as the three monarchs made their way to the city square, where their forces began to muster. Lycia hopped up onto the statue of Luna's founder and hung from the spear. Radric and Fraytor stood on either side of her.

"People of Luna! (The Lunians shouted back energetically) People of Sol! (Cheering) People of Aquaria! (Cheering) Today, we put hatred to rest for good! (Unified shouts) Today, we work towards the restoration of Uçebar's true, natural beauty. (Unified cheering) Our hope is that once hatred has been destroyed in Uçebar, the gods will restore our entire world, not just the kingdoms, to its former glory. The wastelands will become a sanctuary for beauty and abundant with breathable air! (Unified cheering) This is the day of reckoning! This is the day of peace! We will be victorious! We will return home with our heads held high! We will make the gods proud!" The entire city erupted into energetic applause.

"Great speech, love!" Radric said with motivation. She playfully kicked him in the head and hopped from the statue. The three monarchs stood at the front of the vast unified army of three nations. Being it was her kingdom, Lycia stood in the center and held her arm into the sky.

"TO VICTORY!" She shouted energetically as they took off with great speed and began their long journey to the midpoint.

War Against Umbra

The large, unified army reached the midpoint, and the rest of Sol's army and the vanguard energetically greeted them as they arrived. Many of the Solyan and Lunian military members shook hands and respectfully greeted each other for the first time as allies.

"Well, if this isn't the handshake I never expected to receive in a lifetime! What a wonderful feeling this is. Great to have you by my side, Lunian!" An older Solyan sergeant said as he shook the hand of a young Lunian marine. The Solyan medics gathered in a tight circle and began whispering to each other.

"Dude, look at the Lunian medics! I still can't believe they enlist women. Forget only enlisting women!" One grunt said to the rest.

"What's wrong with that?" A second replied.

"Nothing, it's great." His eyes shined with entrancement as he responded and glanced over to the Lunian medics. "Look how cute they are...yet so deadly!"

"Compose yourself, man!" A third said urgently, slapping him on the back of the head. "They're looking over and giggling. You'll ruin this for us all!"

"Hey, we are medics, they are medics..." The first began to speak with excitement. "We are going to be fighting alongside them. We should introduce ourselves, and you know...discuss techniques and what not...it's only polite."

"Techniques, huh? You gonna buy her a drink first, you dog?" A forth playfully elbowed him as he teased.

"No, no, what? That isn't what I meant!" He responded urgently.

"Eh, calm yourself, kid. I'm only kidding." The fourth reassured him. "It is a good idea to go meet them. Lead the way!" He said playfully as he held out his arm. The group of Solyan medics made their way over to the beautiful Lunians and introduced themselves. They were getting acquainted when Radric barreled by.

"That's what I'm talking about!" He continued past them as he shouted with motivation. "Getting along so well and already discussing tactics! You medics are making me proud! Keep up the dedication!" The medics shouted proudly, then returned to their business.

The three leaders convened with their generals. Radric was excited to see Wasukah return to the battlefield.

"Ah Wasukah old friend! Never thought I'd see the day you returned to the battlefield! Think you still got it, old man?" Radric teased.

"You can count on it, my lord!" Wasukah responded energetically as he slammed his fist into his chest. "And I'll have you know, my king, I'm not that old just yet! At least not compared to Lord Fraytor." He said in a semi-low whisper.

"I heard that you scoundrel!" Fraytor playfully shouted. They all laughed, but Wasukah soon became serious.

"I do have some rather disturbing news, however. We did some recon, my king. I know it wasn't part of the plan, but I took it upon myself to do so." Radric nodded slightly. "It appears Lord Maytold has died; we are unsure of how it happened."

"Ha! Well, that sounds like great news to me!" Radric said energetically, slamming his fist into his opened palm. "One less obstacle to…"

"The replacement, my lord…" Wasukah cut him off as everyone began to listen on with great anticipation. "Is your cousin…" Everyone gasped, and Radric felt as if his heart had briefly stopped. Lycia placed a compassionate hand on his arm, but he quickly pulled away, storming off into the wastelands. Lycia went to follow him, but Natia took hold of her arm. Lycia looked back with a sad expression on her face.

"Let him go, majesty; he will be alright." She said softly. Lycia looked back to where he once was, but he had already vanished.

"I understand this must be hard for the king, but what's worse is there's more." Wasukah continued looking to Fraytor. "Karakus has been turned into a demon of shadows, much like the one who wiped out our entire force in the past." They all gasped, and Lycia shook her head frantically with sadness and disbelief.

"We know how to defeat the shadow demons now, though!" Lycia said as her sad frown still road her face.

"Please explain, my queen," Wasukah responded.

"When we faced the demon, it seemed all but invincible. Regenerating as fast as we injured it. But my young colonel, Boyox, discovered that without the light from Mana or the artificial sun to cast a shadow…it had no regenerative powers."

"Excellent, this is most helpful, my queen; thank you!" He responded energetically. "I just don't know how the king will handle having to be a part of killing his own cousin. My lord Fraytor. I feel you are the only one the king will listen to right now. Please go help our king; bring his head from the clouds. We are in dire need of his great strength." Fraytor nodded and made haste in the direction Radric took off in.

While Fraytor searched for Radric, tactics and strategy were discussed back at the encampment. Fraytor eventually caught up to Radric who was standing at the mouth of a familiar crevasse. He knew Fraytor was there, and before Fraytor could say a word, Radric started speaking calmly. He wore a smile with his gaze to the gapping ravine.

"Do you know what this place is, old friend?" He asked. Fraytor stood by his side and gently shook his head as he began to peer into the deep fissure. "This is the location of my first battle with Lycia...the place where I fell for her. That day is when I knew I needed to work towards peace because I knew I had to be with her. I knew I wanted her by my side and not as my enemy."

"So why tell me this? What's on your mind, ol' boy?" He inquired with a gentle smile.

"But never would I have thought that to end evil and hatred in this world...I'd have to kill my own cousin." Radric continued weakly as his smile diminished. "The last living piece of flesh and blood from my ancestors." Fraytor kept his smile as he placed a compassionate hand on Radric's arm.

"Come, my friend, it is best not to worry about this. Especially as we wait outside the gates of hell itself." Fraytor encouraged. Radric nodded, and they both made their way to the encampment. Upon seeing him return, Lycia slowly approached him with a sad look in her eye. Radric smiled warmly as he reached out for her hand.

"My love, we are by your side; we will see this through with you!" She said, placing her hand in his.

"No, I must be the one who faces Karakus," Radric said sternly as his smile faded. "I am the one who has failed him. I am the one who didn't detect the evil brewing in his heart before it was too late. I must be the one to silence him."

"But Radric, please, you mustn't put a burden of such magnitude on yourself." She said, clinging tighter to him. "It isn't your fault that he made the choices he did."

"Please, Lycia...he is my cousin...the last of my living relatives. I should have seen the change in him and helped him before it was too late. I have to be the one to kill him. I have to be the one who sets his soul free." He replied calmly. Lycia moved closer and wrapped her arms around one of his as she rested her head against him.

"I understand, just please, don't forget that we are in this together now. We are a real family. You, me, and our darling Onceli." She replied warmly as she gently massaged his arm. Radric looked to her with a warm smile and placed a soft kiss on her forehead.

"You and Onceli are my strength. With that, I will never fail."

"Alright then, no more mushy stuff! Time to prepare for battle." She said playfully as she released him. He chuckled as he watched her skip away.

"My king, there was one more thing I never got to tell you." Wasukah began to explain. "I'm sorry to burden your heart with this, but it cannot wait. Karakus is not just the new ruler; he has been turned into a shadow demon." Radric clenched his fist tightly as his fiery eyes burned with rage.

"Umbra will pay for this! Forgive me, cousin, but it shall be I who puts your soul to rest for eternity."

Later, within the encampment, Colonels Axaiyan and Boyox had their first interaction after the plans were discussed. Axaiyan was staring down Boyox with a burning gaze from where he sat. Boyox couldn't help but notice, occasionally looking over and meeting his gaze throughout the entire gathering. Boyox walked over to him and held out his arm to shake his hand with a smile.

"Greetings, fellow colonel. Something been in your eye the past half hour?" He inquired playfully. Axaiyan scoffed and slapped his hand away. "Come on, we are friends now, are we not? This is no way to treat a brother in arms." Boyox continued to impishly pester as he wore a cheeky smile. Axaiyan stood with a blunt frown as he looked down on the tiny Boyox.

"Child, it escapes my understanding how you hold the rank of colonel but don't speak to me as if we are equals." He responded condescendingly.

"Aww, isn't that cute? You're jealous of my fast progress, ay, old man?" Boyox said, his grin growing.

"Old?! I'm quite young to be a colonel myself." Axaiyan shouted back defensively.

"Yeah, but not as young as me. Making you jealous, and us naturally rivals." Boyox continued to tease. Axaiyan became furious and cocked back his arm, but before he could deliver the punch, a powerful hand took hold of his wrist.

"Come now, Axaiyan, is this any way to behave when speaking with our newly formed allies?" Radric said playfully, then released his hand. "Besides...this is the man who defeated that ghoul that has always haunted you. You know, the whole demon in the wastelands that you couldn't beat? Yea, he defeated it with the power of his mind. How 'bout that, huh? And you mock him for his age..." Axaiyan was stunned in disbelief as the king's words seemed to pound him into oblivion.

"Muh...my king. That was...incredibly low! How...why would you ever say something so terrible to me?" Axaiyan responded weakly. Radric fell into a spell of his signature laughter, but before it could go on very long, Lycia hopped up and took hold of his ear and dangled.

"Really? You still do that?" She said in disbelief as she began to drag him away. "Dear Mana, that is so embarrassing! Oh, and just give away our position, why don't ya! With your dumb, extremely loud, fake laugh. Hmph!" Boyox returned his hand to Axaiyan with a playful smile.

"It will be much easier for you if you just shook my hand... friend." Boyox teased.

"We—are not—friends," Axaiyan responded bluntly as he reluctantly received Boyox's hand.

"Whatever you say..." Boyox turned and began walking away, holding his hand out in a stationary wave. "Pal!" Boyox pestered. Axaiyan stormed off in a fit of anger, unamused by Boyox's antics.

"What an absolute stiff! I freaken love that guy! Is that how others viewed me through my little power act? Huh, maybe that's why he amuses me so much, cuz for him it's actually legit." Boyox thought to himself as he struggled to contain his amusement.

The wastelands and Umbra were still engulfed in gloom and reliant on the artificial sun. To remain inconspicuous, Radric forced the sun to set at the time he normally would. They did their best to blend with the shadows; however, Umbra is the goddess of darkness. It didn't take long for the fell guards of her demonic domicile to take notice of them.

"They have spotted us!" Fraytor shouted. "Forget the slow stealth. Full force men, attack!" Several evil minions of Umbra burst from her gates as the guards from atop the wall showered them with arrows. The unified Uçebians held out their shields, repelling most of the arrows, but some of them were getting cut down. The medics immediately sprang into action. They smashed large stakes in the ground with giant shields attached to them. Quickly hoisting them up, they protected themselves and the wounded as they rendered aid. Radric let out an enormous battle cry as he channeled a powerful flame torrent, effectively destroying the archers on the wall. Lycia and Fraytor ran by his side as they continued their assault on the ground troops. The Umbrian marines left trails of shadow in their wake as they ran, leaving the unified Uçebians disoriented. However, with Radric, Lycia, and Fraytor in the front, the Umbrians' numbers quickly diminished as the unified Uçebians suffered few casualties. Radric rained fire from the sky, brightening the areas of shadow while roasting the Umbrians. The air was becoming stained with red as blood was evaporating into the air from the heat of Radric's flames. Lycia burst from her clothes, morphing into her powerful wolf form. She clawed, slashed, and crushed her enemies with her powerful jaws. The Umbrians were almost completely defeated when a demonic voice projected over the battlefield.

"Well, well, to think anyone would have the gall to defy Queen Umbra." A familiar yet foul voice called out.

"Karakus! How dare you speak of that foul demoness as a queen?" Radric shouted. "Think about what you are doing! We could have peace; why would you sell your soul like this?" The demonic voice laughed as it began walking into view. Everyone gasped at the nightmarish Uçebian that now stood before them. It appeared to be Karakus with glowing red eyes and an indescribably sinister-looking face. His skin was black as shadow and lacking in texture, generating a miasmic smoke.

"My dear Radric, there will never be peace in this world. Not as long as a single soul still harbors hate within them."

"Karakus, please, it isn't too late. Stop this before there is any further bloodshed. Come back to us and live as the gods intended." Radric pleaded desperately.

"As the gods intended, huh?" Karakus frowned as he responded bluntly. "Well, how did they intend, *noble king?* Has life been anything more than war since as far back as we can remember? Who's truly against the "intended" order of things then, huh?"

"Is that what you truly believe?" Radric shouted. "That there is nothing more to life than war...than death...than hate? Come now, Karakus, we have had our differences with Luna, but this is not you! Snap out of it!"

"How observant!" Karakus responded with a laugh. "You are

right Radric, I am not Karakus! He is gone! He willed his soul to me and allowed me to take refuge in his body. He let me in for my power, but I now control his every action and thought."

"It can't be!" Radric's eye's widened with fear and disbelief as he suddenly felt like he was being crushed under the aura of a deity.

"That's right, peasant! You stand be for me, the great Umbra! Goddess of deception, darkness, and despair! I will be the one who finally puts an end to this pathetic thought of peace and return Uçebar to its proper order! Consumed in hate and chaos... ravaged by war!" She burst towards Radric, wielding a demonic sword. "And I'll start with you!" A loud clang sounded as their swords met, and the battle for Uçebar truly began. Lycia and Fraytor shouted to Radric as they ran towards him.

"Stay back! I must be the one who faces her!" He shouted as he continued to battle the Umbra.

"Don't be a fool, Radric; this is not just your cousin anymore! You face the dark goddess herself!" Fraytor shouted as he continued towards him.

"Fraytor is right, Radric. Let us assist you on this one!" Lycia shouted as her four giant legs propelled her forward.

"No!" He shouted sternly.

"Why, what do you have to prove, Radric?!" Lycia shouted. "We all know you are the most powerful being on Uçebar! Stop trying to act so tough, and allow us to help!"

"You think this is about Pride?" He shouted as he continued to fend her off. Lycia and Fraytor came to a kidding halt. "I refuse to lose anyone else I care for at the hands of this evil witch. I can't even bear the thought! I may be the most powerful being... but I do not possess a fraction of the strength to lose another loved one...not by Umbra...and not while she uses my cousin as her puppet!"

"How cute!" Umbra cut in. "The great king fears for the life of his little friends. So nobly willing to take on a goddess all by himself. Your affection and care for them is your weakness, Radric. Bear witness...look how easily you will lose focus during our little battle." She materialized a shadowy spear and chucked it at Lycia.

"Lycia! No!" He shouted desperately, but Umbra took hold of him with a shadow-like whip, preventing him from rushing to her aid. Lycia quickly dodged out of the way.

"See Radric! I could have easily killed you if I wanted. Your concern for her left you completely helpless! Don't you understand, you don't have a chance. All I would need to do is keep attacking her as I fought you, and you would all but be defeated. You are weak, Radric! And once you are dead, there will be nothing stopping me from destroying your friends! Then, I will reshape this world. Filling Sol and Luna with new people and reteaching them the hate I instilled in your ancestors so long ago!" The Uçebians gasped in utter disbelief.

"It...it was you. All this time! We slaughtered each other for nearly a millennium...because of you!" Radric shouted, fueled with the rage of a thousand lifetimes. "No! NO! I will not fail!" He severed the hold she had over him with her whip and lunged his sword at her. "I do it for everyone! For Lycia...Fraytor...my darling little girl...and the people of all our nations! We will have peace!" He drove his sword deep into Karakus's heart, but no injury was caused. Umbra laughed as she jumped up, passing through his sword and kicking him to the ground.

"Pathetic mortal! Don't ever let the thought of defeating me cross your mind. I am not bound to your realm. I cannot be defeated!" She shouted triumphantly. Lycia and Fraytor began running towards them again in an attempt to render aid.

"I don't care how the odds are against me, witch!" Radric shouted with fury. "I will find a way to stop you; it is my destiny to liberate Uçebar from your tyranny."

"Hmph...very well, young king. I guess you didn't heed my teaching on your biggest weakness. Perhaps it would be more fun to slaughter your friends first...and make you watch!" Suddenly, two shadow demons materialized from the nothing, intercepting Fraytor and Lycia. Blood sprayed from Fraytor's chest as a shadowy claw pierced through him like rotted bark.

"Fraytor! No!" Distracted from the fight, Radric looked to Fraytor with indescribable agony in his eyes. Umbra lunged at him, and he quickly shifted his gaze as he fended off the attack. He grabbed his sinister foe's head with his massive hand and hurled her into the great walls of her kingdom. She quickly came to her feet, unphased, but stood idly by to take in all of the sorrow emitting from Radric's heart. He ran to Fraytor, who was slowly falling to his knees. Radric caught him before he fell to his face. The shadow demon vanished into the gloom with a foul grin. Tears filled Radric's eyes as he rested Fraytor on his lap, and their gaze met.

"Come now, ol' boy." Fraytor trembled as he wore a weak smile, struggling to speak. "I'm old and lived a full and peaceful life. Please don't waste your tears on me."

"You damned fool, I told you to stay back," Radric said weakly but soon wore a tender smile. "But then I guess it wouldn't be like you to listen now, would it?" Fraytor chuckled weakly as he slightly coughed up blood.

"Just promise me, ol' boy...promise me that you won't lose your head over this. Keep a clear mind and do what we set out to. Stop Umbra and save Uçebar."

"You can count on it, old friend. Rest in peace, be free of this world...I will avenge you!" The moment was broken as Radric heard Lycia shout. The second demon cut deeply into one of her large legs as she was distracted by the sight. The severity of the injury forced her to change back to her Uçebian form. In her normal body, it resulted in a deep wound in her left arm.

"Lycia! NO!" Radric shouted as he looked over in horror. He began to sprint to her rescue. He released a large fireball at the demon, but suddenly, Umbra appeared in front of him and absorbed the blast. She began laughing maniacally as she bound his body with rope-like shadows. She floated up and took hold of his face, forcing him to stare at Lycia.

"Now, Radric, you will watch your beloved die!" Lycia was on the ground, bound by Umbra's magic, powerless to defend against the demon's next attack. It gripped its sword and went to drive it into her heart.

"Mother Mana, I implore you, my goddess! Please hide your light!" Radric pleaded into the night sky. In an instant, the world went dark. As Mana's light reemerged, Axaiyan stood with his sword deep in Karakus's heart. Umbra began laughing sinisterly as she kicked Axaiyan to the ground. Umbra stood over him with her sword before his face.

"Fools, did you truly believe that trick would work on me?" Radric let out a sigh of infinite relief, and Umbra looked at him with confusion. She matched his gaze and noticed Boyox with his sword in the body of the shadow demon. The demon burst into a black cloud of smoke and vanished from the world. Boyox smiled as he handed Lycia her clothes, keeping his eyes from her exposed body. A medic ran to her side, tending to her wound and helping her clothe herself.

"Ah, so I see. That attack wasn't truly meant for me." She said calmly. "It matters not; you all will still die! Savor this short victory as long as you can!" She lunged at Radric. He dodged out of the way, escaping her shadowy bonds, and charged her as their swords met.

"Please, Radric, let us help you!" Lycia shouted desperately as she returned to her feet.

"No, I must do this alone! And you are injured."

"But you can't do this alone! Please, love, let us help you. I

cannot bear to lose you, but think of Onceli! She is just a child.
She would never understand. And if we fail, she will eventually
be in Umbra's path. Stop being so damn foolish; together, we
have the strength to stop her."

"Ugh, very well! But please, be careful. I just thought I lost you
a few seconds ago. I couldn't bear it if I truly did."

"Marines, with me! We must defeat Umbra; we'll do it
together!" Lycia shouted. The marines shouted as they sprinted
forward and formed a circle around Umbra. Radric hopped back,
falling into the formation. Lycia winced and fought against the
pain in her arm with valiant determination.

"Fine, then you will all die together!" Umbra shouted as the
circled closed in around her. They attacked her from all sides,
but it was to no avail. Their attacks passed straight through her.
Umbra slashed off the head of an Aquaria. Two Solyans fell while
grasping the gaping holes in their chest as she stabbed through
them. A Lunian fell after having both his legs severed. Body parts
began flying as Umbra effortlessly vanquished more and more of
the unified force. The circular formation jumped back, creating
distance but keeping Umbra surrounded.

"What do we do majesties? We face a goddess, and we are
but mere Uçebians." General Natia said weakly. Radric's eyes
widened as he came to the realization that this fight could not
be won by sheer force or determination, and he fell to one knee.
The surrounding military members gasped with horror.

"Please, sir, you can't give in! We will find a way to defeat
her." Lieutenant General Relic shouted.

"What's this? Do you wish to yield to me, *great king?*" Umbra
said sarcastically with an amused chuckle. Suddenly, Lycia fell
to one knee as well.

"No, my queen! What are you doing? We can't give in!"
Boyox shouted in desperation. Soon, all of the Solyan marines
fell to one knee.

"That's it, give in! It's hopeless! I am the queen of this world! Bend to my will!" Umbra shouted victoriously. Soon, the other Uçebians began to understand. This was no surrender. It was a plea. A plea to the gods, for only a divine being could stop another. Soon, the remaining marines fell to their knees, silently pleading to their respective gods for help. Umbra threw her hands into the air, laughing victoriously, but she was interrupted as a large hole tore open in the sky. Gi's intense light blasted down upon Umbra. She released a loud shriek of agony as she was ripped from Karakus, leaving a floating, sinister-looking spirit. Karakus began to return to normal and fell to his knees.

"What is this! It can't be!" Umbra shouted. Suddenly, Onox, god of Aquaria, caused a deep body of water to form underneath them. A giant wave crashed over them, engulfing both Karakus and Umbra. Gi and Mana's light merged together and began solidifying the water. Radric burst forward and dove into the water that had not yet become solid. He swam with all his might towards Karakus.

"No, just leave me, cousin. I know I deserve this, and the gods clearly feel I do as well. Just let me go…" Karakus said weakly.

"Shut up! I am bringing you home, you hear me!" Radric shouted valiantly. The water around Karakus began to solidify. Radric pleaded with the gods to have mercy on him, but the process continued. Radric powered forward, finally reaching him, and grabbed hold of Karakus. He began pulling him from the solid water and swimming towards the edge with Karakus resting in his other arm. He reached the edge, and Lycia took hold of his hand to assist him out of the water. Without the strength of her wolf form, she couldn't manage to pull him free. Many others began to rush to their aid to assist her. Suddenly, Umbra grabbed Karakus's feet and began tugging at him, with the other half of her body trapped in the solid water. She pulled harder, determined to take Karakus with her.

"No, you shall not have him, witch!" Radric shouted as he pulled with all his might, but it was to no avail. Radric himself started getting pulled in, along with Lycia and all those helping her.

"Let go, my love. I'm so sorry, but there's nothing we can do for him. But we can for you! Please, let go!" Lycia shouted desperately but with compassion.

"How can you say that? He's my blood. I have to save him!" Radric shouted as he glared at her angrily.

"Forget it, cousin, leave me," Karakus said weakly as Radric looked back over to him. "I'm sorry for betraying you. I'm sorry for betraying everyone. Please, cousin, forgive me before I pass so that my soul may rest."

"Never! I won't give up on you!" They began getting pulled in deeper as more of Umbra was absorbed.

"Please, cousin, just let me go. I appreciate all you've done for me. I'll never forget all the times we've shared together. And hey, maybe in the next life...I'll finally get the jump on you." He smiled weakly, but Radric remained staring in despair. "Please, cousin...forgive me...then...let me go."

"I—I forgive you, Karakus...rest in peace...my dear cousin," Radric responded after a heavy sigh, then released Karakus's hand.

"I love you, Radric! Hey...tell my niece I love her too!" He wore a warm smile as he was dragged down with Umbra. Lycia and the others pulled Radric from the water just before it finished solidifying. Onox created four giant waves, taller than even the great walls of the four kingdoms. They surrounded the area where Umbra was trapped. Mana And Gi worked together to solidify the massive walls of water, creating an unbreakable, supernatural prison to trap her.

"This is not over! It never will be! So long as there is darkness left in this world...So long as there is a shred of hatred, I will return!" Umbra shouted as the final wall sealed around her.

Everyone shouted victoriously and celebrated...all but Radric. He remained on the ground with Lycia by his side. He slammed his fist into the dirt, silently weeping. Lycia crawled over to him and embraced him from behind.

"I'm...I'm so sorry, my love, truly. I wish I could have helped you save him." She said compassionately. Radric placed one of his hands tenderly over hers.

"Thank you, Lycia, but his soul is at peace. At least in knowing that, I can be happy for him." They slowly came to their feet and made their way over to the others.

Boyox walked over to Axaiyan and held out his closed fist as he bore a joyous smile. Axaiyan scoffed, lightly slapping Boyox's fist away with the back of his hand. But with a slight grin, Axaiyan walked away.

"I hope he never comes around; this is just too fun! It's a definite now. He is exactly what I used to pretend to be." Boyox thought to himself with a playful chuckle. Lycia ran up to him and threw her arms around him from behind, slightly startling him. She shook him back and forth playfully.

"Oh Kerny, I'm so happy! We did it! It's finally over. Now you can be with the one you love!"

"Praise Mana!" Boyox said with a warm smile as he shut his eyes. Radric was still not getting into the spirits of celebration as he made his way to Fraytor's body, where all of Aquaria had sorrowfully gathered. The others slowly joined as well, and the celebration came to a quick halt. Before they could properly morn the deaths of all their fallen, Radric looked to the sky with horror and dismay behind his eyes. The gloom of the wastelands began to return, and Gi retreated behind the smoggy clouds.

"What's going on?" He exclaimed. "With Umbra gone, how could the gloom possibly persist?" Everyone looked up in shock.

"My king, it is possible some evil still remains behind Umbra's walls. Perhaps we should go purge the kingdom." Wasukah suggested.

"But wait, we said we would try to spare the civilians, didn't we?" Lycia said anxiously.

"My queen..." Wasukah continued with his gaze to the ground. "Something still upsets the gods; we have to do what we must...if it will restore our planet."

"Come, we enter the kingdom...now!" Radric responded sternly.

"But—" Lycia began to protest.

"But— our goal is to keep the innocent alive," Radric said valiantly, interrupting her. "We shall seek out what evil still remains and remove it." Lycia smiled and embraced his arm. "Onwards, comrades, step lightly. We can tend to our fallen once we have finished our mission."

They made their way through the gates to witness a horrific sight. The kingdom was in a disastrous state. Beat up buildings, barely able to stand. Fires burned throughout as rubble and trash littered the ground. Hundreds of civilians lying on matted, dirty drapes littered the grounds. Their clothes were torn, and many looked sickly or injured. Worst of all, piles of dead bodies burned throughout the streets. The Umbrians looked over to them. Fear erupted in their oppressed hearts as they saw the armies of the three other nations entering their kingdom in battle gear. Those with the strength to move ran and cowered behind anything they could find. Lycia fell to her knees and wept gently.

"How long...How long have these poor people been suffering like this? There are so few of them left...look at all their dead! This...this is horrible." Lycia spoke weakly.

"Please, citizens of Umbra, do not be afraid!" Radric said calmly, raising his voice enough for all to hear. "We are here to save you!"

"But of course you are!" A man hiding behind a large pile of rubble shouted back sarcastically. "Every new king, every new general...all promising a change that never came! What difference will you make? Ha, next thing you know it, we'll be slaves. Well, I'd rather die here than fall for any more empty promises and lies!"

"Please, citizens, leave this place of fell darkness. I promise, I only want what is best for you." Radric spoke compassionately. "Look upon the insignias we all wear. We all bear the mark of a different nation, even Luna and Sol have come together for peace. It's over now, we can all finally live together, as Uçebians." Before any further discussion could continue, the medics rushed towards the sickly Umbrians and knelt by their sides, wearing warm smiles.

"Please, let me help you. Here, have some water." A Lunian medic spoke tenderly as she aided an elderly woman.

"Bless you, child. I can't remember the last time I had clean water." Several hiding members began to emerge, apart from the citizen who didn't trust them. Slight chatter began to break out, and smiles of hope painted the faces of the poor Umbrians. Lycia slowly stood to her feet and slowly began to approach the fearfully hiding man.

"No, no! Stay back! I want no part in your lies! Leave me to die!" He shouted frantically. Lycia continued towards him with tears streaming from her kind and loving face. "What's this? Tears? Don't take me for a fool; you are evil! There is no good in this world; there never was! There never will be! Stay back!" Eventually, he backed himself into a wall and began to tremble with fear. Without a word, Lycia embraced him tenderly, resting her head against his chest. He remained stiff and motionless. Her skin began to glow with radiant luminescence.

"Is she a goddess? So beautiful...her light, it's as if she is warming my soul with her glow." He thought to himself, lost in her mystique. He slowly returned her embrace, wrapping his arms gently around her.

"Please, you must trust us. Come and be free, come be happy." She spoke tenderly.

"It's...it's just hard to comprehend the thought of peace and happiness." He began sobbing as he struggled to speak. "I've never known such emotions. I just don't know if I can believe such things can exist."

"Then don't take it from me, good citizen. Come and experience it yourself. Enjoy life the way the gods had always intended for us...before the darkness of Umbra robbed that life away. We vanquished her...we have taken that life back...come with us and experience it for yourself."

"Is this what...hope feels like?" He thought to himself. He released her and fell to one knee.

"Forgive my despair, my queen. You have filled my heart with an odd sensation, a feeling I never thought possible. So...this is hope. This feeling...is hope. I guess it couldn't hurt to believe life could be better."

"Then on your feet, citizen, come join your new family." She said with a warm smile as she held out her hand to him.

Soon, the entire military was scouring the kingdom for any oppressed citizens they could find, remaining on guard for whatever evil may still lurk within the shadows. Suddenly, a voice called out to Radric and Lycia from the darkness as a man ran up to them and fell to bended knee.

"Your majesties, a thousand blessings, and thanks for freeing us! I cannot begin to thank you for what you've done. But I may have some useful information for you, and I could use your help with something."

"Rise, good sir, please enlighten us," Radric responded. He stood to his feet energetically and began running back into the city.

"Quick, great ones, follow me. There is something I must show you!" He shouted back to them as he continued.

They followed closely behind until they reached a dark and gloomy stairway. He proceeded down into the deep darkness and disappeared. Radric held out his arm, stopping Lycia from continuing.

"Something doesn't feel right about this Lycia...I don't like it." Lycia nodded her head, and they readied their battle stance. They heard footsteps quickly running towards them from the bottom of the stairs. They drew their weapons and stood alert and ready.

"Hey!" The mysterious man shouted. Radric wrapped his arm around Lycia and hopped back. "What are you two doing? Please follow me!"

"What are you up to, Umbrian?" Radric inquired sternly.

"I assure you, my king, there's no need to worry. I promise this is not a trap." Lycia lowered her guard and tried to proceed, but Radric took hold of her arm. Lycia looked up to him with a confident smile.

"Can't you feel his genuine aura? Come, Radric, let's follow him."

"That is just like Umbra though Lycia, deceptive and highly believable. We must use caution." She nodded, and they proceeded down the steps. The mysterious man was waiting for them with a warm smile.

"Lord Radric, would you mind pushing all your weight at—" He held a torch to the walls and looked at them intently as he searched for a very slight indent. "Ah yes, right here if you wouldn't mind, my king." Radric reached out and pushed, but nothing happened. "Come now, Your Majesty, show me the strength of your lineage! Show me the strength only a giant could muster!" Radric grunted heavily as he pushed with all his might, and the wall began to slide forward. A few heavy pushes followed, and there was enough room for them to proceed down yet another dark stairwell. The mysterious Umbrian charged forward, encouraging them to follow. Radric and Lycia made their way down the stairs cautiously, not knowing what to expect.

The Chosen

When they reached the bottom, Radric and Lycia could not understand what they were seeing.

"What is this? The room is illuminated by that glass rod on the ceiling! Is it like the artificial sun of Gi?" Radric inquired.

"No, my dear king." The Umbrian chuckled playfully. "Afraid that light is of no importance, this is what I really wanted you to see!" Radric and Lycia looked toward where he pointed and once again witnessed a sight that they could not comprehend.

"A door? But...what is it made of?" Lycia inquired softly. "A shiny silver rock? And how does it glow with colorful light?"

"This can't be real! That door looks like it is from another word!" Radric exclaimed in disbelief.

"Now that I have you here, I know I can trust you! My name is Ontoni. I'm a being that has been cursed with immortality." Radric and Lycia gasped.

"Cursed? But is that not a blessing?" Lycia responded in a confused manner.

"Watching your loved ones die of old age, sickness, starvation, war...and remaining through it all...Immortality becomes very lonely, believe me, my young queen. By this time in my life,

I have learned to avoid making any new connections...to avoid the pain of loss. I have been around since the birth of Uçebar."

"That's impossible!" Radric exclaimed.

"I know how that must sound, but I was selected by Father Gi to guide this world. It eventually led me to be the keeper of this door and seek out the chosen."

"The chosen?" Radric responded.

"Yes, dear king. In the ages of Old Uçebar, there were strange technologies that I couldn't possibly be able to explain to you. You just wouldn't be able to comprehend what I am telling you. But all you need to know is this. When Old Uçebar fell, this technology vanished from the face of the planet. The Uçebians fell into disarray, no longer knowing how to survive without it. The room behind this door is the only remaining piece of tech that has survived the millennium. Father Gi came to me in a dream and explained why I had stopped aging, what my mission was, and showed me a vision of this door and how to get to it. Eventually, the kingdom of Umbra was founded, and the main city was built over this mystical room. I have remained in Umbra, waiting for this very moment. Guarding the secret of this door. This door will only open for someone of genuine valor and unparalleled moral character. Selected by the gods to make the ultimate decision that will decide the fate of Uçebar forever."

"What do you mean, decision?" Radric responded with intrigue.

"Behind this door is a room filled with ancient technology. Whoever is allowed inside may choose to learn this technology from its creator himself and give the gift of technology back to Uçebar...or they can decide to destroy it forever. Lord Radric, Queen Lycia, I believe one of you to be the chosen! To be the Uçebian I have been waiting to find for over a millennium."

"What do we do to try to open it?" Radric inquired.

"Just stand before it. If you are the chosen...it will open."
Ontoni said, stepping to the side and holding out his arm.

"Go ahead, Radric, perhaps it is you." Lycia nudged him with
a warm smile.

"Nonsense, dear, it couldn't possibly be me." He responded
weakly.

"I've been corrupted by a demon, and you are the one who
first sought me out. If it weren't for your actions...we wouldn't
be standing here now. No, it must be you." Radric's eyes grew
wide as she stepped back. He slowly began making his way to
the door. When he reached it, he fell to one knee and waited.

"Nothing happens, Ontoni, what should I do?" He whispered.

"Patience, king, trust in the gods!"

"*You who kneel before the door.*" A strange voice began to fill the
room. "*Know this, only the chosen shall enter.*"

"Who is this? Is this a god? I see nothing, but I hear a voice."
Radric said, becoming slightly afraid.

"It is an artificial intelligence. It is a being that does not contain a soul which was created by an Uçebian. It has the capac-
ity to look into your soul and evaluate your value. But that isn't
important now, please continue to be patient. The fact it is
speaking to you at all is very encouraging!"

"*Know this—*" It continued. "*Alone, you are unworthy to enter
here, but there is great character within. Perhaps a piece of you may
be missing. Search yourself and find that which is missing in you. Only
then may you enter this place.*" Radric's eyes grew with confusion.

"A piece of me is missing? What could that possibly mean?"
He thought to himself. Suddenly, he looked at Lycia and understood what the voice meant. He held out his hand to her with a
warm smile, beckoning her over to him.

"Come, Lycia. The piece missing from me...is you!" Lycia's
cheeks flared a bright red as her skin began to glow. She walked

up to him and joined his side as she fell to her knee. They waited anxiously for a few minutes before the voice finally returned.

"Yes, indeed. You have found that which was missing in yourself. Alone, you are unworthy to enter this sacred place. But with her by your side, you are whole. Together, you are the chosen."

"So...not one...but two make up the chosen. How could I have been so blessed that they both happened to show up here together!" Ontoni thought to himself as his eyes filled with joyous tears. Suddenly, Radric and Lycia heard Ontoni grunt, and a thud sounded as he fell to his hands and knees. They looked over to see him breathing heavily and gripping his chest.

"Ontoni, what's wrong?" Lycia said, running over to him.

"Fear not, majesties...it would seem my long journey has finally come to an end! You have given Uçebar hope, you truly were the chosen. Therefore, I am no longer needed. I have succeeded in my mission. I have found the chosen! Now..." He began sobbing heavily with a bright smile of relief on his face. "Now, I can finally rest. It's finally over. This long, treacherous life of loneliness and pain. I can finally be with the ones I love. Thank you, Radric of Sol and Lycia of Luna. You have freed my soul and are one step closer to saving our world. Choose wisely, and may the gods always favor you." Ontoni faded into nothing, and Radric and Lycia smiled warmly to see him finally at peace. The strange door began to glow with brighter colored lights, and the voice returned.

"Now chosen, enter, and decide the fate of your world." The door opened, and Radric took Lycia's hand as the proceeded into the mystical room. They were overtaken by awe and wonder. All the shiny surfaces, whirring sounds, and flashing lights paralyzed them with disbelief.

"An...Uçebian made this? How could this be?" Radric said softly. Lycia ran around like a small child filled with excitement.

"This is so amazing! Can you believe what we are seeing,

Radric? This is like a fairytale, look how beautiful this place is. We should try to share this with the world! Imagine what we could do for everyone."

"Easy, Lycia," Radric said with a slight chuckle. "This could very well be the evil that is preventing the gloom from passing."

"Aww, but look at this, it is so wonderful...I can't bring myself to believe something so beautiful could be evil." Lycia said with disappointment. Suddenly, a large rectangular mural began to flash with bright lights, and an image of an elderly Uçebian man wearing strange clothes appeared inside it.

"Greetings, my friends. If you are seeing this, then I am no longer alive." The man spoke.

"Impossible! The mural not only moves...but it speaks!" Radric said with disbelief.

"Don't be afraid, this is not any fell sorcery, I assure you. It is simple science, honestly. My name is Doctor Ulysses Hawthorne. I am the founder of the technology you find yourself surrounded by. I only sought to better Uçebian life with my vast intellect. I wanted to make life easier, more comfortable. But I never realized the horrors that would come from my work. The once peaceful, loving nature of the Uçebian heart became filled with greed. I fear this ravenous avarice gave birth to a dark entity of immense power. It fed on the despair of the innocent and the avarice of the greedy. It grew stronger the more Uçebians turned to darkness."

"Umbra! So this technology...was the reason for her birth! The greed from the possibilities this technology offered became her strength, her life force." Radric said.

"This room contains all my research and how to harness this technology." Hawthorne continued. "My dream is that one day, the parasitic greed feeding on the hearts of Uçebians will die. Giving way to truly benefit from this technology. It is my hope that when someone enters here, the world will be ready for my inventions and my wisdom. If that is the case, I happily share my vast knowledge with you. If, for any reason, however, you feel there is still a shred of greed and hate in this world...destroy it all! To my left is a large purple sphere, a button in proper terms. Put your weight onto this button, and you will gain access to all my research and teachings. To my right, a large black button. Placing your weight on this one will cause everything to be destroyed forever. If you choose to destroy this place, leave immediately. You will have seven hours before everything explodes, but don't wait...just leave and put the nightmare to rest. Choose wisely and be at peace, my friends." The image of the doctor faded, and Lycia and Radric remained motionless, pondering all they had just heard. Lycia eventually snapped to her senses and ran to the black button.

"Let's do it, Radric, let us destroy this place! If it was what gave Umbra her strength in the first place, we can never let this technology return to our world. This may be the final step towards the restoration of Uçebar." She said with determination in her revealed eye. Radric smiled and quickly joined her. Radric placed his massive hand on the button, Lycia placed both of her tiny hands over his, and with a hopeful stare into the other's eyes, they pressed down. An alarm began to sound, and red lights flashed aggressively.

"Evacuate the area, evacuate the area. 420 minutes remain before total destruction. Repeat, evacuate the area." Another strange voice filled the room.

Lycia and Radric joined the others and explained what happened to the commanders. The injured and weak were carried, and everyone quickly began making their way out of the kingdom of Umbra. Fraytor and the other deceased Uçebians were laid to rest before they proceeded toward Luna.

Uçebar's Rebirth

The morning was upon them, but Radric was too focused on leading the people back to Luna to raise the artificial sun. Suddenly, a massive explosion filled the air, and a giant cloud of smoke erupted into the sky. Everyone looked back in awe. Immediately following the eruption, the ground quaked, and a large tear tore through the gloom in the sky. It grew wider with every second, revealing the once-hidden, baby-blue sky. Before the sky had fully opened up, the Uçebians heard a strange yet beautiful melody floating on the breeze. They looked around in awe at where the sounds emitted. Gracefully gliding by them were dozens of blue birds singing peaceful lullabies as they floated by.

"What...are those?" An Umbrian asked.

"Those dear citizens, are songbirds. Some of the many true creatures of Uçebar, not creatures of darkness." Radric responded with great excitement. The smog continued to crack until the sky fully opened, and the gloom of the wastelands completely vanished. The Umbrians looked up in disbelief as joy filled their once sad and oppressed hearts. Never before could they have imagined such beauty to exist. They were all suddenly cradled in the loving, warm embrace of Gi as his light gently massaged the ground. Soaking in the majestic beams, the dry, cracked dirt of the wastelands began to morph before their very eyes. Lusciously thick, green grass sprouted from the once-dead earth. A fresh breeze rolled through, filled with clean and welcoming air. Radric closed his eyes and took a deep inhale as his daydreams finally became reality. Flowers of all colors began to sprout up from the ground, and the lifeless trees began to erupt with glorious lime-green leaves. Mana appeared in the sky, floating beside Gi. She cast her loving luminescent light on to the sick and injured Umbrians. Immediately, their pain and suffering washed away, and they became filled with energy and new life. Lycia fell to her back, cuddled in the soft grass, and joyous tears rolled down her cheeks.

"Radric, tell me this isn't a dream!" She said, grasping firmly at the fresh green blanket and ripping it up from the ground. Radric fell by her side and stared into the crystal sky as Lycia released her grip, allowing the grass to gracefully float away on the breeze. Small creatures began running around them, playfully nibbling at their boots and clothing.

"This is truly amazing!" The originally skeptical Umbrian shouted into the sky. "So...this is happiness? I never could have imagined anything could feel this good...this freeing! My friends, we have the king and queen to thank for this." He fell to bended knee, weeping joyous tears. "Your majesties, you have given us new life! There are...no words...just nothing that could even begin to express my thanks for such an amazing gift!" Radric and Lycia smiled warmly as they bowed their heads slightly. Eventually, the rest of the Uçebians fell to their knees as well, in veneration. Lycia took Radric's hand tenderly.

"It really is over...isn't it?" She asked gently.

"No, dear," Radric said with a smile, gently shaking his head. She looked up to him with confusion, and he remained with a smile, glancing down at her. "This is just the beginning. The beginning of a new life for all Uçebians!" She smiled and nodded slightly before they proceeded on their journey home. They made many more stops than usual along the way to take in the wonders that had sprung up from the ground. They were within a few hours from Luna when they stopped and huddled around a beautiful spring. Radric stood in front of it and looked at his fellow Uçebians.

"From this day forth, my dear friends, the wastelands shall know be known as "The Great Prairies of Uçebar!" Everyone cheered in excited approval. Several Uçebians hopped into the cool crystal waters, splashing, laughing, and absorbed in true bliss. Eventually, they continued on their journey home.

When they finally reached Luna, everyone was waiting for them outside the gates. As they came into view, Onceli charged towards them as fast as her wobbling little legs could carry her.

"You did it, Mommy and Daddy!" She shouted as Radric and Lycia sprinted towards her." Look how beautiful everything is now!" Lycia scooped her up, and Radric scooped up Lycia, forming their group hug. Elizya slowly made her way to Lycia, tears streaming down her face. Lycia slid from Radric's embrace, gently passing Onceli to him, then flew into Elizya's arms and began to glow brightly.

"See, Mother, I told you...everything would be alright."

"I'm so glad, dear daughter." She responded softly, resting her head atop Lycia's. "We can finally live normal, happy lives. It is finally over."

Boyox looked around but didn't see Uahka amongst the other Uçebians. He ran into the main city and still couldn't find her. He finally made his way to his house and released a shocked gasp as he found it abandoned. All their belongings were gone, and so was Uahka.

"What's going on?" He thought to himself as he peered into

the window. Suddenly, he felt a pair of tiny arms wrap around him from behind. He leaned into her embrace and closed his eyes, wearing a warm smile.

"Come, my dear Boyox, I have a surprise for you." She released him and took his hand as she began running towards the city. She guided him to the center of the city, where a small blue house stood. It had a beautiful garden filled with lush greens and many different vegetables that had sprouted up instantly.

"Is this...is this *our* house?" He asked with his eyes wide. She leaned against his shoulder, and he wrapped his arm around her waist. She nodded gently as she cuddled closer to him. "And your garden, things have actually grown. No more twigs and dead bushes!"

"Yes, it is as we always dreamed, only better." She replied with delight. "The people warmly welcomed me into the city and offered us this house as an engagement present." He smiled wide, and she released a slight giggle as he lifted her up and began to carry her into their new home.

A few days later, not only was their wedding held, but Radric and Lycia's as well. A massive celebration of all the nations present was held in the city of Luna for the long-awaited peace and the union of the two couples. At the conclusion of Boyox's wedding, Axaiyan walked up to him in an awkward manner, refusing to smile and not making direct eye contact.

"Here, I wanted you two to have this." He said bluntly as he held a small box out. Boyox received the gift with a look of surprise in his onyx eyes. Boyox opened it to see an arrangement of shiny stones of many colors and shapes, resembling polished glass. "I found these in a lake just outside the kingdom. I wanted to go for a swim but kept feeling them at my feet. I thought they were beautiful and figured it would make a nice wedding gift." He looked over to Boyox with a stern face. "Don't think this makes us friends, though!" Boyox smiled wide and held out his fist. Axaiyan smiled slightly and gently pressed his fist into Boyox's.

"Woah, so the edge lord can smile! There is a decent guy in that angry body after all, huh?" Boyox teased as their fists remained united. Axaiyan scoffed and looked away as he dropped his fist. Uahka embraced him tenderly, resting her head against his stomach.

"They are so beautiful, thank you so much." She said softly. Axaiyan smiled and received her embrace.

At the conclusion of Radric and Lycia's wedding, Elizya approached them and placed a necklace around Lycia's neck. Radric fell to his knee so she could reach him, and she placed one around his as well. They each reached down and grabbed the medallions that how rested against their chest and stared with wonder. Lycia's was made from the finest silver and shaped like a dire wolf. Radric's was pure gold and shaped like a phoenix.

"They are beautiful...thank you!" Lycia said with misty eyes. Radric remained silent as he stared with wonder and slight sadness as it reminded him of Octonia.

"Don't worry, big guy, there's no need for words," Elizya said as she teared up. "You are part of the family now. Speaking of which..." She knelt down in front of Onceli, who stood beneath her parents. "Don't think I forgot about our dear princess." Onceli became excited as Elizya placed a gorgeous medallion around her tiny neck. Onceli's was divided in half: the left side was a moon made of silver, and the right was a sun made of gold.

"These are just, so perfect, Mother! How did you make these?"

"Just enjoy them, dear; that is a secret," Elizya responded playfully. Onceli wrapped her arms around Radric's legs, and he scooped her up.

"We are a real family now, Daddy! Just like Mommy said we would!" Radric smiled warmly as he stared into Onceli's multi-colored eyes.

"We are, indeed, my sweet girl!" He said as he playfully "booped" her little nose, causing her to giggle. Wasukah approached Radric and punched him in the arm playfully.

"Well, my friend, you have done it! Peace has embraced Uçe-bar as it once did in the olden days! Can't wait to return to Sol and begin our new lives!" Radric smiled as he handed Onceli to Lycia.

"I'm not going back to Sol, old friend." He said warmly.

"But sir, what do you mean?" Wasukah said with a look of great dismay. Lycia backed away with a warm smile.

"Kneel, general!" Radric shouted in a manner of pride.

"My...my king?" Wasukah weakly uttered. Radric stood as he was, waiting for him to do as he said. Wasukah slowly fell to bended knee and bowed his head to the ground.

"This man that kneels before me is a loyal friend! A gallant warrior whose valor knows no bounds! I trust this man with my very life! I trust him...with the lives of my people! I, Radric Wartox, Son of Montec Wartox, ruler of Sol! Dub thee Wasukah Graysbond as the new king of Sol!" Wasukah let out a slight gasp. "Now rise Wasukah, first of his noble line, and king of Sol!" Wasukah slowly stood to his feet, and Radric fell to bended knee before him. Soon after, everyone in attendance followed his example. Wasukah looked around in awe as everyone rendered him proper honors. He looked up as Gi's majestic light shined on him in the form of acknowledgement, granting him the strength and wisdom to rule. Everyone slowly came to their feet.

"But my king...I don't deserve this honor; I could never accept." Wasukah said weakly.

"Nonsense, my friend!" Radric boomed with a powerful laugh. "You have been a most loyal friend to me. A courageous and noble warrior. I look to you as if you were my own brother. I trust none other than you with the protection of our people." Wasukah's eyes quivered slightly, growing misty. "Besides, I can't be king of both Luna and Sol...and my place is here now. Oh, and Wasukah..."

"Yes?" He replied softly.

"No need to refer to a fellow king as "my king," anymore." Wasukah nodded and smiled warmly. The crowd erupted into cheers, and Axaiyan and Gorg lifted him up onto their shoulders.

"Long live, King Wasukah!" The crowd began chanting as Axaiyan and Gorg paraded him through the streets. They finally placed him down and congratulated him warmly as the celebration continued on.

The end of a great day finally came to a close, and Gi returned ownership of the sky to Mana. The Uçebians of other nations departed for their respective kingdoms, followed by the Umbrians who chose to join them. Wasukah and the other Solyans carried off the great stone of peace to be placed in the center of Sol, and Radric and Lycia placed theirs in the center of Luna. Radric placed his hand on the stone tenderly as he viewed their marks. He smiled warmly as a slight tear fell from his fiery yet calm eyes.

"This stone represents the peace we have always dreamed of, Lycia." She embraced him tight as they marveled over the stone.

Happiness and harmony loomed over the Uçebians as their trip through the Great Prairies was a much nicer journey than once before, through the wastelands. Boyox and Uahka departed to explore the Prairies to find a beautiful and peaceful spot for their honeymoon. Radric and Lycia needed no such venture, for they had everything they could ever want right there in Luna. They made their way into the palace and tucked their little girl into bed. Radric began energetically reenacting the story of how he and Lycia met. Onceli loved the story, but eventually, her tired little body succumbed to the need for sleep. Radric made his way out to the balcony to gaze upon the stairs that sparkled gloriously alongside Mana. Lycia soon joined him and matched his gaze.

"I never imagined..." Radric began to struggle to speak as he wept. "That I would stand out here, staring into the true sky. It is still so surreal." Lycia began to glow brightly but let out a heavy yawn. She began tugging him towards their chambers. They cuddled face to face.

"You know Lycia...this is truly all thanks to you." He said warmly.

"What are you talking about?" She began playfully. "If you hadn't snuck into my kingdom all those years ago, we never would have been able to make this happen."

"Had you never come into my life, I would not have found the strength or even the desire to sneak into this kingdom. Only you could have inspired me so." Lycia kissed him tenderly and closed her eyes as she cuddled close to him.

"You are a truly noble man, my dear Radric. I am eternally grateful to Mana for bringing you to me." He let out a happy chuckle and closed his eyes as they both drifted into a peaceful sleep.

This peace and tranquility would continue for many years. Though unity still prevailed, the three kingdoms still remained as a tribute to the gods who defended their freedom and returned their world to them. The Uçebians of this generation, and many following, would come to experience life on Uçebar as the gods had intended for them. In peace and harmony and as one unified people.

THE END

ACKNOWLEDGEMENTS

This journey would not have been made possible with out the support of my family and friends, as well as the tutelage of my mentor.

I would first like to sincerely thank Paul Caranci, who provided me with valuable information on the road to getting published. He spared no detail about the process and warned me about certain road blocks I would need to look out for along the way. He also ensured to let me know about the potential mistakes I could make that would cripple my chances of being successful. Paul taught me about and encouraged me to join our local writer's association. By being a part of that team I'll have a better chance to reach the public. He also steered me into the direction of Stillwater River Publications.

Which leads me to my next acknowledgement. Stillwater River Publications worked with me on tailoring a publishing package that best fit my specific needs. They were very professional, yet personable, and very friendly. They taught me a lot about what to expect and how I can better prepare myself. Without their professional services this dream would have never become a reality.

Now I would like to acknowledge a very good friend and business partner so to speak. Nelson Navarro Navarro has been the artist I've been working with since 2017. He is the talented hand that brought my characters to life for this book cover. Nelson is unlike any other artist I've ever worked with. He takes the time to read through my very detailed descriptions of the characters and backgrounds I desire. Never have I experienced a better representation of what I imagined for my book covers. Sometimes I would picture things that either wouldn't work or could be improved on and he would make his professional suggestions to me before going forward with the changes. In fact, the Luna Sol Amat logo attached to the title was his own creation that I never asked for and it truly adds the finishing touch. I couldn't have done this without him.

There have been a small few that have read my stories, but four in particular truly helped me to get to this point.

Starting with Austin Townsend, a military brother of mine, who was the first individual to have ever completed one of my books. He provided me with very positive and encouraging feedback as well as constructive criticism that led me to an important realization. I rushed the ending and I'll never forget his words. "I couldn't put it down, but you ruined it with the ending. It seemed rushed." So I rewrote the ending and he took the time to read it through, completely, for a second time, even while being on active duty. Afterwards letting me know that I nailed it. His support and critique gave me the confidence I have to seek publication.

The second person I want to mention is a college friend of mine, Robb Susnik. He was the first and only person, thus far, to read Luna Sol Amat. Robb provided me with a very in-depth and detailed critique of the story. An important take away being that the flow of my story was a little rough and needed to take a more "show don't tell approach." Another being that even if my genre is fantasy, there were some elements of my story that were too ridiculous compared to the tone I was setting. This story wouldn't be as ready as it is without his valuable assistance.

The third is a good friend, and another military brother of mine, Nathan Solares. I never would have imagined myself seeking publication. The first story I wrote was merely something I did for fun while I was in the military. He was also on active duty with me and still took the time to read through my book. Upon finishing it, he said something to me that I've never forgotten. "Are you planning on publishing this? Cuz you should." The thought never crossed my mind, but ever since I have been working tirelessly to reach this point in my life.

The fourth was another military brother, Deepak Devasthali. At the time, he was the officer in charge of the clinic I was stationed at. His role was probably one of the most taxing, time consuming, and pivotal positions in the command. Even while overseeing clinic operations, mentoring his subordinate leaders, and handling mountains of paperwork, he still put in the time to read one of my books. Normally, I would have to go up the chain of command just to speak with him. However, he invited me personally to his office, once a week, to go over the story, chapter by chapter. Giving me some of his valuable and minuscule free time. He provided me with suggestions on how I could improve as well as finding plenty of grammatical errors that I hadn't noticed yet. His support and guidance encouraged me to continue on my journey.

My last mentions are two of the most important components of my life. I definitely wouldn't have got this far without them nor would I be the man I am today without their guidance.

Gail Lynn Faraj-Musleh and Fouad Elias Faraj-Musleh, my parents. Of all the support anyone could receive, of course, nothing can describe how nice it is to have your parents backing you. Nothing can describe how nice it is to know they are proud of you. Even when I felt like giving up, like I would never get published. Even as I failed to get responses from publishers, they were always there, cheering me on and encouraging me to keep at it. I don't know where I'd be without their love and support. The way the raised me nurtured my creative mind and allowed me to even develop this passion. I never would have began writing had they not provided me with the amazing childhood I had. A life that sculpted me into the person I am today. I could never thank them enough for all they've given me.

ABOUT THE AUTHOR

My name is Fouad Faraj. I was born in San Pedro Sula, Hondu-
ras, and raised in North Providence, Rhode Island. Growing up, I
always had a special love for fantasy and fiction. I found nothing
more exciting than to see movies of magical worlds of make-be-
lieve. I also had very vivid lucid dreams where I would, often
times, enter those magical worlds. Creativity has always been
a natural talent of mine, a state where I shine. Playing outside
or in my room with toys would keep me entertained for hours.
Through that time I'd be creating stories and scenarios for my
little characters to be in. As I got older, I never imagined I'd end
up being a writer, but I never lost that excitement for fantasy.

It wasn't until my mid-twenties, when I was serving on
Active Duty in the US Navy, that I found my passion in creative

writing. In fact it was completely by happenstance that I ever had. To cope with the mental stress that came from military life, I'd spend the free time I had immersing myself in worlds of fantasy. I was watching an anime that really interested me, quickly pulling me in. The ending was beyond disappointing and unsatisfying. So, just for fun, I decided to write a better ending. As I went though, I was having a lot of fun and decided to start over from the beginning. It was starting to come together so well, I decided to remove the characters and plot of the anime in order to make the story my own. Several weeks later, I ended up finishing my first book and I could not have been more surprised. My teenage self never would have seen "us," as a writer despite our knack for it and creative spirit.

When I got out of the military, I decided to get a degree in creative writing to help me improve my skills. My first book was good in the sense of storytelling, but formatting and grammar... not remotely. Getting my degree in creative writing helped me to push forward and become a more mature and polished writer.

The funny thing is, through my schooling I always heard this very phrase: "A good reader makes for a good writer." Some were even under the impression that someone couldn't be a good writer, if they didn't love to read. That said, I've only ever read one book apart from my own, my entire life. It was in the third grade, *Max and Me and the Time-Machine*. My classmates laughed at that, assuming I wouldn't get far. "How can you learn how to write, if you haven't seen how it's done?" they'd ask. My response was simple: "How did the very first do it then?" I believed that you didn't need to be a reader to know how to tell a good story and sought to prove that. My stories will do the talking for me, and I have many to share. I'm excited to have opened this door, and hope my stories bring others the same joy writing them brought me.